The Rebellious Tide

The Rebellious Tide

Eddy Boudel Tan

DUNDURN
PRESS

Publisher: Scott Fraser | Acquiring editor: Rachel Spence | Editor: Diane Young
Cover designer: Sophie Paas-Lang
Cover image: unsplash.com/Katherine Gu
Printer: Marquis Book Printing Inc.

Library and Archives Canada Cataloguing in Publication

Title: The rebellious tide / Eddy Boudel Tan.
Names: Boudel Tan, Eddy, 1983- author.
Identifiers: Canadiana (print) 20200310291 | Canadiana (ebook) 20200310399 | ISBN 9781459746879 (softcover) | ISBN 9781459746886 (PDF) | ISBN 9781459746893 (EPUB)
Classification: LCC PS8603.O9324 R43 2021 | DDC C813/.6—dc23

We acknowledge the support of the Canada Council for the Arts and the Ontario Arts Council for our publishing program. We also acknowledge the financial support of the Government of Ontario, through the Ontario Book Publishing Tax Credit and Ontario Creates, and the Government of Canada.

Dundurn Press
1382 Queen Street East
Toronto, Ontario, Canada M4L 1C9
dundurn.com, @dundurnpress 𝕏 f ⊚

To all the Beauties who shared secrets with me in the disco

Petit
Géant

ONE

Young Once

"I used to be beautiful," she said.

It was true. Sebastien grew up surrounded by the evidence of his mother's beauty. Ruby kept most of these faded photographs in boxes stacked on the top shelf of her closet, a hidden archive of tattered prints that spanned decades. Her favourites were trapped in cheap frames throughout their apartment. Sebastien had them etched in his memory, having seen them every day for as long as he could remember.

The young woman was striking. Every image preserved the delicate curve of her neck and the clarity of her eyes. Her hair was worn the same way in each one, a heavy veil black as a nun's habit. She began to smile more with time, as though age softened whatever caused her younger self to be so serious.

"You're still beautiful." Sebastien looked into her yellowed eyes to show he meant it. She laughed, unconvinced. Ruby Goh was no longer the vital woman who stared at them from the photographs. Her body sank into the shallow canyon that had formed in her mattress. A pile of blankets concealed her bloated stomach and swollen legs. She wore her long hair in the same way, but the colour had faded over time.

"I'm fifty-two and I look like I've been dead for years," she said. "There are women my age running marathons. I'm lucky if I can make it to the toilet in time." Her body shook as her laughter became a fit of coughs.

Sebastien handed her a glass of water, shaking his head. "Don't talk like that. The negativity doesn't help."

"If you think I'm still hoping for a miracle, forget it. Positive thinking won't do a damn thing. Sometimes the only thing left to do is laugh or cry. Let me laugh."

A year ago, Sebastien would have argued, but now he knew she was right. The chances of a liver donor materializing in time were slim. He flashed a disapproving look at his mother before moving one of his little black discs across the checkered board.

The only similarity Ruby could find between her native country of Singapore and her adopted home of Québec was their version of checkers. There were more squares and pieces on the board than the more common variation of the simple game. They used to play on a flimsy sheet of cardboard with the squares coloured in with felt pen. Dented bottle caps had been the checkers. When Sebastien started working during high school, he used his first paycheque to surprise his mother with a proper version of the game from the local hobby store. She was thankful for the gift but preferred their makeshift board.

"Bad move!" Ruby let out a gleeful shriek as she thrust one of her white discs over two of Sebastien's, palming the captives.

He grabbed fistfuls of hair and moaned in disbelief. "I didn't see that coming."

She rested against the deflated pillows that lined her headboard and smiled. "I used to play this with your father, you know. He would say the exact same thing."

He looked up, attentive, though it wasn't her first time offering this same glimpse into her past. Ruby rarely talked about his father. This man he had never met was a phantom whose absence still haunted their lives. He lived on in the rooms of Ruby's memory, where he held her face in his hands, kissed the back of her neck. Her mind housed a projection room that played a continuous reel of distant scenes, remembered or imagined, that always ended with his father vanishing before it started from the beginning again.

"I guess you had lots of time to kill on board that ship."

She nodded, the smile lingering along her lips.

"Was he as terrible a player as I am?"

"I would always beat him," she said. Her eyes were alive, less clouded than usual. "That's why he fell in love with me. He wasn't used to losing."

Sebastien had collected shards of information from Ruby's stories over the years to form a picture of his father. The man was charismatic and bold, a young sailor who loved the sea more than any woman. He had the angular features and thick tangle of hair that his ancient Greek ancestors chiseled into stone, traits that were passed on to his son.

There were inconsistencies in Ruby's stories. Sometimes he was a gentle lover who adored her. Other times he was an ill-tempered brute who viewed her as disposable. Sebastien was clever enough to know that both versions must have been true.

"I was young once," she went on, her eyes clouding over again. "And I was beautiful. He promised to take me to France. I couldn't believe it. A poor girl from Singapore sailing away to Europe with a handsome foreigner. It was like a dream."

Sebastien had heard this story before. He used to let his mother indulge herself in the fog of these memories. The older he became, the more he realized the danger of selecting the memories that lived on and those that got buried. Ruby did this ruthlessly as though choosing which photographs to display and which to hide in boxes.

"It *was* a dream," he said, moving one of his pieces aimlessly forward on the checkerboard.

"Excuse me?"

"It wasn't real. He was never going to take you to France."

"He was going to —" she said, but Sebastien couldn't listen to any more.

"You've never been to France because he didn't take you there," he interrupted, his tone steady and factual. "He brought you here to this nowhere town instead. He got you pregnant, then he left. He ran away like a coward."

Ruby shook her head. The two captured discs were still clutched in her hand. "That's not what happened."

"Then tell me. What happened? Why did he leave?" Sebastien knew he wasn't likely to get any answers. These questions always upset her, so he had learned to fill in the blanks himself. He hoped one day Ruby would provide an explanation that would redeem his father. Until then, the young foreign sailor who abandoned his mother would remain guilty. This was Sebastien's own private mythology.

"Things didn't go according to plan," she said as she wrapped a blanket around her thin frame.

"You used to make him sound like some sort of hero. I wanted to be just like him, to sail the world, wake up every day in a different port. But he was no hero, was he? He was selfish and cruel. That's the truth."

He paused, drawing a deep breath. "We don't need him, anyway. We have each other." He offered her a reassuring smile.

"I made some bad choices, but you know what? I don't regret any of them." She placed her hand on his warm cheek. "Those choices gave me you. I will always be proud of that. You should be, too."

Sebastien set the checkerboard on the floor and pulled his chair closer to Ruby's bed. Her hands were silk gloves filled with bones as he held them. "I am proud," he lied. He leaned forward and kissed her on the forehead. "It's late. You should get some sleep."

The last image in the projection room of Ruby Goh's mind was of Sebastien and his father. They were roughly the same age — two men brimming with such youth they seemed immortal — sitting side by side, laughing. The thought made her smile before sleep washed over her like the ocean's tide. She never woke up.

TWO

Surprise

The residents of Petit Géant didn't care for the world outside the town's borders, despite the welcoming signs in English and French at either end of the main road. The hand-painted porcupines on these signs, their paws waving in the air, were meant to make visitors feel welcome. The truth was the locals had always been wary of outsiders.

No one was more of an outsider than Ruby Goh. Imagine the confusion and suspicion the unexpected arrival of the young Singaporean woman must have created thirty years earlier. And she had been pregnant, too, with no husband in sight. The local hair salon was filled with gossip from mouths puckered with distaste.

Ruby gave her newborn son a name that would be considered acceptable by the inhabitants of her new home. The name sounded both strange and beautiful to her ears when she first heard it spoken on the radio. Even so, the young child was excluded no less than his mother. Being the outsider's son was a sin equal to being the outsider.

No matter how much effort Ruby put into helping him blend in, dressing him in sweater vests from the thrift store and trimming his hair with the kitchen scissors, people would still look at him as though he were a wild animal. This little boy with the deep green eyes and bronze skin, with hair as black as his mother's but coiled like a nest of serpents, was like no one they had ever seen before.

Back then, Ruby cleaned the homes of Petit Géant while their owners were busy living their lives. She found a sense of purpose in detergent and disinfectant, taking something neglected and making it sparkle.

The money was barely enough to cover the bills even during the busier months, but she enjoyed the work. She loved having the privilege of spending time in these houses. She would look at the portraits on the walls and admire the fine furniture. Sometimes she'd pretend she lived there, tidying up while her husband worked in a fancy office.

The only place she didn't like to clean was the Villeneuve house. Pierre Villeneuve worked as a councillor at the town hall. His young daughter was Sebastien's age. "She's sweet as a rock," he had once told his mother. But the lady of the house was the reason Ruby dreaded her weekly appointment.

Ruby would arrive with a smile every Wednesday at one o'clock in the afternoon. Overdressed and eager for company, Genevieve Villeneuve would open the door and then follow Ruby from room to room, smoking a cigarette while she supervised. "I just want to be sure you don't feel tempted to take anything," she said on more than one occasion. "I mean,

I'm not saying you're a *thief*, but I've heard stories about that sort of thing happening."

She would offer generous amounts of feedback on Ruby's performance. "I pay you good money. I don't want you getting lazy."

Her favourite topic of conversation, though, was her family. "Chloe and I are so lucky to have Pierre. He works so hard to give us such a good life. I don't know how you single mothers cope. And a wild little boy like that without a father! I just can't fathom it."

Ruby would return home every Wednesday, close her bedroom door, and cry into the red, raw skin of her hands. She knew Genevieve was a silly woman whose opinions didn't matter, but every comment felt like the lash of a whip against Ruby's self-worth. Maybe Genevieve simply spoke what everyone else in town thought.

Sebastien would return from school and sit beside his mother with his little hand in hers. It wasn't fair that women like Genevieve Villeneuve could have such power over women like his mother. "She thinks she's better than you, but she's not," he would tell her.

Ruby would nod and force a smile. "You're right," she would say, not quite believing it.

The weeks went by and every Wednesday was the same. Finally, Sebastien had had enough. One night, when he was nine, he slipped out his bedroom window and walked to the tree-lined streets of the wealthy part of town. The Villeneuve home lay under the moonlight like a sleeping giant. He reached into his backpack. His little hands wrapped around the jagged rocks inside. He didn't stop throwing until the windows were shattered.

Now, many years later, Sebastien heard the sound of broken glass as he cracked the eggs against the side of the frying pan, an echo from the past. He tucked the memory back into a crowded corner of his mind. The eggs spilled from their shells and sizzled in the heat of the pan. Sunny side up, the way his mother liked them.

The cramped apartment with the faded wallpaper and stained ceiling was the only home Sebastien had ever known. It sat directly above the neighbourhood's convenience store in an old two-storey building covered in stucco the colour of traffic cones. The store had been a laundromat when Sebastien was younger. He would sit on the rusted metal steps of the fire escape outside his window and absorb the scent of detergent like a chemical sauna.

It was barely enough space for the two of them, especially as Sebastien got older, but they'd learned ways of simulating privacy. They had their own bedrooms, though the wall they shared couldn't have been made of much more than sawdust and cardboard. Sebastien used noise as a curtain, dialing up the volume of his music when he needed to be alone.

The moon-shaped clock on the wall counted the seconds as Sebastien slid the eggs onto a plate. He crossed the linoleum floor of the kitchen, bumping into their faux-wood dining table along the way.

"Your breakfast awaits, m' lady," he said, in his best English-butler accent.

There was no answer. He glanced at the clock. It was unusual for Ruby to sleep in so late.

"You awake in there?" he asked with two knocks against the door. "Rise and shine, lazy bum."

He held his ear against the door, but he couldn't hear a thing besides the creep of worry that had a way of altering his senses.

"I'm coming in." His fingers wrapped around the doorknob as he paused, afraid of what he'd find on the other side.

He thought about how silly he'd feel for expecting the worst if his mother was asleep in her bed. He held onto that silly feeling as he pushed open the door.

Ruby's bedroom looked exactly as it had the previous night except for the morning light that slipped through the blinds. She even lay in the same sacrificial pose, cupped by the curves of her mattress.

Sebastien set the plate on her desk and stood over the bed.

"Wake up, Mama," he said, although he knew the truth. She was as cold and still as the morning-after remains of a fire.

"Wake up." His voice was less steady the second time. The pain started out dull, but he could feel it blossoming deep within his chest. "Wake up. Wake up." His face was calm as his fingers felt for the missing pulse in Ruby's thin wrist. It occurred to him how funny it was that absence could be felt more strongly than presence.

He drew a long breath and swallowed it.

The checkerboard was on the floor beside the bed where Sebastien had placed it, the game no longer paused but abandoned.

With a loud exhale, he picked up the plate of eggs and walked briskly out of the room. He stood in the middle of the kitchen for several seconds before throwing the dish against the wall with such force that it snapped cleanly down the middle like two halves of a moon. The sound wasn't satisfying. It was flat and blunt, nothing like the music created by the rocks and shattering windows from many years ago.

The pain now clawed at his lungs. He grabbed a chair and lifted it above his head until its wooden legs scraped against the uneven ceiling. With a groan, he swung the chair downward. It crashed against the surface of the kitchen table, creating a pleasing sound. The chair sliced through the air repeatedly until his hands gripped nothing more than a splintered frame of wood.

"What's going on in there?" The shrill words were accompanied by three beats against the front door that led to the hall. "Sebastien? Ruby? Is everything okay?"

"Everything's fine," he shouted back, his voice stuttering. "We're fine, Elise. Sorry for the noise."

His neighbour hesitated, but the sound of her slippers could be heard moments later as she padded down the hall.

He looked at the floor. What remained of the kitchen table resembled the beginnings of a bonfire. The clock ticked steadily as he made his way back into the bedroom.

One look at his mother lying motionless in bed was all he could handle. He walked into her closet and closed the creaky doors behind him. It was cool and dark inside. He'd always found it comforting to curl up in a corner of the closet, although he usually took refuge in his own, not Ruby's. He had forced himself to outgrow the habit. Men mustn't hide from their problems. He knew that. But he allowed himself this relapse into his past behaviour. He wasn't strong enough to resist it this time.

He thought he had been prepared for his mother to die. As the weeks and months had trickled by, he could almost see the life escaping through her pores. He'd remained positive for years, but the hope had drained out of him. Eventually, he knew his energy would be better spent preparing for what was to come.

It wasn't enough. He'd underestimated his capacity to feel. Smashing the kitchen table had been an effective release, but he couldn't ignore the burning in his lungs. He knew it wasn't just grief and shock and loneliness. It was rage. He had kept it hidden inside for years. It was fed by every muttered insult, every Christmas they couldn't afford, every time his mother embarrassed herself trying to fit in with the other townspeople. Most of all, the rage had grown whenever he saw that his mother wasn't also consumed by it. More than anyone else, she had earned the right to be angry.

As he sat on the closet floor with his knees tucked against his chest, he pictured his rage and saw it had a face not so different from his own. It was the face of the man who had left them there, alone, empty-handed, in a town that would never be home.

✥

Kostas Kourakis was his name. Sebastien had made that discovery several years earlier. He'd thought it was a strange combination of letters when he first saw it, an unfamiliar union of hard angles and gentle loops. The sound was even stranger when he said it aloud.

Kostas Kourakis.

Kostas Kourakis.

He'd repeated the name until it began to make sense, until it sounded like it could belong to a person who shared his blood.

His girlfriend at the time, Sophie, was throwing a party. "The theme is *Belle Époque*," she had said. "Just come dressed French."

Sebastien would never normally rummage through his mother's closet, but he had remembered she owned a felt beret that would work with his outfit.

He found a wide rectangular box on the floor of the closet. Inside was something he'd never seen before — a white jacket with brass buttons. A single golden stripe with a diamond shape in the centre was emblazoned on the epaulet of each shoulder. He knew immediately that it must have belonged to his father.

It fit perfectly. Standing in front of Ruby's bedroom mirror, Sebastien saw that the jacket could have been tailored to his athletic frame. It smelled musty, like dust and dampness, and the colour had yellowed over time, but it was in good shape considering its age. As he ran his hand down the inside lining, he felt something sewn into the fabric. Embroidered across a black badge were bold white letters: *K. Kourakis.*

After carefully replacing the jacket where he had found it, Sebastien spent the next several days discovering who his father was. He didn't go to Sophie's party. He locked himself in his room with his laptop and followed the clues.

It didn't take him long to find an officer in the Hellenic Merchant Marine named Kostas Kourakis. This man had dedicated his youth to sailing the world on Greek cargo vessels but had spent the past ten years in greater comfort aboard passenger ships. One look at the man's angular face and deep green eyes told him everything he needed to know.

Sebastien kept this to himself. He certainly wasn't going to say a word to Ruby. Every now and then he would check in on his father online. Kostas had a wife and two young children. They would huddle together closely in each new picture as though protecting themselves from outside forces. Sebastien watched as the boy and girl grew a little older each year. Their smiles always seemed staged.

The itch to reach out to this man shamed him. He had never longed for a father, even though as a child he sometimes wondered why his family was so much smaller than others. Curiosity grew with age, then transformed itself into blame when he became more perceptive of his mother's loneliness.

Still, he'd always refused to let his father hold more space in his consciousness than the man deserved. He would almost believe himself whenever he told Ruby they didn't need that man in their lives.

When Sophie asked if he'd consider meeting this sailor with the strange name, Sebastien's answer was a definitive *no*. He had enough money saved by then for a plane ticket to Europe, but it would have been an irresponsible expense with Ruby's condition worsening. Besides, what would be the point?

And, so, it bothered him that these images on the screen had consumed so much of his imagination. *What would be the harm of sending a little message? The response could be surprising*, he thought to himself.

He resisted in the end. Knowing Kostas was unaware that his forgotten son was watching over him allowed Sebastien to claim some of the power he was never born with.

"I know who you are," he would whisper to the image on the screen. That was enough for him back then.

❖

Now, as he sat in the protective darkness of his mother's closet, he wondered if it was still enough.

Sebastien needed an explanation that Ruby had never been able to offer. He used to dismiss his father as being too weak and too cruel to take responsibility for an unexpected pregnancy, but he knew the truth couldn't be that simple. It didn't fit his mother's stories. A romance with a young foreign sailor. The promise of a voyage to Europe. Then an unexpected separation on a cold Québec morning. That had been the only thing Ruby would say about that day — she remembered the cold.

The only way to learn why that man fled thirty years ago would be to meet him. But it wasn't just an answer Sebastien wanted. There was something darker stirring in his belly.

His hands reached out blindly until they touched the rectangular box in the opposite corner. He pushed open the closet doors with the box clutched in one arm.

The scent was familiar as he pulled the jacket over his T-shirt. He examined himself in the full-length mirror beside Ruby's dresser, not able to deny liking the way the uniform looked on him. The shade of white was sad with age, but the gold embroidery on his shoulders shone brightly. There was a faint spatter of orange drops across the breast, and he wondered if the colour had been redder thirty years earlier.

Dozens of eyes stared at him from the picture frames that lined the shelves and walls. Since his earliest memories, his mother had been a strong woman who loved to laugh as much as she loved to argue. Even as her body slowly betrayed her, she'd never let herself be diminished. But the earlier photographs revealed a more cautious woman, one whose eyes were mistrustful and whose lips refused to lie. She gazed at her grown son wearing the mysterious man's jacket. She knew the truth.

Sebastien picked up one photograph in a pewter frame. Although he'd been very young, he remembered that day at a local petting zoo. The image captured Ruby as she laughed uninhibitedly while her son held a baby goat barely smaller than himself. Relief came to his red, itching eyes as he blinked away the tears.

⟡

Sophie Lamoureux took Sebastien's virginity in her bedroom when they were eighteen. As his face hovered above hers, sweat pooling in the shallow wells of his collarbone and hair draped around his head like Spanish moss, she decided she would love him, despite his background.

Their relationship didn't officially begin until she returned to Petit Géant after several years of university in Montréal. It was her little rebellion, dating Sebastien Goh. She saw herself as the benevolent princess choosing true love with an outcast over the preordained comfort of her mother's expectations. It was a story she loved to believe even more than she loved Sebastien himself.

Reality was less flattering. Their relationship was often punctuated by indefinite separations as frequent as the solstice. Her friends would exchange glances and knowing smirks during these periods of respite. *We knew this would happen*, she imagined them saying. *If only she had listened.*

With every spiteful remark she would later regret, with every ambivalent shrug of his shoulders, she held on tighter. Sophie had given up too much and invested too many years for this gamble not to pay off.

Sebastien had ended things six weeks earlier. "We've tried for years to make it work. It's run its course" is how he had put it. She begged him to reconsider as she'd done in the past, but she knew it was different this time. It was an anticlimactic end to so many years of intensity. If she were honest with herself, she would have known they were doomed from the start. A romance like theirs wasn't meant to last. They never stood a chance.

Today, though, was special.

"He should be here any minute," Sophie said as she scanned the garden, her hands outstretched in front of her as though she were tiptoeing away from a bear.

It was a surprise party for Sebastien's twenty-ninth birthday. A wooden dining table long enough to seat thirty stood in the middle of her mother's backyard. It was set with linen napkins and polished silverware. Spring flowers spilled out of ceramic vases. Champagne was being chilled in silver buckets of ice.

The guests were scattered outside the entrance to the solarium that protruded from the house. The mood was tense. Everyone but Sophie seemed to know this was a bad idea.

The party was being organized weeks before they broke up. She could have cancelled it but instead chose to forge ahead. It could be a chance to redeem herself, to prove her love for him.

She viewed the death of Ruby as another opportunity. It was a tragedy, of course, and Sophie was saddened by it, but it was also a path back to Sebastien. Now more than ever, he needed someone to turn to, and she had gladly allowed him to find comfort in her arms. He sobbed against her neck the day it happened. She wouldn't fail him this time.

After two weeks of grieving, Sebastien would need something to celebrate.

"He's coming!" she whisper-growled, waving her hands as if swatting flies. She could hear his voice from the hall, musical and boyish compared to her brother's baritone. The guests took their positions.

The town hadn't changed much over the course of Sebastien's young life. Even now, he felt like a child as he walked along the main street. He used to stand at the window of the same ice cream shop that he passed now, imploring his mother to treat him to a pastel swirl atop a waffle cone like the ones the other kids got to enjoy. Instead of giving in, she would remind him how much more affordable it was to buy the plastic bins of freezer-burned Neapolitan.

He walked past the bar that got him drunk for the first time, at the age of eighteen, where he had slammed back nine bottles of Blanche de Chambly before getting into a fist fight with a boy who called him a fag. Sophie had pulled him away when it was clear the other boy wouldn't be getting off the floor without help.

"Pas de Papa." French for "No Father," that's what Sophie used to call him when they met in primary school. It caught on and soon all of Sophie's friends, precious and white like porcelain dolls, repeated the name until it evolved into the snappier version of "Pas Papa." It wasn't until high school that Sophie warmed up to Sebastien, when lacrosse and puberty had moulded his body into a different shape. The insults had become less vocal by then, but they persisted in whispers while he was kept several arms' lengths away from being included.

Sebastien didn't care. From boyhood to manhood, he never cowered in the face of their abuse. He learned to like the isolation. It came with a certain freedom. He understood that he simply didn't belong there. He may have been born and raised in Petit Géant, but it was never home. How could it be? It was three hundred kilometres from the ocean.

Sebastien walked past the bar and stood in front of the photography shop where he still worked. "Cameras! Art! Portraits! Passports!" claimed the candy-striped awning above the door. Sebastien had advised against the reckless use of exclamation points, but Jérôme, the shop's owner, insisted on the "excitement" they evoked. Sebastien paused across the street, considering popping in to say hello, but decided against it and continued walking.

"A smart boy like you could work wherever you want," Ruby used to lecture him. "Why waste your life taking pictures of people in that shop? You should be famous."

"I could find a better job," he would respond with a shrug, "but that would probably mean moving to Montréal." That would be enough to shut her up. It was an empty threat, of course. He would never leave his mother behind.

Sebastien shoved his clenched fists into the pockets of his pants, letting the memory pass through him like a chilly wind.

He strolled along the same route he used to take when Sophie lived with her parents. The houses he passed increased in size and decreased in visibility, hiding behind impenetrable hedges and wastefully wide lawns, the closer he came to the Lamoureux family home. He marvelled at how little the neighbourhood had changed over the years. Its residents weren't known for embracing change.

The house stood at the end of a sloping street that wound its way through a grove of maple trees. He'd thought it was a castle on his first visit as a teenager. Its bay windows and broad balconies had intimidated him with their extravagance.

He climbed the steps of the veranda and pressed the doorbell. Sophie had claimed she simply wanted to cook him dinner for his birthday, but his stomach rumbled uneasily when her brother answered the door with an uncharacteristically warm smile. "Keep your shoes on," he said, leading Sebastien through the quiet house and into the glass solarium.

Sebastien jumped as he walked through the door amid the screams of "Surprise!" He stood there with his eyes wide, unsure of how to react, before turning to Sophie. She wore a floral dress and the pendant he'd given her once upon a time. Her hair was a cascade the colour of a robin's breast.

"What's going on?" he asked.

"Happy birthday!" she squealed with a smile as big and bright as the sun.

Dinner was served after cocktails. Sophie instructed Sebastien to sit at the head of the table beside her. He forced a smile as often as he could bear and laughed when everyone else laughed.

These weren't his friends, though. Most of them hadn't attended Ruby's memorial service. He doubted Jérôme had been invited. This wasn't his life they were celebrating. It was Sophie's party. Her touch was evident in every detail. He tried to fight the resentment that crept beneath his skin.

"You shouldn't have done this," he said in a hushed voice, his eyes fixed on his plate.

"Don't be silly." Sophie took a sip of wine, leaving a cranberry-coloured mark along the rim of the glass. She patted her lips with a napkin. "We always celebrate your birthday."

"You should've known I wouldn't want this."

Her hands fell into her lap, the napkin clutched between her fingers. "You've never been good at showing gratitude."

"It's just so soon."

She turned her chair to face him and reached beneath the table for his hand in one fluid motion.

"A little distraction is what you need right now," she said. "Remember what I told you on your twentieth birthday?"

"That was nine years ago, Soph."

"I said you could lock yourself in your room, or you could choose to move on. You'll get through this, too, but only if you get yourself out of your apartment."

It was a memory he preferred to forget. Now that it had surfaced, it was like an unreachable itch. He knew she was right, though. Locking himself in his room wouldn't be an option this time.

"Excuse me," he said, placing his napkin beside his plate. He could feel her watching as he made his way to the door of the solarium.

Sophie looked around the garden, feeling satisfied. The bubbly chatter and clinking of glasses felt like affirmation of the party's success.

When the chair at the head of the table remained empty ten minutes later, she started to worry. Another five minutes passed and she knew something was wrong. The caterers were clearing the dishes from the main course when she stepped into the house.

"Sebastien?" she called out, her voice echoing throughout the halls. Her heels clicked assertively on the hardwood as she checked the powder room. It was empty.

She searched every room on the main floor before she found the note pinned to the kitchen fridge by a magnet shaped like a seashell. The jagged handwriting was unmistakably his.

I'm sorry. I have to go. You won't see me
again for a while.

Civitavecchia
to
Athens

THREE

The Glacier

Seagulls soared overhead in undulating patterns. They would form perfect concentric circles, their outstretched wings frozen in the air, before darting across the sky in every direction. Of all the new things he had seen since leaving Petit Géant two months ago, these birds brought him the most joy.

The sun beat down on Civitavecchia, the clay-coloured port town outside Rome. Heavy beads of sweat made the journey from Sebastien's forehead to the base of his neck.

The dock was alive with the sights and sounds of the sea. Everyone moved with purpose. Sailors stamped out cigarettes and hurried across the concrete. Merchants sold balls of deep-fried dough to hungry travellers armed with suitcases with indestructible shells. Smoke and salt were infused in the air, but he liked the scent.

The hiking backpack he sat on was stuffed with almost everything he owned. An elegant woman in sunglasses dropped a handful of coins in the cap on the ground in front of him. He realized he looked like a beggar. "*Signora!*" he called out, wanting to return her money. She quickened her pace. He pocketed the change.

Fuelled by rage and a desperation to flee everything he knew, Sebastien had spent the last two months fixated on a plan. He had a purpose now. It brought him to Civitavecchia and, more specifically, to the *Glacier*.

It wasn't a real glacier, of course. It was a ship. Towering above him like a steel behemoth, its hull was white like snow. A thousand eyes stared down at him — panels of blue-tinted glass held in place by silver bolts. The ship exhaled a thin plume of smoke from the pyramid-shaped funnel at its summit several decks above him.

"Sebastien?" A woman in a turquoise pantsuit stepped off the gangplank that led to the ship's crew entrance. A silk scarf decorated with golden anchors was tied around her neck. It was his first time hearing a South African accent. "Sebastien Goo?"

He stood up and waved before slinging the heavy backpack over his shoulder. She smiled brightly as she approached, her heels unsteady on the concrete dock.

"It's Goh," he corrected her with a smile. "Like 'Go home.' Not Goo."

She held her palms to her chest with her mouth open, embarrassed. "I'm so sorry!"

Sebastien laughed. "It's fine. It happens all the time," he lied.

The woman introduced herself as Claudette, manager of the photography department. She led him up the gangplank into the belly of the ship. Two uniformed men in blue shirts and dark pants stood guard. One of them made small talk with Claudette while the other checked Sebastien's passport and employment papers. The guard handed back the documents and gave him a decisive nod.

"Thank you, sir," Sebastien said with an overly enthusiastic smile. The guard jerked his head in the direction of the metal detector beside him. An X-ray machine devoured the backpack before spitting it out on its conveyor-belt tongue.

"Why is this ship called the *Glacier*?" Sebastien asked, as he followed Claudette through a maze of steel corridors. "Seems like a strange name for a Greek ship sailing the Mediterranean."

"It used to do the Baltic route. I guess they didn't bother to rename it."

She stopped abruptly at a door painted the same ivory colour as the walls. "This is your cabin," she said as she knocked.

The door opened seconds later to reveal a man in his early thirties, wearing nothing but a pair of orange soccer shorts. A fresh layer of sweat coated the well-defined lines of his torso. His close-cropped hair was the colour of sand.

"And this," Claudette said, her cheeks blushing, "is your cabinmate."

"Welcome aboard!" The man took Sebastien's hand in a crushing grip. "I'm Ilya. Sorry for looking like such a beast. I was just doing a quick workout." He pivoted to grab a towel, revealing constellations of little round scars across the otherwise smooth skin of his back.

"I'll let you boys get acquainted," Claudette said. "Ilya, be a doll and give Sebastien a tour of the ship. Sebastien, I'll come by in three hours to brief you on your first assignment."

"My first assignment?"

"The captain's cocktail party. You'll be taking photos."

"Cocktail party?" Sebastien hadn't known what to expect on joining the staff of a ship, but he didn't imagine sipping a negroni with the captain.

Claudette let out a pretty laugh and looked at him as if he were a puppy learning to swim for the first time. "This is no oil tanker. This is the *Glacier*."

✦

The *Glacier* was a 90,000-ton floating hotel that offered guests the same grandeur they'd expect to find in any European capital. "It's a luxury liner, not a cruise ship," Ilya explained an hour later as they marched through the winding passageways of the staff quarters. "At least that's what they want us to call it. *Cruise ship* is a dirty word here. It's more or less a cruise ship, though, but with a superiority complex."

The two men were dressed in identical uniforms the staff members wore while visiting the upper decks of the guest quarters. The gold buttons on the turquoise blazers were embellished with anchors. Their white pants had perfect creases ironed down the fronts. Sebastien tugged at the collar of his shirt. He wasn't used to being strangled by a necktie.

A gold badge was pinned to the lapel of each jacket. His cabinmate's badge said:

Ilya Tereshchenko
Fitness Trainer
Ukraine

He glanced down at his own badge.

Sebastien Goh
Photographer
Canada

Ilya strolled through the corridors like he owned the ship, explaining every stop along the tour with the flair of a maestro. He seemed to know everyone they passed, swapping smiles and air kisses.

"We call this Styx," Ilya explained, sweeping his arms outward as though revealing the grand prize of a game show. The wide passageway was the main artery in the lower decks of the staff quarters, stretching from one end of the ship to the other. "There are seventeen decks on the *Glacier*. The top fourteen are where paying guests wine, dine, and sun themselves into a stupor. The bottom three are where staff and crew live. These lower decks we call Hades — the underworld. Styx is the river that runs through it. In Greek mythology, the newly dead are ferried down the River Styx but only if you've paid the toll."

The *Glacier's* version of the River Styx was a social hub for the ship's staff and crew. There was the cafeteria ("The food isn't too bad, if you're a zoo animal"), the staff bar ("The crew bar on C Deck usually gets wilder"), the staff purser's office ("Uma will be your favourite person. She's the one who pays us in cold, hard cash"), the computer lounge ("Since they installed Wi-Fi everywhere, nobody goes here except for the Filipino Mafia"), and the medical clinic ("As many free condoms as you need!").

Over a thousand people worked aboard the *Glacier*. They lived on the three lower decks of Hades, ordered by the ship's strict social hierarchy.

Located just below guest quarters was A Deck, where the ship's white-suited officers lived. An exclusive wing near the stern was home to the captain and his commanders. If the officers were the upper crust of *Glacier* society, the commanders would be the aristocracy. "You need a special key card to enter, unless you make friends with one of them," Ilya said with a mischievous twinkle in his eyes. "Their cabins are much nicer than ours. They don't have to share with a mate. They have portholes so they can look outside and not feel like they're rotting inside a coffin. There's even carpet!"

Directly below the officers was B Deck, home of Styx and all members of staff, including Ilya and Sebastien. This was the realm of the turquoise-suited middle class comprised of people holding titles deemed respectable, such as massage therapist and art auctioneer. They generally came from wealthier countries. "As staff, we get more privileges than crew. We can hang out in the guest areas when we're off duty as long as we're dressed appropriately and wearing our name badges. Crew aren't allowed to do that. We can go to the crew bar, but crew can't enter the staff bar. Class division is a cruel reality here, I'm afraid. It's sickening, but I guess we're the lucky ones."

Near the bottom of the ship were the crew quarters of C Deck. This was for the lower class of servers, cooks, bartenders, housekeepers, and deck cleaners. Most of them came from countries in Asia and Eastern Europe. "They work longer hours and get paid worse than staff. Plus, guests and officers treat them like servants." Ilya shook his head in disgust. "Most have families back home. The money here is better than it is there. They deserve more respect."

"It sounds a lot like the real world," Sebastien said with a shrug.

"You're wrong, my friend." A devilish smile returned to Ilya's lips. "This is as far from the real world as you can get."

After Claudette rattled off instructions for Sebastien's role in the evening's festivities, she hurried away down the corridor. "Don't be late!" she called out, wearing a fitted gown that seemed out of place in the stark surroundings of the staff quarters.

"Ready to see the world above Hades?" Ilya asked, adjusting Sebastien's necktie.

They went up a set of stairs and stepped through a nondescript door. There was no doubt they were now in a part of the ship designed for the guests. Even the air felt cleaner and cooled to the perfect temperature.

In contrast to the utilitarian aesthetic of the decks below, the setting was opulent. The soles of their shoes sounded more dignified against the marble floor. The richly upholstered lounge chairs looked more comfortable than their cabin beds. Windows stretched from floor to ceiling to reveal the indigo sea outside. The ship's forward motion cut across the surface of the water, creating waves that rippled toward the edge of the earth.

"What's with these statues?" asked Sebastien, examining a life-sized replica of a Greek sculpture. It was a man with blank, pupil-less eyes and a calm expression on his face. Every muscle of his nude body was flexed to flaunt his physique, although his manhood was nothing to brag about. Similar statues of ancient Greek men and women were lined along the hall. The unusual thing about these sculptures was that they were covered in a translucent blue glaze.

"They're frozen," Ilya said. "We're on the *Glacier*. Get it?"

"Clever."

"You'll see this classical-ice-age motif all over the ship. The *Glacier* is owned by one of the richest shipping families in

Greece. This was their attempt at making the country's heritage relevant in the Baltic. I suppose it's better than ancient Greece post–climate apocalypse."

"They'd have to change the name from *Glacier* to *Puddle*."

"Dork," Ilya said with a laugh.

Sebastien couldn't hide how awestruck he was when they reached the atrium. The entire centre of the ship was hollowed out so that, looking up, he could see the twilight sky beyond the glass ceiling dozens of metres above. All of the interior guest decks had open terraces with lounges and gardens that hung overhead. Two elevators travelled through glass tunnels from top to bottom. He'd never seen anything like it.

The Agora was the ship's central lobby at the base of the atrium. Guests in evening wear sipped cocktails in the lobby bar. A tuxedoed man charmed the keys of a grand piano while a voluptuous chanteuse serenaded the room in front of a vintage microphone, the kind Marilyn Monroe held to sing "Happy Birthday" to the president. An impressive Y-shaped staircase led to Adriatic Deck's circular balcony above the Agora, where Sebastien and Ilya stood.

"We're not in Hades anymore," Sebastien said, turning to Ilya.

"Don't be fooled. They're mere mortals like us."

❖

The captain's cocktail party was always held on the first night of a new sailing, known as embarkation day. It was the only social event at which the ship's reclusive captain would be expected to make an appearance, albeit briefly and begrudgingly. The *Glacier* had sailed away from Civitavecchia to begin an eighteen-day circuit around the western Mediterranean. After returning to Italy, it would carry on eastward to Greece.

Various venues throughout the ship were used to host the welcome-aboard event. That evening it was in the Odeon, a cavernous theatre that dominated the forward end of the guest quarters. A chandelier hung from the ceiling like an array of icicles, a senseless design choice given how precariously it swayed whenever the ship listed. The orchestra level and balcony were lined with rows of plush turquoise seats.

Sandwiched between these two levels and almost parallel to the stage sat the mezzanine, the centre of the party. Sculptures and leafy plants were scattered throughout the open space. The backlit bars that lined the perimeter were already crowded with people impatient with thirst.

"Thank you kindly," Ilya said with a smile as he snatched two flutes of prosecco from a tray held by a waiter. He clinked the glasses together before handing one to Sebastien. "*Yamas!*"

"I'm on duty."

"You're taking photos of drunk people. You should blend in."

Claudette's instructions were to get guests to pose for photos they could purchase later at the portrait gallery above the Agora. It wasn't difficult. All he had to do was hold up his camera, and people would eagerly get into position, baring their bleached teeth and thrusting glasses in the air.

It was easy to spot the staff members who had the privilege of enjoying the party. Generally younger than the well-heeled guests, they also wore name badges like the one pinned to Sebastien's blazer.

The officers looked elite in their formal uniforms of collared shirts and jackets studded with gold buttons. Every article of clothing on their bodies was a brilliant shade of white. Their shoulders were adorned with black epaulets that proudly, or not so proudly, displayed their rank with golden stripes. Four stripes were worn only by the captain, and the number descended from there. The guests were drawn to the uniforms like flies to honey, eager to shake hands and have their photographs taken with these alluring men of the sea. The officers themselves seemed bored, clustering together so they could sip their drinks in peace.

"They're all Greek," Ilya said under his breath as he gestured to the officers, "and take themselves far too seriously."

One of the younger officers walked by, eyeing them with suspicion and curiosity. He strutted across the room with curt, confident steps, yet the effect was self-conscious, as though he were trying to prove something. His chest was held outward a touch too proudly, his chin a degree too high.

"Nikos Antonopolous," Ilya said. "Deputy security commander. Thinks he's hot shit because he has two stripes and gets to bark orders at the security guards like they're a pack of dogs. I don't think I've ever seen him smile. Also, a total closet case."

"Really?"

"Don't be fooled by the macho exterior. He got drunk once in the crew bar and tried bringing me back to his cabin. I politely declined. He's had it out for me ever since."

Nikos stood at the other side of the room flanked by fellow officers. Sebastien caught him glancing back at them.

"You weren't interested?"

Ilya laughed. "Interested? Sure. But men like that aren't allowed to like other men. I didn't leave homo-hating Ukraine to hook up with guys like Nikos. He's a classic Greek tragedy."

When he was sure Nikos was no longer looking their way, Sebastien held the camera to his eye and pointed it in his direction. The viewfinder displayed a blur of white and gold. With a twist of the ring around the lens, the brooding features of the man's face came into focus. Sebastien froze.

Standing beside Nikos was a man telling a story. His hands waved in the air as everyone around him listened intently. There were three golden stripes on the epaulets of his white uniform. He looked to be in his midfifties, but there was a youthful vanity about him. Neither tall nor large, he held himself proudly with a set of square shoulders. A thick tangle of hair rippled from his angular face, unnaturally black and hardened in waves. His story seemed to reach its climax, and he laughed. Sebastien could hear it clearly from across the room. The man laughed thunderously until there were tears in his eyes.

It was his father.

"Are you okay?" Ilya put his hand on his cabinmate's shoulder and gave him a little shake.

"Who's that man?" Sebastien asked, shuffling behind a sculpture of a frozen Greek Olympian holding a discus. "The older one with the three stripes?"

Ilya poked his head out from their hiding spot to get a better look. "That's Kostas, the hotel commander. He's basically the top boss, besides the captain, of course. The captain's usually holed up in Olympus — that's what we call the navigation bridge — and Kostas runs the show down here. Most of the staff and crew ladder up to him."

"What's he like?"

Ilya shrugged. "He's what you'd get if you mashed together Santa Claus and George Clooney, with a dash of Genghis Khan. He can be charming but then turn in the blink of an eye. I only know this because he attends my kickboxing class twice a week. He surrounds himself with his white-suited cronies and doesn't mingle with the commoners. You'd be better off with him not knowing your name."

"Who's he with?" Sebastien pointed his head discreetly toward another middle-aged officer standing beside Kostas. The man was slimmer and several inches taller. A humourless expression was his face's default. Even when he smiled, his mouth simply lengthened horizontally instead of curving upward. Like Kostas, he wore three stripes on his uniform.

"That's Giorgos, the deck commander. Engineers, officers — all the technical people we need to actually sail the ship — they report to him. He doesn't talk much. As much fun as a bag of sand."

Ilya looked puzzled as Sebastien started to walk away. "Where are you going?"

He held up the camera. "I'm going to meet them."

The clamour of the party dissolved into a hallucinatory fog. Sebastien's legs went numb as they pulled him forward, through the hazards of the crowd, to his father.

This is it.

He swallowed the rage that was creeping up his esophagus until it was safely hidden beneath the ribcage. His pace slowed as his head felt light. His eyes were fixated on the smile on his father's cleanly shaven face. It was the same face he'd studied over the years from the safety of his bedroom, the same face that would visit him in his sleep.

Seeing Kostas Kourakis in a three-dimensional form, moving and talking like a sentient being, meant that Sebastien would have to give up control. His father could no longer continue existing as a property of his imagination.

Sebastien stood paralyzed in the middle of the mezzanine floor, surrounded by the man's voice from six metres away. He was so close, but his consciousness was dimming. The collar of his shirt tightened around his neck.

Tearing his gaze away, he pivoted and collided with a waiter. A silver tray fell to the floor with a loud clatter, spilling several glasses of orange liquid all over Nikos and his crisp white suit.

"*Gamóto!*" the young security commander wailed. The sound of shattering glass followed like exclamation points.

"I'm so sorry," the waiter said, horrified. Nikos fumed, but he didn't say another word. His accusing eyes shot to the waiter, then Sebastien, before he stormed off toward the exit.

"Nikos, relax! It was an accident!" Kostas called out to him.

Sebastien couldn't help glancing in the man's direction. Their eyes met, and for a second he couldn't look away. An unsettling current passed through his body, and he wondered if his father felt it, too. With a shake of the head, he overcame the paralysis and made his retreat.

❖

The blood rushed through his veins like a geyser through a pipe. He felt so alert he was dizzy.

Ilya was recounting the entire scene that had ended in Nikos becoming a human dishcloth, but Sebastien couldn't focus on the words. The carpet swayed beneath their feet as they left the Odeon and entered the casino.

The flashing lights and dinging noises made his head feel like it was going to erupt. The slot machines sounded like hammers crushing carnival lights and police sirens.

"I need some water," he said, interrupting Ilya as he was describing the look on Nikos's face.

A raised lounge overlooked the gaming tables from the centre of the casino floor. It was styled like a circular temple, complete with Ionic columns that stretched up to the ceiling. Sebastien thanked the bartender as he reached for the glass.

"Are you okay?" Ilya asked, watching his cabinmate down the contents of the glass in a single swallow.

They perched themselves at a counter facing the casino floor. Sebastien wiped his lips with the sleeve of his turquoise blazer. "I'm good now. My head just hurts. That's all."

"I read somewhere that nine out of ten headaches are caused by dehydration," said a petite woman seated beside him at the counter. Like the rest of the casino staff, she wore a button-up vest over an emerald-green shirt. Her hair was pulled up into a bundle of dark curls. Wisps of steam rose from the mug in her hands.

"I guess I chose the right remedy." Sebastien smiled as he held up the empty glass. He glanced at the badge pinned to her vest.

Diya Sharma
Gaming Attendant
India

"Meet my newest cabinmate," Ilya said to the woman. "Sebastien, this is Diya. She's the queen of blackjack."

"I hope you're saner than Ilya's last cabinmate," she said, shaking Sebastien's hand.

Ilya groaned. "Let's not think about him."

A flash of white caught Sebastien's eye. Three officers entered the casino from the hall that led to the theatre. In the middle was Giorgos, the deck commander with the unsmiling face. He sauntered past the blinking lights and crowded tables at an arrogant pace, slow enough to make clear he had the authority to simply be present and supervise.

Giorgos halted at the roulette wheel, and his eyes drifted toward the bar. Sebastien thought the commander was looking at him before he realized the attention was on the woman by his side. Giorgos and Diya glared at each other across the casino. She turned away.

"I need to get back on the floor," she said. Her face, which had appeared tired but kind a second earlier, was now alert and tense.

"It was nice to meet you," Sebastien said with a wave.

She gave him a hurried kiss on the cheek. "Welcome aboard."

❖

Relief swept over Sebastien like a breeze as they descended the stairs into the underworld. As glamorous as it was on the passenger decks above, he didn't belong there. It was all smoke and mirrors. Fake statues. Warm champagne. Everyone on their best behaviour.

There were no forced smiles here in the lower decks of Hades. It wasn't pretty, but it was real.

"Are you ready for our final stop of the evening?" Ilya asked, with a devilish look in his eyes.

"As long as it involves a cold beer."

They followed the stairs past the staff quarters to C Deck, where the less-privileged crew called home. A steady bassline reverberated throughout the narrow corridors. Ilya led him through a door with a sign that declared the location in twisted tubes of neon light: Crew Bar.

The crowded room was dimly lit and filled with smoke. Sebastien thought something must have caught on fire before he realized the only thing burning was a battalion of ciga-rettes. A man with locs piled high on his head stood behind a DJ booth as reggae blasted through the speakers.

"This place is ours," Ilya shouted as he made his way through the crowd, kissing cheeks and waving to calls of his name. "On the upper decks we're squeaky clean. Wholesome, even. It's all a show for the guests. It's what they pay good money for. They want to talk to us. Flirt with us. Fuck us. Abuse us. All we can do is smile. But down here, this is where we remember who we are."

A slender man in a nude-coloured leotard approached. His skin was flawless, but he looked like a stylized raccoon with dark makeup around his eyes. The man and Ilya leaned in to kiss each other on the cheek, but their lips manoeuvred to meet at the last second. The man's hands disappeared beneath Ilya's turquoise blazer before their bodies drifted apart. He didn't say a word as he vanished into the smoke.

"He's one of the dancers who perform in the theatre," Ilya explained. "Very friendly."

It wasn't hard to notice the attention Sebastien was attracting as they made their way to the bar. Eyes darted in his direction. Mouths came up for air from their glasses. Voices lowered mid-conversation.

"You're fresh meat," Ilya said. "Enjoy it while you can. You won't be fresh for long."

Seated throughout the crew bar were the various tribes of the underworld. It was the one place on board where it didn't matter if you were crew or staff or officer. The rigid rules of *Glacier* society were loosened by free-flowing liquor and the human need to connect. Although the tribes intermingled, most didn't stray too far from their distinctive circles.

There were the dancers — beautiful creatures who were

treated like celebrities. They wore the same costumes they performed in during the captain's cocktail party, mostly feathers and sequins and skin. Ilya's friend in the leotard seemed to have more than one person to warm his hands. "The dancers are a lot of fun, but they're full of drama," Ilya said with a shake of the head. "They also survive on a diet of vodka and avocado. I see them in the gym every day. If they gain more than ten pounds, they're gone."

The cleaning crew dominated the area of the bar with the foosball tables. They cheered loudly as they played, spinning the rods as though they were on *Wheel of Fortune.* "We call them the Filipino Mafia. They run an entire black market of pills, drugs, whatever you want. They'll also cut your hair for ten euros." He pointed to his own head. "Not bad, huh?"

Members of the spa team clustered on couches in the corner. Made up of massage therapists, beauticians, naturopaths, and fitness trainers like Ilya, they were mostly young and less cynical than the rest of the staff. "They have the best stories, if you ask me. The things they see in those treatment rooms ..."

They settled into an area filled with a mix of others — entertainers, shop attendants, shore excursion guides, even a tailor. Claudette, Sebastien's South African boss with the pretty laugh, was chain-smoking while a bartender who appeared to be ten years younger gently kissed the side of her neck.

"I know it's only your first day, but does anyone catch your eye?" Ilya asked. "What do you like? Ladies? Lads?"

Sebastien laughed. Subtlety wasn't Ilya's strong suit. "I'm open to anything, really," he answered. "I don't usually know what I like until I see it."

He sat back and surveyed the room. He saw a piece of himself in everyone there. The lives they left behind weren't good enough. They came from different parts of the world, each of them with a different story, but something common brought them here to this ship. Together, they formed a family of outsiders. They found refuge from reality in the middle of the sea.

A mob of white entered the bar. Among the six officers, Nikos was the only one not in uniform. He wore slim black pants and a loose green sweatshirt. He no longer looked untouchable.

"And the *malákas* have arrived," Ilya muttered into his ear. "That's what we call the officers — *malákas*. I think it means *jerk-off* in Greek."

"They can't all be that bad."

"They're not. But they're not all that good, either."

The crowd parted to make way for Nikos and the five others. Sebastien watched as they ordered a round of beers from the bar. With bottles in hand, they huddled around a high-top table against the wall.

"I'll be back," Sebastien said before being swallowed by the dense crowd. The officers were clearly surprised as he joined them at their table a few minutes later holding two bottles of beer. The conversation they were having went quiet. Nikos examined him with the same combination of curiosity and suspicion he'd shown earlier.

"Sorry to interrupt," Sebastien said. "Nikos, I just want to apologize for what happened upstairs. I didn't mean to bump into that waiter."

The young commander cocked his head to the side but remained silent. The other officers continued to stare, not knowing what to make of this stranger's brazen interruption.

Sebastien held one of the bottles above his head. Without a word, he tilted it toward himself and let the frothy liquid pour over his hair. It spilled down his face and onto his chest, soaking his shirt and blazer. He placed the other bottle on the table and pushed it toward Nikos. He looked into the amber eyes as he held out his hand.

"Now we're even."

No one moved. They stared at Sebastien while his arm hovered above the table. After a heavy silence, Nikos's lips curled upward in a reluctant smile. An abrupt laugh escaped him, and soon the other officers were laughing. He grabbed hold of Sebastien's hand and gave him a slight nod.

Ilya looked dumbstruck when Sebastien returned to his side, dripping beer. "What the hell was that?"

Sebastien wiped his face with a paper napkin and squeezed it over the empty glass in his cabinmate's hand. "You'll see," he said. "I have a feeling that man is going to be useful."

FOUR

Bang Bang

The *Glacier* sailed steadily to the island of Sicily. Two weeks had passed since Sebastien walked up the gangplank from the clay-coloured port of Civitavecchia, and he was getting into the swing of his new life at sea. Even the unsteadiness of the swaying floor beneath his feet no longer fazed him. He preferred the constant motion over the rooted inertia of Petit Géant.

Most mornings would introduce a different port, storied places like Barcelona and Málaga. He would take the elevator all the way to the open-air Sunset Deck where he could admire each new destination. Every morning brought a different view, just as he had dreamed as a child. There were sandy coves and hills cloaked in mist, cities with earthen rooftops and gleaming towers of glass.

Despite the ship's perpetual motion, most days followed the same routine. Breakfast would be served in the cafeteria. Staff would head into port to explore while crew would remain on board to clean cabins, scrub decks, and prepare for the evening's festivities. The *Glacier* would set sail just before sunset. Once the horn sounded from the pyramid-shaped funnel, staff would be on duty to entertain the guests as the ship came alive again.

The evening sun flooded the atrium with honey-coloured light. Sebastien's photo station was set up on the Adriatic Deck balcony overlooking the Agora lobby one level below. It was filled with music and chatter, but the lounges began to empty as people made their way to the dining hall for the late seating.

Guests had two options for having their photos taken. They could pose in front of the balcony with the atrium unfolding behind them, or they could choose from a selection of canvas backdrops. One depicted a stereotypical Greek island scene, complete with whitewashed walls and pink bougainvillea. Another was a night-time view of Athens with the Acropolis lit up like a birthday cake. The most popular backdrop was the open sea with the *Glacier* floating in the distance. Sebastien was surprised by how many people opted for a fake view over the real one.

"Smile!" he said, snapping a large Italian couple in front of their chosen backdrop — sunset over Santorini, another favourite. There was no one else waiting in the queue, so Sebastien was relieved to see the couple hurry off to dinner.

He leaned over the balustrade and observed the Agora below. It was quieter now, but a few dozen guests from the early dinner seating were scattered throughout the lounge.

The laugh was instantly recognizable as it echoed across the atrium. He followed the sound to see his father standing on the other side of the circular balcony. Giorgos stood there, too, his stern face an odd contrast to Kostas's cheerful smile.

Sebastien lifted the camera to his eye, adjusting the lens to home in on the two commanders, like the crosshairs of a rifle.

He pressed the trigger.

Bang.

Bang.

He kept his eyes fixed on his targets as he crossed the deck to the other side of the balcony. They stood at the railing beside fan-shaped plants in a cauldron-sized pot. He crept behind the foliage until he could hear the men's voices. They were too focused on their conversation to notice him.

"We need to deal with him," Giorgos said, his voice taut as a violin string.

"He doesn't know anything," Kostas said. "He's a harmless cabin cleaner. What could he possibly do?"

"He could tell someone."

"Then what?" Kostas's tone was tinged with impatience. "Who would believe him?"

The men were silent as two guests in evening gowns walked past.

"We need to be more careful," Giorgos said moments later, his voice quieter.

"What do you propose we do? Throw him overboard?" Kostas laughed so abruptly that Sebastien bolted upright at the sound.

The two commanders made their way to the grand staircase that led to the Agora below. Sebastien gripped his camera as he followed several paces behind. They lowered their voices, and he could no longer hear what they were saying.

A quartet of jazz musicians played from a circular stage in the middle of the lobby bar. The wail of the saxophone and rattle of the drum drowned out other sounds.

Kostas and Giorgos paused on the landing where the three flights of stairs converged. With his gaze distracted by the two men, Sebastien's feet flew out from under him as he slipped on the top step. Panicked, his hands reached for the railing but grabbed only air. He tumbled down the staircase, an avalanche of limbs, before crashing on the landing in a heap.

It took him a moment to realize that the white objects beside his head were shoes. Dazed, he looked up to see the faces of the two commanding officers. The atrium's glass ceiling hovered high above them.

"Are you okay, young man?" There was concern in the creases around his father's eyes.

No words came to Sebastien, but he held their outstretched arms as they helped him to his feet. Several guests stifled laughs in the lobby bar, but he barely noticed them.

"That was quite the fall," Kostas said. He smiled, but it was more friendly than mocking.

"I'm not known for my grace," Sebastien said, adjusting his uniform. It was true, despite his athletic prowess. His mind tended to focus on one thing at a time, and it was often out of sync with his restless body. He had been clumsy ever since he was a child.

Giorgos displayed no emotion as he examined the stranger, but Kostas chuckled warmly.

"I'm no gazelle myself," his father replied. "Watch out for these slippery floors. They can be deadly."

"I will." He paused. "Thank you."

Sebastien turned to walk away when Kostas stopped him. "You're new, aren't you?"

"I started two weeks ago. I'm a photographer." He held up the camera that was loosely strapped around his neck, hoping it was still intact.

"It's good to have you aboard."

It's good to be here, Father.

It was clear he didn't realize who Sebastien was. There was no glint of recognition in his eyes. Kostas would never guess that this young man could be his son because it had never been important to him. Ruby and her unborn child were just a forgotten part of his past, something unfortunate and insignificant that happened many years ago.

Sebastien didn't want him to know — not yet. It wasn't the right time. He had even considered changing his surname before coming on board to avoid the risk of it giving him away. Now he could see he had nothing to fear.

Even so, Sebastien hadn't been prepared for Kostas to be kind. This development agitated him. He used to have complete control over his perception of his father. His imagination had assigned a personality riddled with flaws and failings. Kindness hadn't been one of them.

"It's good to be here, sir."

He noticed for the first time what looked like a scar that began at the base of his father's forehead. The jagged seam of skin trailed above his right ear before disappearing behind thick waves of hair. Sebastien found it strangely comforting. It was a reminder of how much there was to uncover about this man.

"Since you're here, why don't you take our photo?" Kostas suggested.

"Absolutely." Sebastien held the camera to his eye, framing the two commanders with the Agora behind them. One man beamed while the other stood begrudgingly, but there was one thing they shared, something Sebastien hadn't possessed in a long time. It was conspicuous in the way they held their shoulders and tilted their chins.

Pride.

❖

The darkness of the cabin wrapped around Sebastien while he lay in his bottom bunk. He listened to the rhythmic breathing of Ilya, a man easily seduced by sleep. It sounded like a whistle caught in the wind.

There was a reason there were no windows in the staff quarters. B Deck was the second-lowest level of the ship, so the view would have been like looking through the glass door of a washing machine. The officers on A Deck had the privilege of living above sea level.

Sebastien didn't mind the confinement. It reminded him of his bedroom closet thousands of kilometres away, a protective cocoon. The darkness also helped him sleep more easily, though tonight was different.

He pictured his father's smiling face every time he closed his eyes. An instance of kindness was far from enough to forgive that man — hatred still simmered inside Sebastien like hot oil — but it was an unexpected crack in the image he had sculpted over the years.

Numbed by the spinning thoughts, he rubbed his face with his palms before reaching for his phone. Blue light washed over the space around his bunk. There was one new message from Sophie. His thumb hovered over the screen, a curious hesitation, before he decided to read what she had to say.

It was nearly identical to her previous messages, filled with "I wish" and "why can't you." He had sent her a brief response when he first landed in Europe, confirming that he was fine and she had nothing to worry about. He had been vague about the details. This was his burden to carry, not hers.

Guilt pecked at him for leaving his birthday dinner so abruptly three months earlier, although a part of him also felt justified. In the end, he was grateful for what Sophie had done. She had convinced him, in her own indirect way, to take control. Just as she had said, he wasn't going to achieve anything locked inside his apartment. She had a way of giving him what he needed. It was a power she had always possessed.

The screen went dark as the phone shut off. He was half a world away from Petit Géant, and he wanted to keep it that way. Thinking about Sophie brought him closer to that cruel town and the memories that lived there.

His mother gave him a disapproving look from the picture frame on the desk beside his bunk. He could see it despite the darkness. The photo had been one of her favourites. She was as young as Sebastien remembered her being, her long hair blowing loosely in the wind.

"Don't look at me like that," he said in a whisper that was barely audible. "I'm here because of you."

The cabin walls creaked as the waves battered the hull outside. The sounds echoed throughout the ship as though it were hollow.

❖

When Sophie and Sebastien were eighteen and still fumbling their way toward love, they convinced their parents to come together for dinner.

The Lamoureux and Goh families held positions on opposite poles of the town's social sphere. Marcel and Marie

Lamoureux knew Ruby as the single mother who cleaned their friends' houses and worked as a cashier at the Prix-Mart. They didn't approve of their daughter's new friendship with this woman's son, but they didn't see themselves as the kind of people who would forbid their children from associating with those they held in lower esteem.

The dinner was Sophie's idea, of course. Sebastien knew what her family thought of him and his mother. A dinner party wasn't going to change that.

Ruby fussed over what to wear for days. "What do people like that wear to dinner?" she had asked as though Sebastien would know. She ended up choosing her favourite dress — a cheap replica of a traditional Chinese silk cheongsam that was red with gold trim.

It was her first time in the Lamoureux family house, the largest in town. She was uncomfortable, dishing out more compliments than were needed. "What do you call these beautiful things?" she said at one point, referring to the drapes that framed the windows. Sebastien found himself embarrassed by how visibly impressed she was by things that were ordinary to everyone else.

Sophie had spent the entire day cooking a three-course meal. The table was elaborately set. Her mother would correct them whenever they picked up the wrong piece of cutlery. "There are so many forks and spoons," Ruby said with a nervous laugh.

Partway through the meal, Sophie's father boasted about his daughter's prospects after graduation. "She's narrowed it down to two schools, but she really could go anywhere she wants. What about you, Sebastien? What are your plans for university?"

Sebastien looked across the table at Marcel, knowing he was aware of the answer. "I won't be able to afford it. And I don't like the idea of taking out a loan. I'm going to apply for a few scholarships and hope for the best."

"Hope for the best," Marcel repeated before taking a sip of his wine. "What about you, Ruby? Where did you study?"

She blushed and shook her head. "I was never the school type."

"The school type." He let the words linger in the air. Sophie shot him a disapproving look but kept her mouth closed as she chewed.

"How old were you when you gave birth to Sebastien?" Sophie's mother chimed in.

"Twenty-three."

"So young." She looked around the table with a sympathetic expression. "It must have been very hard for you, raising him all by yourself."

"Yes. It was hard." Ruby looked down at her plate. She didn't know what she was eating.

When they returned to their apartment after dinner, Ruby kissed him good night and went straight to her room. She sobbed quietly, trying to stifle the sound, but he could hear it through the wall.

His face was hot as he lay in bed, agitated by how casual the condescension had been during dinner. It seemed like the evening was designed to emphasize the absurdity of the Lamoureux and Goh families sharing a meal together. He'd been prepared for pity, suspecting that Marcel and Marie viewed the invitation as an act of charity, but he hadn't expected cruelty.

There was something else pressing against the inside of his skull, something stronger. He didn't want to feel this way about himself, but it was undeniable.

Shame.

FIVE

Better Odds

"How do I look?"

Ilya examined his cabinmate with a discriminating eye. A white bedsheet was pinned around Sebastien's waist and slung over one shoulder like a sash. A handmade crown of leafy twigs was embedded into the curls of his hair. Holding a plastic trident on loan from the theatre's prop storeroom, he spun around in the centre of their cabin so Ilya could view all angles.

"Like a god," Ilya said. "What about me?"

He wore a pleated white skirt that ended at the thigh, borrowed from one of the dancers and belted by a thick band of leather. The only article of clothing above his waist was a red cape tied around his neck by a golden tassel.

"Like a stripper."

Sebastien laughed as Ilya punched him playfully in the stomach.

They had spent the day exploring the ancient city of Palermo before returning to the ship to cobble together their last-minute costumes. The *Glacier* sailed eastward from the island of Sicily. It would take two full days at sea before they reached Athens, completing the eighteen-day circuit around the western Mediterranean. Once there, two thousand new guests would board for the next sailing.

Days at sea were gruelling for the staff and crew. They meant longer hours, irritable guests, and a heightened sense of captivity. With two full sea days ahead, the most reliable way of keeping the residents of Hades from descending into madness was throwing a party.

In contrast to the stuffy events that were held for guests on the upper decks, these gatherings were characterized by debauchery. The staff and crew's preferred method of letting off steam involved outrageous costumes, shots of ouzo, and risky sexual behaviour.

The crew bar that evening was transformed into a nightclub version of Mount Olympus. Flowing white curtains were draped over Ionic columns. Vines spilled out of baskets hung from the ceiling. A thin layer of artificial fog floated through the room. The decorations were borrowed from the set of the theatre's upcoming production, a modernized retelling of Homer's *Odyssey*.

Dominating an entire wall was a gigantic mural of Zeus holding a jagged bolt of lightning. The theme for the evening was plastered across it in glittery paint: Gods & Goddesses.

Sebastien and Ilya arrived as convincing versions of Poseidon and Heracles, impressive considering the little time they'd given themselves to prepare. The crowd in the crew bar displayed similar combinations of sheets and skin.

"He's wearing even less clothing than you are," Sebastien said to Ilya, pointing to a minotaur in a fur loincloth. "Unless you count the horns on his head."

"We'll see who's more naked by the end of the night," Ilya said with a smirk.

A striking woman sang from a pedestal against the far wall while her Grecian gown billowed around her body. The alluring voice permeated the crowd like humidity. Sebastien knew her only by reputation. Contessa Bloor was the ship's star. She performed five nights a week in front of crowds eager to give her standing ovations. Radiant as Medusa, her hair was braided elaborately around golden snakes.

Kostas and his officers were clustered in front of the stage. They often came to these parties to partake in the hedonism rather than to police it. It was in their interest to allow the crew this outlet for their angst, to keep them pacified. The officers never dressed up for the parties — they didn't want anyone forgetting who was in charge — though their uniforms were less conspicuous than usual given the profusion of white throughout the room.

Sebastien stared at the uniformed men on the far side of the bar. "Grab me a beer, will you? I'll be right back."

"As you wish, master," Ilya said with a theatrical bow.

Contessa's song came to an end, and the officers cheered loudly from the base of the stage — all but Giorgos. He stood with his arms crossed over his chest and eyes fixed intensely on the woman in the spotlight.

Sebastien weaved through the sea of togas toward the stage. He hadn't seen his father since the previous night, when he'd tumbled down the staircase in the atrium. Now that the initial contact had been made, he felt bolder. This could be another chance to speak with him. It was a party, after all.

Kostas stood near the centre of the white-suited crowd, the gold stripes on his shoulders glinting beneath the spot-lights aimed at Contessa. Sebastien couldn't get a good view through the mob of officers, but he'd already learned to recognize the shape of his father's hair and the proud angles of the man's stance. Standing at the edge of the crowd, he watched as Kostas pulled aside a younger officer. They retreated to a quieter, darker corner of the party. Sebastien followed close behind, trying to be discreet, despite apologizing for every jostled shoulder and stomped foot.

He sidled along the wall, stationing himself at a high-top table where he could hear his father's voice. It was more hushed than usual, though still heavy with authority.

Sebastien cursed under his breath when he realized he didn't understand their words. They were speaking Greek. It looked like Kostas was delivering orders of some kind, but the younger officer's narrowed eyes and tight lips hinted reluc-tance. The two men looked in the same direction, trying to spot something, or someone, in the crowded room.

They turned to face each other. Sebastien watched as Kostas reached inside his white jacket, retrieving what looked like a small paper envelope. The younger officer hesitated before accepting it and shoving it into his pants' pocket. Kostas said a few brusque words, gave him a nod, and disap-peared into the crowd.

Sebastien didn't know what he had just seen, but the offi-cer didn't seem pleased. His thick brows pulled toward each other above eyes that couldn't stop darting from side to side. He coughed into a closed fist, then headed through the mass of bodies.

The air was dense with artificial fog and cigarette smoke as Sebastien followed the officer's close-cropped hair. Contessa's voice boomed through the speakers, this song livelier than the last. The dance floor was a blur of skin and loosening fabric that pulsated to the beat of the music.

The young officer reached a counter slick with spilled liquid. Glasses went up and down in an endless choreography of flexing arms. He prowled over to a group from the cabin-cleaning crew. They had their backs to the officer, laughing and shouting while one of them told a story with erratic hand movements.

Clearly nervous, the officer leaned against the counter in a pose that was meant to appear casual. With a quick scan around and a shake of the wrist, he emptied the contents of the little envelope into a glass filled with clear liquid. The powder formed a white cloud before dissolving into nothing. He buried his hands in his pockets and slunk away.

We need to deal with him.

The words Sebastien had overheard Giorgos speak the previous night echoed through his memory. Recalling Kostas's response sent a shiver along his skin.

What do you propose we do? Throw him overboard?

One of the Filipino men in the group reached for the glass with the invisible substance. His hair was styled like Elvis Presley's from the 1950s. The top three buttons of his linen shirt were undone, revealing a small gold crucifix that dangled from a thin chain around his neck.

Sebastien hurried over to him. "Hey, buddy!" he said loudly, locking their hands together. He smiled widely and lowered his voice. "Just pretend you know who I am."

The man's confused expression transformed into a laugh as he wrapped his arms around Sebastien. "What's going on?" he asked, playing along.

"Put down your glass. Don't drink it."

The artificial smile on his face faltered. "Why? It's only water."

"Don't look, but there's an officer watching about twenty feet behind you. I saw him spike your drink with something."

"Fucking *malákas*." The man shook his head. "I should have known."

"Why are they after you?"

He tapped his knuckles against the countertop and glanced at the floor. "Look, I appreciate you warning me. But the less you know, the better."

"Tell me what's going on," Sebastien said.

"Whatever you do, don't tell anyone what you saw." He walked away, the glass still held in his hand. Sebastien watched him pour the tainted water into a garbage bin.

"There you are." Ilya appeared with two bottles. "I've been searching for you everywhere."

"Sorry," Sebastien said, taking one of the bottles. They clinked the glass necks together before tilting them into their mouths. He looked past Ilya's shoulder. The young officer with the close-cropped hair was no longer there. "Something strange is going on."

"How do you know Dominic?"

"Dominic?"

"Filipino Elvis. The guy you were just talking to."

"That's the thing. I just saw —"

He was interrupted by a sharp voice that pierced the drone of conversation around them. Everyone at the counter turned to see what was causing the commotion.

In a nearby corner, partially hidden by a white curtain draped from the ceiling, were two people Sebastien recognized but had never seen together. Diya, the curly-haired blackjack dealer he'd met his first night on board, held her hands defensively in front of herself while Giorgos, the deck commander with the unsmiling face, towered over her.

The surrounding chatter went quiet long enough for them to hear her words.

"Back off," she said, her tone blunt as a lead pipe.

Even beneath the dim lighting, the anger was evident in the tight muscles of Giorgos's face. "Who do you think you are, speaking to me like that?"

"You're vile." She spat out the words like venom.

An indignant noise spread through the crowd as Giorgos grabbed Diya by the wrist. She grunted, trying to twist out of his grip. When it was clear he wasn't letting go, she pounded on his chest with her fist. He yanked her by the arm until she fell to her knees, her white dress twisted around her legs.

"Let her go!" Sebastien demanded.

There were scattered shouts in Diya's defence, but nobody stepped forward to help her. Their fingers itched to act, weight shifting forward in their bodies, but something stopped them. The uniform Giorgos wore acted like a fortified wall. It symbolized the height between his station and theirs.

Giorgos glanced at the few dozen people watching the scene unfold. He was clearly humiliated by the unwanted attention, but he refused to let go of Diya's wrist. Sebastien was shaking, unsure of what to do. He looked around frantically: everyone was in a similar state of conflict. Even Ilya, normally not one to think before acting, was frozen.

For a moment it appeared as though nobody would be willing to stand up to the commander. Then one man came forward.

"Get your hands off of her." Dominic's order was delivered with authority, despite his smaller size and status. His glare didn't waver as it fixed itself on Giorgos's eyes, which hovered several inches above.

"Do you know who you're speaking to?" Contempt simmered in Giorgos's low voice. "You jungle rat."

The surrounding crowd erupted with rumbles of disgust. Diya seized the distraction to wrench herself from his grip. Her hand flew through the air and landed against the commander's cheek like a paddle on the surface of a lake. The sound rang through that corner of the room, and it was followed by a stunned silence. Everyone's expression reflected the one on Giorgos's face.

Before anyone could act, his palm swiped forward and struck Diya's left ear. Her head jolted to the side against the blow.

Dominic lunged, seizing Giorgos by the lapels of his uniform. They pushed and pulled, clenched in each other's arms. Dominic twisted to one side, throwing the commander onto a table filled with empty glasses. With a roar, Giorgos picked himself up and leapt forward. The two men wrestled across the floor, colliding into stools and tables, as onlookers stepped back to make way for them. Sebastien jumped in and tried to pry them apart until Giorgos fended him off with a punch to the chest. Soon Giorgos and Dominic were entangled in the white curtain that hung from the ceiling, their limbs flailing as they tumbled to the floor.

Dominic had Giorgos pinned to the ground, his fist held in the air. It was about to fall like a hammer when Sebastien pulled him from behind. The cabin cleaner and the deck commander climbed to their feet.

"That's enough," Sebastien shouted, standing between them. Giorgos stood up straight and adjusted the cuffs of his white uniform, reminding Sebastien of how he looked in the viewfinder of his camera.

Nikos, the young security commander with the cocksure attitude, arrived a second later with two of his guards. The onlookers that encircled the scene protested while the blue-suited guards grabbed Dominic by the arms. He didn't put up a fight as they escorted him away.

"Nikos, that man didn't do anything wrong," Sebastien said, his eyes wide and his voice fraught. He glared at Giorgos, who was slipping away through the crowd. "We all saw the deck commander assault a woman. The man you took away, Dominic, was just trying to help."

Diya appeared at his side. "It's true," she said. "Giorgos hit me. If anyone is taken away, it should be him."

The young commander's amber eyes darted from Sebastien to Diya to Sebastien again. His eyebrows angled downward in skeptical arches. "You both saw what happened?"

They nodded.

"Then come with me."

❖

They followed Nikos to the administrative section of A Deck. His office was sterile and tidy. There wasn't much in the cube-shaped room except for a desk, computer, cabinet, safe, and a few neatly stacked folders. His only personal effects were a black vinyl jacket that hung behind the door and a few paperback novels on top of the cabinet; a mix of science fiction and classics, judging by the titles.

Nikos spoke efficiently, but he wasn't as cold as he'd been that first evening. There was a depth in his eyes that hinted at more beneath the hard exterior. *He looks so young*, Sebastien thought. *A boy trying hard to be a man*. In reality, they were the same age.

Nikos took notes as Sebastien and Diya recounted what had led to a cleaner and a commander wrestling on the floor.

"Thank you both for your time," he said as they wrapped up. "I'll share the report with Kostas. We'll be sure the appropriate actions are taken."

Shortly afterward, as Sebastien, Ilya, and Diya huddled together in her cabin on B Deck, they didn't know what to make of Nikos's remarks. It was three in the morning, and they were still wearing what remained of their costumes from the party. Diya drank tea from a ceramic mug that said *Kiss Me I'm Irish* in fat green letters.

"What does that mean, 'appropriate actions'?" she asked.

"I guess Kostas makes the call in the end," Ilya said, trying to be hopeful but knowing better.

Much like Sebastien and Ilya's, Diya's cabin was a rectangular box no more than nine square metres with two bunks affixed to the far wall, a narrow desk with a chair, a cabinet for hanging clothes, a safe, and a skinny door leading to the shower and sink.

"Giorgos has been harassing me for weeks," she said. "He is truly despicable. What I told Nikos is just the tip of the iceberg."

"Why didn't you tell him everything?" Sebastien asked, recalling how terse her answers had been.

She shrugged. "There's no point. Nikos already knows. It wouldn't make a difference what I say. Giorgos is one of them. He can do whatever he wants. He's protected."

Sebastien understood. It was the same reason he hadn't mentioned the white powder sprinkled in Dominic's glass, or whose jacket pocket that powder had come from. They couldn't trust Nikos. He was one of them, too.

"How did it start?" Ilya asked. He was sitting on the floor

with his back against the wall, his red cape draped over himself like a blanket.

"Gambling," she said with a snort. "The officers put on these secret gambling parties every now and then in one of the lounges on A Deck. They asked me to be their dealer a while back. I guess they're too proud to shuffle their own cards, the pompous pricks. I couldn't say no. Most of the commanders are usually there."

"Sounds delightful," Ilya said with a frown.

"Just picture a room crowded with drunken *malákas* and their egos, Greek pop music from two decades ago, and enough cigarette smoke to suffocate a small village."

"I think I saw a horror movie once that started out like that," Sebastien said from his spot by the desk.

Diya took a sip of tea, her eyes tired. "It wasn't so bad at first. They were obnoxious, but they never treated me poorly. Giorgos was even kind in the beginning, before he got too friendly. It started with a hand on the shoulder, which I let slide. Then the hand drifted lower as the weeks went by. I kept telling him to stop, but he would just laugh it off. I felt like a mother scolding a child."

"Doesn't he have a thing going on with Contessa?" Ilya asked.

"Wait, what?" Sebastien was genuinely surprised. "Contessa Bloor, diva of the *Glacier*? There's no way."

Diya nodded. "Believe it or not, it's true. Their forbidden love affair is the worst-kept secret on the ship. The distinguished deck commander and his beautiful American songbird. It wouldn't be such a big deal if it weren't for the fact that Giorgos is married. He has a son, too."

"What is a woman like Contessa doing with a lifeless coatrack like Giorgos?"

"It's the uniform," Diya said with a resigned shrug. "It drives women mad. I've seen his wife. She's gorgeous. I heard she's coming aboard in Athens for a couple weeks. Poor thing. She'll probably be cooped up in one of the guest suites while her revolting husband lives like a bachelor below decks."

"I guess one affair isn't enough for him," Sebastien said.

Diya pulled a blanket around her shoulders. "It never is for men like him. He's been following me around for weeks, watching me. Then tonight he cornered me in the crew bar. I told him I didn't want anything to do with him, but he wouldn't let me go. I couldn't take it anymore."

"I'm sorry," Ilya said. "We should have stopped him as soon as he touched you."

Diya grabbed him by the hand. "The only person who did something wrong was Giorgos. Don't put any of the blame on yourself."

"We just stood there, helpless." Sebastien hugged his arms around himself, ashamed.

"I wouldn't want either of you risking your positions on board for me." She gave them a reassuring smile. "Besides, I can take care of myself. I've faced worse men than Giorgos."

"Who could be worse than that vulture?" Ilya asked with a look of revulsion.

"My husband."

The two men were silent as they waited for her to continue. She hesitated, looking at the floor, then drew a deep breath.

"I thought I could love him at first, even though Rajan wasn't like the romantic men in the Bollywood movies I used to watch as a girl. Marriage was never important to me before I met him. I had just earned a mathematics degree, and I was too busy with my work. Then he came into my life and made up his mind. He was going to make me his wife. I just let it happen.

"It wasn't until the second year that he hit me for the first time. We argued often about my work. He was embarrassed by what people would think, that it would look like he couldn't provide for us. It was the same argument for months until one day it escalated. The slap left a mark on my skin, but it was nothing a little makeup couldn't fix."

Sebastien and Ilya cringed. She paused for some tea.

"Every day was different, depending on his mood. There were days of affection, and there were days of complete silence. Then there were days when Rajan would pin me to the floor with his hands around my neck — he'd learned how to leave minimal evidence.

"He didn't want to hurt me. It wasn't about the pain. All he wanted was control. Sometimes I thought he'd actually strangle the breath out of me just to prove that he could. I felt myself diminishing as the years went by. No words came to mind when I tried to describe myself. I had lost my identity.

"Rajan wanted a son, but there was no way I was going to let that happen. I already had a father and a husband. I couldn't bear to be owned by another man. I packed a suitcase when he was at the office one day, then I walked out the door. It was so easy. I could have done it years earlier. I guess sometimes we build our own cages."

Every muscle in her body was limp with exhaustion, but an indignant flame flickered in her eyes.

"I figured I'd have better odds of happiness somewhere far away. I took a train to Goa, one of the only parts of India where gambling isn't outlawed. I went to nearly every casino and put my math skills to work. Chance and luck aren't the same; everything is an equation. It took me a week to win enough to fly to Europe and survive for a few months. Then I found a job here. The *Glacier* is home now."

The men exchanged glances, impressed by Diya's ability to reclaim her life.

"What happened to you was terrible, but you're free now." Sebastien placed his hand gently on her wrist where Giorgos's grip had been. "You can forget about him."

She flinched at Sebastien's touch. "I thought so, too, until Giorgos turned his attention to me months ago," she said, relaxing the tension in her arm. "I see a piece of Rajan behind his eyes. Men like that share something the rest of us can't understand."

The door burst open as Diya's cabinmate stepped into the room, nearly tripping on Ilya's outstretched legs on the floor. She was an Irishwoman named Briana with an abnormally loud voice. Her white dress had streaks of purple down the front. A crown of plastic laurels was tangled in the knots of her hair.

"Bad news," she said, shutting the door behind her. "Dominic's been fired."

"No." Diya's hands hovered in front of her mouth. "They can't do that."

"They can," Briana said, her voice filling the narrow room. "They have him locked up in his cabin as we speak. He'll stay there until we dock in Athens. Then he's gone."

Sebastien shook his head in disbelief. "They're evicting him for standing up to assault? What about Giorgos?"

"I told you," Diya said, her face heavy with guilt. "Nothing will happen to him. He's protected."

An image flashed through Sebastien's mind — a young officer with close-cropped hair pouring a mysterious powder into a glass of water. Dominic's words from earlier that night repeated themselves in his ears.

But the less you know, the better.

He could hear his father, too, speaking to Giorgos in the atrium, unaware they were being watched.

He's a harmless cabin cleaner. What could he possibly do?

"We arrive in Athens in two days," Sebastien said, looking at everyone in the cabin. "We still have time to figure out a way to save Dominic."

"You're right," Diya said. "We can't let this happen."

Sebastien tried to appear strong, but he couldn't deny the ripple of apprehension beneath his skin. Something unpleasant was in the air, and he sensed that it might be worse than he could imagine.

SIX

I Know What I Saw

The water was glass the next morning as the *Glacier* travelled onward to Athens. Floor-to-ceiling windows displayed a panorama of the sea to everyone in the fitness centre, on the sixteenth deck, directly below the navigation bridge.

Working out was the last thing Sebastien cared to do this morning — there were more pressing things on his mind — but he had a plan.

He leaned forward on the bench he straddled and dropped the dumbbell to the floor. The walls around this corner were covered in mirrors. From here, he could see the entire gym behind him.

The ship's dancers occupied an entire row of cardio machines that faced the windows. They ran and pedalled furiously, despite the hangovers, desperate to stay below the ten-pound threshold that could end their *Glacier* careers.

Behind them, Ilya was coaching a client as she performed a series of complicated movements on the matted floor. "Push ... Harder ... You got it ... Nice work!" he said, cheering her on. She was struggling, judging by her flushed skin and sweat-drenched spandex, but able to muster the energy to flash a flirtatious smile Ilya's way as she swung a kettle bell between her legs.

Good luck with that, Sebastien thought, chuckling to himself.

Just past Ilya was the target. Nikos was seated on a rowing machine. The muscles in his arms flexed and relaxed as he pulled the cable rhythmically. His black shorts ended at the thigh, revealing a set of impressive quads. It wasn't exactly a coincidence to find the young security commander here. The officers kept strict workout routines. Ilya knew them all by heart.

Nikos wrapped up his session exactly when expected. Sebastien waited a minute before following him into the men's locker room.

A pattern of Greek keys formed golden spirals across the tiled walls of the shower. There were twelve nozzles spaced equally apart, but Nikos was the only person there. The taut muscles of his body were wrapped in steam and spray. A round emblem of black ink was etched into the planes of his chest. The two men nodded to each other silently.

The officer was shy, his body turned away at an angle and his head tilted forward.

Sebastien held his head back as he washed the shampoo from his hair. He lathered the soap slowly over his chest, feeling every contour of his body, before his hands made their way farther down. Nikos glanced over at him, then looked away. The covert glances continued until their eyes met.

They faced each other and watched as their hands slid over their bodies. The warm water rinsed the soap off their skin. Not a word was spoken. Their eyes conveyed everything they needed to say. They had nothing to hide now.

Nikos was breathing heavily when Sebastien turned off his shower nozzle. He flung the towel over his shoulder and disappeared around the corner.

Ten minutes later, Nikos emerged from the locker room wearing black joggers and a sweatshirt. His hair was still damp, and his gym bag was strapped over his back. He was surprised to see Sebastien waiting for him on a bench outside the entrance.

"Nikos." The two men stood and looked at each other, inadvertently recreating the scene in the shower, though this time they were clothed.

"Sebastien," he said, chin tilted down and hands clasped around the gym bag's strap across his chest.

"Can we talk?"

Nikos nodded as they walked through the sliding doors to Sunset Deck's outdoor promenade. Sebastien doubted he would ever tire of this view. The sea stretched out around them. The salty air stroked his skin. The rest of the world could be burning and they would have no reason to care.

"It's about Dominic." He detected a flash of relief and disappointment on Nikos's face. "What he did took courage. He doesn't deserve to be evicted for it."

"I heard about Kostas's decision. It's unfortunate."

"We can't let it happen."

Nikos paused by the railing and turned to face him. The morning light chased the shadows from his skin, and there was a glimpse of the man he could be. "What do you want from me?" The tone wasn't hostile. His voice was soft. He genuinely wanted an answer.

Sebastien stepped closer until he could smell the soap on Nikos's skin.

"I want you to help me."

✣

His father was a proud man. You could even say he was something of a narcissist, judging by his office. The enviable life of Kostas Kourakis was on display in the many frames that covered his walls. There were certificates embossed with seals. A few medals lined the shelf. Most of all, there were the photographs.

An image of Kostas shaking hands with someone distinguished.

A solitary portrait of Kostas as a young man.

Kostas on his wedding day, holding his bride by the waist.

Kostas with his children, a protective hand on each shoulder.

Kostas beamed in every single one, evidence of his satisfaction.

Sebastien observed every detail from the upholstered chair. His father sat behind a desk only two metres in front of him. They were alone together for the first time in their lives. Son and father, hunter and hunted.

Nikos had come through. All Sebastien wanted was his help to secure a private meeting with the elusive hotel commander, a man who didn't take appointments. Perhaps Nikos was an ally after all.

"Tell me about yourself," Kostas said. His smile was warm, but he had a restless face. The features shifted as easily as the surface of the sea. He glanced at the name badge on Sebastien's lapel. "Goh. An interesting name."

"It's from my father's side. He's Chinese."

You're my father, Sebastien thought. *I'm your son.*

"You don't look like any Chinaman I've ever seen."

"My mother's French-Canadian," he explained.

My mother you abandoned.

"Exotic."

"You have a beautiful family." Sebastien's eyes darted to the wall of staged smiles behind Kostas. One photo in the centre flaunted the four of them on the prow of a yacht. They were dressed in matching linen outfits with the wind in their hair. He cringed inside.

Kostas twisted around in his chair as though he had no idea what was behind him. "Ah, yes." A proud smile swept across his face. "You might meet them soon. They're coming on board in Athens for the two-week sailing to Cannes. A few of the other officers' families will be here, too. It should be fun."

Why did you leave me and my mother?

"Fun." Sebastien couldn't tell how convincing his smile was as something violent churned in his stomach. "Will they be staying here below decks?"

Kostas laughed as though the idea was absurd. "In Hades? Oh no. They'll be in one of the guest suites. Far too many corrupting influences down here."

"Of course."

Kostas reclined in his chair, clasping his hands together against his stomach. "So, Nikos tells me you have something important to say. What is it that you want?"

I want to know what happened thirty years ago.

I want to know if you ever think about her.

About me.

He hadn't planned to confront his father so soon, but something changed when he saw the kindness on Kostas's face in the atrium the other day. Perhaps redemption would be possible once Sebastien learned the truth. Now that they were so close and alone, he found himself barely able to hold back.

But first, there was another matter at hand.

He leaned forward, fixing his eyes on his father's. "It's about Dominic. I saw everything that happened in the crew bar last night." He paused, aware of the controversy the following accusation could stir. "Giorgos was making a woman feel uncomfortable," he said, choosing his words carefully. "She told him to stop, but he became angry. He grabbed her by the wrist. It looked like it was going to get worse until Dominic stepped in. He was only trying to defuse the situation, to help the woman being intimidated."

"Yes, yes. I've read the report from Nikos."

"I heard that Dominic has been fired over this."

"He attacked a commanding officer," Kostas said, his words blunt in delivery and sharp in meaning. His eyes appeared to possess a darker shade of green than earlier as the lines of his face hardened. "According to the report, this woman struck Giorgos. He was then attacked by Dominic, who grabbed him by his uniform and tackled him to the floor. Giorgos did nothing to provoke this behaviour. He was the one being assaulted."

"That's not what happened," Sebastien said.

"There's no evidence of Giorgos harassing this woman."

"There were at least thirty people who saw what happened. Talk to them!" The air in the room felt suddenly warmer. Beads of sweat formed along his forehead.

"I doubt any of them will come forward." The corners of Kostas's lips curled upward ever so slightly. "As for you, I'm willing to dismiss your previous statement as a temporary lapse in judgment. It was dark. You'd had one too many drinks. You can't be sure of what you saw."

Diya was right. You're protecting him. You can't be trusted.

"I know what I saw," Sebastien responded.

And I saw what you gave that officer to put in Dominic's drink. Now I just need to find out why.

Kostas leaned forward, placing his palms on the surface of the desk. "Be careful, Mr. Goh. An accusation like that can be dangerous."

Sebastien felt the sting of shame on his cheeks. He hated himself for failing to predict this would have been the inevitable outcome. He hated his father more.

He wanted to lay bare his identity, to demand answers about what happened thirty years earlier, but he buried the words beneath his tongue. It was clear that he couldn't trust a word from the man's mouth. The truth wasn't going to reveal itself in a conversation. It would have to be uncovered another way.

"Understood, sir."

"Good, good." The smile returned to Kostas's face as though it had never left. "Is there anything else you want?"

I want you to be punished.

I want you to lose everything.

I want you to know it was because of me.

"Nothing at all," Sebastien said with a smile of his own.

He couldn't deny the pleasure he felt. There was power in knowing what his father didn't.

❖

Dominic's cabin was in the depths of C Deck. The air was thicker and warmer than it was above. The constant clash of sea against steel could be heard through the ship's hull.

Nikos led Sebastien through the labyrinthine passage-ways of the crew quarters until they came across a security guard seated outside a door. He was smoking a cigarette and scrolling through his phone. Nikos barked a few words in Greek, sending the blue-suited guard scurrying away.

"I can't believe he's being imprisoned in his own cabin," Sebastien said, shaking his head in disbelief.

"I'm just following orders."

"I know," he said apologetically. "That wasn't a jab at you. I'm thankful for your help. You didn't have to do any of this for me."

Nikos offered a shy nod. He gave three firm knocks on the door before inserting a key card above the handle. With a tilt of the head, he gestured for Sebastien to go inside. "I'll wait out here."

The cabin was a similar size to Sebastien's, but there were four bunks instead of two. Dominic lay in one of the bottom bunks wearing basketball shorts and a grey, hooded sweatshirt. There was a book in his hands. Hearing the door open and close, he climbed to his feet to greet his unexpected visitor.

"What are you doing here?" he asked.

"I wanted to talk to you about last night," Sebastien said, taking a seat on the opposite bunk. "This is cruel, locking you up alone like this."

Dominic offered him a bag of greasy potato chips. "At least I get to spend my final hours on the *Glacier* in peace." He swept his arms outward. "They relocated my cabinmates."

"I tried pleading your case to Kostas. It was no use."

Dominic shook his head, wiping crumbs from his lips. "Thanks for trying, but you're right. There's no point. He's not going to listen."

"What you did was brave. The rest of us just stood there like mannequins. You showed that arrogant *maláka* that he can't just do whatever he wants. There are people on board who won't put up with it."

Dominic nodded along, but his eyes drifted thoughtfully to the cabin floor. "He'll get away with it, though. They always do."

"Perhaps this time. But things change."

"I saw him pull Diya to the ground, and I couldn't take it." Dominic's nostrils flared with anger. "He's twice her size. What kind of man treats another person like that?"

"A coward," Sebastien said. "A powerful, protected coward."

"Exactly." Dominic ran his fingers through his hair, which was no longer firm with styling gel. "I don't know what I'm going to do for work now, but at least I'll see my family again."

"What are they like?"

"I'm here because of my brother and sister. Our parents died years ago. I come from a part of the Philippines where there isn't much opportunity. Most people I know have ways to make a living that aren't exactly legal, some of them shadier than others. I don't want that for my family. I work here so they can get an education without worrying about money. What I get paid as a cleaner may not seem like much to you, but it felt like winning the lottery when I got this job. Free room and board, payment in euros. I was lucky."

"I know how you feel," Sebastien said. "I didn't grow up with money, either."

The two men looked at each other from across the cabin, feeling a little less different than they had earlier.

"They're both in school now," Dominic went on. "My sister is studying business, and my brother wants to be a nurse.

I'm so proud of them." He cradled his forehead in his hands. "I don't know what we're going to do now."

"It's not over yet. We still have time to change Kostas's mind."

He shook his head. "It won't change a thing."

"We need to try. We can't let the commanders control us like this."

"Do you think I'm being evicted because of what happened last night in the crew bar? People don't usually get locked in their cabin when they're fired. This is different. They want me gone."

"Why?" Sebastien's voice lowered, signalling for Dominic to do the same.

"I told you last night — the less you know, the better. You don't want to get mixed up in this."

"What did that officer put in your drink?"

"I don't know," Dominic admitted. "Cocaine, probably, or MDMA. I know what would have happened if I drank it, though. They would have taken me to the medical clinic to get me tested for drugs. Not only would they have a reason to throw me off the ship, it would also hurt my credibility."

Sebastien looked intently into his eyes, his tone more forceful. "Tell me why they're after you."

Dominic hesitated, touching the gold crucifix that hung from his neck. "I was cleaning cabins in the officers' quarters four days ago, the wing behind the locked door where Kostas and the other commanders live. I saw something I wasn't supposed to see."

"What was it?"

"Now they know. They've been watching me ever since. If I hadn't stood up to Giorgos last night, they would have found another reason to get rid of me."

"Tell me what you saw."

After another hesitation, Dominic leaned forward with a cautious look in his eyes.

"Cabin A66. They're hiding something they don't want anyone to find. Something bad."

The two men sat upright as the door flung open. Nikos motioned for Sebastien to leave. "Time's up."

SEVEN

Free Dom

As Dominic remained locked in his cabin the following morning, the corridors of B Deck and C Deck were covered with posters printed on cheap photocopy paper. The text was big, black, and bold.

Time is running out to stop the unfair
eviction of Dominic Mendoza.
If you want to help, meet in the computer
room today at 12:30.
Bring friends.

Sebastien, Diya, and Ilya didn't know how many people to expect. There hadn't been much time to plan anything other than to spread the word by mouth and poster. By 12:35 the computer room was so crowded that everyone had to stand. They came from all areas of the staff and crew, from the spa to housekeeping, but the majority wore the grey uniforms of Dominic's colleagues in the cabin-service crew.

The energy in the room was a combination of uncertainty and impatience. A small group of dancers stood in one corner, exchanging stories from the previous night in the crew bar. Some housekeepers huddled together nearby, fidgeting with their hands and glancing around the room. Scattered throughout the crowd were flimsy keyboards and the black screens of old computer monitors, relics from a simpler time.

The hum of conversation diminished when Sebastien and Diya stood on a table in the middle of the room. They were opening their mouths to speak when a knock sounded on the door.

Ilya opened it to reveal Contessa Bloor, the ship's star. Everyone was surprised to see her.

"Sorry," she mouthed silently as she made her way to an empty spot against the wall.

"As you all know, we arrive in Athens tomorrow morning," Sebastien began, shifting attention from Contessa back to himself. "Our friend, Dominic Mendoza, will be forcefully removed from the ship, his home, for defending a woman from an abusive man."

Diya's face was tense. "Giorgos is the one who should be punished, not Dominic," she said. "But the commanders are the ones in power. They think they can get away with anything. We need to show them that isn't true."

She glanced at Contessa, who looked away. There were scattered cheers and nods of affirmation throughout the room.

"Someone stuck a note on my cabin door yesterday," she went on. "It said 'Good girls keep quiet.' I wanted to laugh when I read it, but then I remembered this isn't a joke. It's our reality. They think we're that easily intimidated."

"We can't let Giorgos and his protectors erase what he did from our memory," Sebastien said. "We must show them we know the truth. They need to understand that if we can't get justice for Dominic and Diya, there will be consequences."

✦

When the meeting came to an end, Contessa slipped out the door. She was walking down the wide passageway of Styx when someone called her name from behind. Startled, she spun around to see Diya, the petite blackjack dealer, hurrying over to her, a bundle of curls bouncing atop her head.

"I know this must be uncomfortable for you," Diya said, her tone gentle, "given how Giorgos is involved."

Contessa was about to feign confusion, then realized there was no use in denying it. Her affair with Giorgos had been going on long enough that it was no longer a scandalous secret. It used to bring her a delicious sense of pride when people discovered she was sleeping with the mighty deck commander. Now it made her feel sick.

"I probably know more than anyone that he's no gentleman," Contessa responded.

"Why did you come?"

She had wondered the same thing, but she gave Diya the same answer she'd given herself. "I just want to help."

✦

It was quiet on A Deck that evening when Kostas Kourakis tidied his office. He'd always been an orderly man. "A mess in your hands shows a mess in your mind," he liked to tell his young son. He faced his wall of photographs, but the memories didn't interest him. The frames would often move to the swaying of the ship. He wanted to be sure they weren't askew.

Five loud knocks sounded against the door in quick succession. Upon opening it, he saw it was Giorgos.

"You need to come down to B Deck," the deck commander said, his face drawn even tighter than usual. "Now."

They hurried down a narrow staircase that led to the staff quarters below. Kostas heard the noise before they stepped through the door.

The main thoroughfare of Styx, the wide passageway that spanned the length of B Deck, was a carpet of black. Hundreds of staff and crew were seated along the cold steel floor, blocking the entrances to the staff cafeteria, purser's office, medical clinic, and computer room. They were dressed entirely in black. Several of them had messages scrawled across their bodies in jagged lines of red paint.

FREE DOM

Sebastien and Ilya were in the middle of the floor. The dancers sat among the housekeepers. Musicians linked arms with servers. Even the ship's head concierge and maître d' were there, surrounded by cleaners and bus boys. There were no uniforms or class distinctions. They were united in the message on their bodies.

Diya's voice boomed through the intercom speakers that were mounted along the ceiling of Styx. She stood by the door of the purser's office, the microphone in her hand attached to the base station on the wall by a coiled cord.

"This ship isn't just a job," she said.

Cheers rumbled along the passageway, echoing across the metal walls.

"This ship certainly isn't a vacation."

They shouted in agreement.

"This is our home."

The noise of the crowd was thunderous when Kostas and Giorgos appeared through the door. The volume grew even louder when everyone saw them standing there, confused and unnerved.

"The hotel commander has arrived," Diya declared through the microphone. Kostas straightened his stance, adjusting the jacket of his uniform. Giorgos glared at her with a savage look on his face, but she had already decided she wouldn't acknowledge his presence.

Sebastien watched as Giorgos's stare travelled from Diya to another familiar woman. Contessa was surrounded by members of the Filipino Mafia, her clothing splashed in red paint and her hair tied behind a black baseball cap. The anger in Giorgos's eyes intensified when he saw her there, cheering along with everyone else.

Diya turned to face Kostas. "We are here to show support for Dominic Mendoza. With all due respect, sir, your decision to evict him is wrong. There are dozens of people here tonight, including myself, who witnessed the courage that man showed in the face of an outrageous abuse of power." She didn't want to look at Giorgos, but she couldn't help herself. Her gaze drilled into his, unyielding as a beam of steel. "Dominic should be applauded for what he did, not punished. He came here to the *Glacier* to provide a better life for his family. What we're asking of you is simple: Reconsider your decision. Allow Dominic to remain on board. And show us all that you care about our safety and our dignity."

The once-raucous crowd was now silent. All eyes were on Kostas, the hotel commander with the power to choose between right and wrong. His move.

Sebastien didn't realize he was holding his breath. He remembered what Dominic had told him the previous night — the fight in the crew bar was merely a convenient excuse to throw him off the ship. If it hadn't happened, the commanders would have found another way to get rid of him. The protest was futile. Kostas wasn't going to have a change of heart.

But it wasn't just about freeing Dominic — not in Sebastien's mind, at least. This was about defiance. Sebastien wanted to chip away at his father's power until there was nothing left.

After a moment's hesitation, Kostas adjusted his jacket and marched toward Diya with long, unhurried strides, as people shuffled out of his way to form a path. He took the microphone from her hands and cleared his throat.

"You ungrateful little children. Get off the floor. This is absurd."

His words took a second to be understood, but the reaction was fierce. Insults and pleas surged in his direction in equal measure.

"I don't take demands from any of you," he said, his voice blaring through the loudspeakers. "Remember who you work for."

Briana, the Irishwoman who shared a cabin with Diya, charged toward Kostas, her strawberry hair blowing behind her like wispy flames. She stood in front of the commander with a finger pointed in his face.

"We have a right to protest," she said.

Kostas glared at her with rage in his eyes. The tone of his skin deepened into the colour of wine. It was a feeling Sebastien recognized.

Without warning, the anger on the hotel commander's face dissolved into laughter. The sound rumbled through the speakers and along the walls. "A right to protest? What makes you believe that?" His eyes blinked, and his face hardened. "This is my ship. You have no rights unless I say so. You are powerless."

The passageway was filled with indignant cries. Briana's arms shook as she absorbed his words. With a snap of her lips, she ejected a bullet of saliva that splattered across Kostas's chest.

"Nikos, take this woman away!" he shouted in disgust. "Anyone not standing in the next few seconds will be dragged out."

Sebastien followed his father's gaze and saw Nikos for the first time that night. The deputy security commander stood near the back of the crowd, an island of white in an ocean of black.

Unsure of what to do at first, Nikos gestured to his blue-suited security guards to follow Kostas's orders. He unhooked the two-way radio from his waist and called for backup.

The mass of people on the floor huddled more closely together. The shouts were deafening as the guards made a few weak attempts at breaking the chain of linked arms. One guard tried dragging a Russian bartender by the ankle, but she kicked him in the chest. "Don't touch me!" she roared.

Several officers arrived on the scene in their bright white suits. They roamed through the seated crowd, demanding people get to their feet.

"Hold onto each other!" Sebastien shouted.

"Free Dom!" Ilya cried. It wasn't long before the rhythmic chant echoed throughout the hall. The demonstration had escalated in a way that nobody had quite imagined, but they weren't about to move.

Nikos marched down the passageway and grabbed Briana by the arm. She twisted out of his grip. Two guards chased after her as she bolted away, pushing aside a few curious onlookers.

When it was clear the security guards weren't going to use force to remove the protestors, Kostas held the microphone to his mouth. "If you want to play these silly games, so be it." He looked at Nikos and the other officers. "Shut down the electricity on B Deck. No lights. No sound. They can sit in the dark if that's what they want."

The stark fluorescent lights went out seconds later and the hum from the speakers went dead. The darkness was tinted red by emergency lights that ran along the floor. Styx truly resembled its namesake.

After a collective gasp spread down the hall, everyone cheered as Kostas and his officers made their exit. The crowd of staff and crew clustered on the floor hadn't got the outcome they wanted. They hadn't won. Perhaps it was the adrenalin surging through their bodies, passing from one person to the next by touch, but it still felt like they had accomplished something with this little act of defiance.

As the cheers died down, a voice as pure as rain began to sing. It was Contessa. Soon the darkness was filled with voices as the crowd sang and hummed along.

"Can we talk?"

Sebastien looked up to see Nikos standing above him. With a furtive glance at Ilya, he nodded and climbed to his feet. The young security commander led him through the doors of the staff cafeteria. The smell of chicken parmigiana lingered in the air.

"Did you have something to do with this?" Nikos asked when he was sure they were out of sight.

Sebastien could barely make out the serious features of the face before him in the darkness, but the hushed tone was tinged with anger.

"Yes." No other words came to him.

"This was a bad idea."

"What were we supposed to do, Nikos? Nothing?"

"You could be in a lot of trouble. All of you."

"Did you hear what he said?" Sebastien startled himself by how distressed his voice sounded. "He doesn't give a shit about any of us. We're beneath him. Disposable."

His body trembled as Nikos's hands reached out and held his arms. He shook them off, but they held him again more firmly. He grabbed the front of Nikos's jacket in both fists, pulling toward him roughly until he could feel the warm breath on his face. They struggled back and forth, clutching each other, locked in a rigid embrace.

"What are you going to do?" Nikos said, his voice deep and dark. "Hit me?"

He flinched as Sebastien's cheek brushed softly against the side of his nose. Their faces hovered closely together, a magnetic push and pull. Their lips met, as if reeled in by each other's breath, softly at first, gently. Their bodies gave in to the pull as they pressed together.

Every muscle in Nikos was tense with restraint, but he couldn't deny himself any longer. As the voices sang and their lips burned, nothing else mattered in that moment but Sebastien Goh.

Athens
to
Palermo

EIGHT

House of the Heel

Sebastien leaned over the edge of the ship's railing. Twenty-first-century Piraeus was a different place than the war-ravaged stronghold it was once. The port town outside of central Athens hissed with life. Ships of all sorts pulled in and out of the harbour, leaving paths of white foam that criss-crossed each other in the waves. Streams of sailors, travellers, and workers hurried across the docks. The morning sun glinted off glass buildings that jostled against the edge of the sea. Although it was now a place of modern industry, one of the busiest ports in the world, Piraeus wore its history in its faded facades and cracked pavement. Wars, plagues, victories, defeats — Piraeus had seen it all.

The staff and crew of the *Glacier* felt defeated. They crowded onto the outdoor bow, the arrowhead-shaped deck reserved for crew, and leaned over the side with Sebastien. They wanted to get a glimpse of Dominic as he disembarked onto the crumbling concrete of Greece.

The high from the previous night hadn't survived the dawn. Their rebellion might have woken them from their apathy, but they hadn't won. Dominic was still being sent away. The commanding officers had made their message clear.

You are powerless.

The words repeated themselves endlessly in the tunnels of Sebastien's mind. They confirmed everything he had imagined his father to be. Cold. Cruel. A man who was hollow on the inside. How else could he have done what he did to Ruby Goh?

At least everyone saw what's behind the mask of smiles, he thought. *They won't be so easily manipulated now.*

The staff and crew of the *Glacier* had risen that morning to a message from their overlords. It was posted along every corridor of the lower decks, printed on the same cheap photo-copy paper as the signs Sebastien had used to gather Dominic's defenders. This time, the words were different.

> *In response to last night's misconduct on B Deck,*
> *staff and crew will not be permitted onshore*
> *while we're docked in Athens.*
> *ACTS OF INSUBORDINATION WILL NOT*
> *BE TOLERATED.*
> *REBELS WILL BE DISMISSED*
> *IMMEDIATELY.*
> *Questions or concerns can be raised with*
> *your staff purser.*
> *Regards, Your Commanding Officers*

Standing beneath the morning sun, Sebastien wore the dejection on his face. They had failed Dominic, and it hurt. But there was something else. He kept picturing his father from the previous night, dismissive and uncaring, and tried to reconcile the image with the kind-faced man who helped him to his feet in the atrium. His face flushed at the realization that he'd been fooled. The feeling that eclipsed all others was hatred.

"There he is!" someone shouted. Their eyes followed the pointed finger to see a man walk off the gangplank. He wasn't more than a black speck in the distance, but they could tell it was him by the blue specks on either side. He was being led away by Nikos's guards. Shouts and applause rumbled across the deck. Dominic looked up toward the noise. A hand waved in the air until the blue specks prodded him onward.

I'm going to get justice for you, Sebastien thought. *And it will begin with finding what you saw in cabin A66.*

Following Dominic was Briana. The reward for her courage was immediate eviction. She also had an escort of guards leading her to the gates of the dock.

"Tell your secret boyfriend to rein in his pack of dogs," Ilya said, with his arms dangling over the railing. He saw Sebastien was in no mood to joke, and the smile faded from his lips. "You did everything you could. You know that, right?"

"It wasn't enough." He pushed the hair away from his eyes to see the sincerity on Ilya's face. He wanted to tell his friend the truth — that Kostas was his father — but he held it back. He didn't want to implicate Ilya unless it became necessary.

"For all we know, nothing we could have done would have been enough," Ilya said. "But we couldn't just stand and watch. We had to do something, so we did."

"All we did was piss off the *malákas*. You heard Kostas. We're powerless. Maybe he's right."

"He's wrong." Ilya turned so they stood face to face, eye to eye. "What happened last night meant something to people. It meant something to *me*." He scanned the wind-swept deck around them. It was filled with people of different colours wearing uniforms that represented contrasting social stations, but something intangible now bonded them together. "This isn't just a job," Ilya went on. "This is our home. The commanders keep us numb with parties and privileges, but the truth is they dominate us. We give up a piece of our freedom when we board this ship. Last night was a sign that we do have power, because now we know we're not alone."

As if on cue, three Filipina housekeepers in grey uniforms approached them, looking both shy and excited. "My name is Rosa," said the woman in the middle. She had a plump figure and a friendly face. Her palms were placed against her pale pink apron. "We want to thank you both for everything you've done. Dominic was our friend. We didn't save him, but seeing how much support he had last night …" Her words trailed off as her face welled with emotion. "For so many people from the staff to care about a crew member, for Contessa Bloor to be there for his cause, it was unbelievable. We've never seen anything like it."

Sebastien didn't know what to say. "I'm happy we did what we could to help. I just wish it had made more of a difference."

"It made a difference to us," Rosa said. "It isn't easy being crew. We're treated like we don't matter because we're at the bottom. We don't have any of the influence the staff have. So when we work together, people like you make us stronger."

Ilya flashed Sebastien a look that said "I told you so."

"We will remember this," Rosa said. "You have friends in the crew."

A saxophone moaned through the atrium later that afternoon, a melancholy sound to welcome the new arrivals.

It was another embarkation day. Out with the old passengers, in with the new. Sebastien leaned against the balustrade of Adriatic Deck in his turquoise blazer, the gold buttons glinting in the pale light, with his camera strapped around his neck. He was supposed to take photos of the guests as they stepped on board, but his motivation diminished with every second that went by. He watched the endless stream of people enter the ship while thoughts swam through his mind.

Tonight would be the captain's cocktail party. The same staged smiles. The same excuse to forget about all that was wrong in the world. Except this time there would be three new attendees allowed in the elite officers' circle.

He remembered the photograph of Kostas's wife and two children holding one another on the prow of a yacht, the wind tossing their hair. He conjured the images he had examined over the years of this happy family and their proud father. The elegant wife with the pointed nose who rarely looked directly at the camera. The daughter whose languorous limbs implied complete satisfaction with her place in the world. Most of all, he imagined the son. The boy with the deep green eyes and wild tangle of dark hair.

"They're coming on board in Athens for the two-week sailing to Cannes," Kostas had told him in his office the other day. "It should be fun."

He repeated the words under his breath. "It should be fun."

Adriatic Deck was quieter the farther he got from the Agora. The smile on his face felt more forced than usual as guests stopped him for questions. He needed to get away from them.

He ambled along the halls of the shopping arcade, avoiding eye contact with people passing by. The windows displayed merchandise in square frames of light as recorded music spilled from hidden speakers. He nearly tripped over his own feet when he reached the bank of elevators near the ship's stern.

Standing there were the woman and two children whose faces had been haunting him all day — the wife, daughter, and son of Kostas Kourakis. The boy and girl had aged since the most recent photograph Sebastien had seen, but they were instantly recognizable. The daughter was almost as tall as her mother and had the same placid look in her eyes. The son was a miniature version of his father.

The woman wore a chic white skirt and a hat with a wide brim. The bright orange colour of her blouse reminded him of the stuccoed walls of his old apartment building in Petit Géant.

They hadn't noticed him standing there. He was about to spin around and retreat in the direction he came from, but something stopped him. With a slow inhale, he stepped toward the elevators.

"We'll see him later for dinner," the woman was telling her son. Their hands were held tightly together.

"That's what you said about lunch." The boy's tone was petulant. "He was supposed to take us to that place by the port for Jewish doughnuts."

"He had work to do. And those aren't doughnuts. They're rugelach."

A musical chime announced the arrival of an elevator. Sebastien stepped inside with the family of three. He pressed the highest button on the panel, which was level sixteen, Sunset Deck. The woman's manicured hand, cuffed by golden bangles, reached out for the button two levels below. The Kourakis family was staying on Riviera Deck.

They avoided looking at each other's reflections in the mirrors that covered the walls of the elevator, except for the little boy. There was a flash of surprise on his face when his deep green eyes met Sebastien's.

"Kristo," whispered his mother with a hand on his shoulder. "Don't stare."

Listen to your mother, Kristo.

There was silence as they climbed upward through the ship. The air was heavy with the woman's perfume, a distinct fragrance of wildflowers and spice. Sebastien felt drunk from the scent.

The chime sounded as the elevator doors slid open to reveal the seafoam-coloured carpet and rose walls of Riviera Deck, where the most luxurious suites could be found. The woman nudged her two children into the hall.

"Enjoy your stay," Sebastien said, his voice buoyant.

It should be fun.

She turned around and offered a hesitant smile. "Thank you," she said before hurrying down the corridor. The boy craned his neck to get another look at the strange man behind him. Sebastien held up his hand and waved as the doors closed.

❖

The electric lights of Piraeus flickered on as the sun dipped behind the hills in the distance. The port town was serene compared to the bustle of the morning. The docks were almost deserted. A hush had fallen over the streets.

Sebastien watched as the shore drifted farther and farther beyond reach. The glow of Athens hovered over the east like a protective shell. He stood on the stern of Sunset Deck, sixteen levels above the churning sea below. From here, the waves looked like ripples in a pond.

A man appeared by his side, startling him from his thoughts. He smelled like earth and warm skin. Nikos didn't say a word. He leaned against the ship's railing, his shoulder touching Sebastien's, and looked across the gulf to the disappearing shore. His eyes were brighter in the twilight.

A few minutes passed in silence before Nikos tilted his head toward Sebastien. "I'm sorry for what happened to your friend."

Sebastien hesitated before responding. "I'm sorry, too."

"Do you blame me?"

"For what?"

"For having to follow the orders."

Thoughts circled his mind, but he knew Nikos wasn't the enemy. "You're just doing your job, like the rest of us." He inhaled deeply, letting the salted air fill his lungs. "This ship felt like home when I arrived on board a few weeks ago. I thought I'd finally found a place where I belonged. Now I'm not sure."

"You do belong here," Nikos said, tilting his head closer. "Meet me on Riviera Deck in ten minutes. Walk to the very front. Portside. You'll see a set of locked doors at the end of the hall. Knock." With that, he was gone in a flash of white and gold.

Riviera Deck was a seafoam-carpeted loop around the entire ship lined with identical doorways that led to guest cabins. Frosted-glass lamps shaped like scallop shells punctuated the rose-coloured walls between doors. The centre of the deck was the atrium, with a balcony that hung dizzyingly above the Agora lobby below.

Just as Nikos had said, at the end of the hall on the forward section of the ship was an unmarked set of double doors that weren't numbered like the others. He knocked quietly.

Nikos appeared, grabbing him by the hand and pulling him inside. The room was egg-shaped and softly lit. Enormous white sheets were draped along the walls and over pieces of furniture. The bottom half of the curved wall was made of teak panels like the floors of the outdoor decks. The top of the wall was a mosaic of jagged fragments of coloured glass that were lit from behind. Three steps led to a stage that spanned the front of the room.

"Where are we?"

"I like to come here when I need to be alone," Nikos said with a shy smile. "It's a temple. At least, it used to be. They designed it to be a place where anyone could come to worship. Muslim. Christian. Buddhist. Jew. It was always the emptiest room on the ship. It's funny how easily people forget about their god while on holiday." He let out a quiet snort. "It's closed to the public now, to be turned into a venue for small wedding ceremonies. The renovations are suspended for a few weeks. Until then, I'm one of the only people on board with access."

He held a key card in his hand. It looked identical to the rectangles of plastic everyone used to access their cabins, but it was black instead of white.

"No way," Sebastien said. "Is that a skeleton key?"

"I don't know what that is, but it does get me into almost every room and corner of the ship. See? Being deputy security commander has its perks."

"Why did you bring me here?"

Nikos stepped closer. The machismo evident weeks ago had vanished. Standing in front of Sebastien was just a man who didn't know how to be loved. He was nervous, unsure. He struggled with his words. "I guess —"

Sebastien didn't let him finish. Their mouths pressed against each other. He stripped off the officer's jacket and threw it against the wall. Nikos pulled the shirt over his head. Their chests heaved as the heat of their bodies filled the room. Soon, the floor was littered with their uniforms and the differing statuses they represented. They were made equal in the exposure of their skin.

The two young men collapsed onto a mattress of white sheets bunched together on the floor. Their bodies rocked to the rhythm of the ship as it swayed against the waves. Nikos exhaled so violently when he came, it was as if his lungs were emptied of everything that had once suffocated him.

They lay on sheets that were damp with sweat, tangled in each other's limbs. Nikos kissed Sebastien's shoulder and held him tightly. "I've been wanting to do that for a long time."

"Me, too," Sebastien said, shifting his body so their foreheads touched. "That is, ever since I learned you were just pretending to be an arrogant prick."

Nikos responded with a playful shove.

"Have you always liked men?" Sebastien asked.

A faint shadow fell over his face. "I'm not supposed to. Love between men isn't understood where I come from. People say it's getting better in Greece, but it doesn't seem that way to me."

"Your family doesn't know?"

Nikos gave him a sardonic look. "My father took me to a whorehouse when I was fifteen. He told me it was time to become a man. It's a common thing for fathers to do in my village. Nothing would bring them more shame than to see their sons do what we just did."

"You're just going to hide it for your whole life?"

"I'm used to hiding. It won't be so bad. I love women, too. I'll find a wife one day, settle down. Make my family happy."

Sebastien felt the sadness that had crept into Nikos's eyes. He kissed him. "Do what makes *you* happy. Don't worry about them. Your father sounds like an asshole."

Nikos laughed, and he looked beautiful. Eyes squinted. Lines creased into his cheeks. Lips pulled over teeth. Sebastien wanted him to look that way forever.

"You're not wrong about that. At least I don't have to see him much anymore. That's what drew me to the sea. I could get far away from him and my village, where it's so dry you can't even have a meal outside without it getting covered in dust. He didn't think I would make it on my own."

"Look at you. You command an entire security team for a ship of three thousand people. You proved him wrong."

His face flushed. "With a little help, of course. I met Kostas when I was just a deck cadet. I guess he saw something in me. I wouldn't have moved up the ranks as quickly as I did without him."

"It helps to have friends in high places," Sebastien said. He hoped the tensing of his muscles went unnoticed. "That dusty old village is far away. You can be yourself here."

Nikos's eyebrows pulled toward the bridge of his nose. "I know the *Glacier* might seem like a carefree utopia in the crew bar. Be who you want to be. Love who you want to love. I wish it were true." His gaze drifted past Sebastien's shoulder. "It's different in the officers' circle. The commanders want the staff and crew to feel safe, but the truth is they're disgusted by people like us. They think it's a disease that afflicts the weak and immoral. A corruption of character. I'd lose my rank if they knew."

Sebastien's skin went warm. He had no doubt in his mind who was cultivating this belief.

"What about you?" Nikos said as he combed his fingers through Sebastien's hair, tucking a few tangles behind his left ear. He touched the black metal stud that was pierced through the earlobe. "Have you ever been in love with a man?"

"Sure, but I love easily. It's a character flaw. I've been in love with women, too. One woman, to be exact. It ended not long ago."

"What happened?"

"Nothing. Everything." He paused in thought. "It was doomed from the beginning. I realized one day that I had used her. I needed to feel redeemed, and she gave that to me. But she used me, too."

"Love is complicated."

Sebastien ran his fingers along Nikos's chest. Below his right shoulder was a circular tattoo with concentric rings. It had caught his eye the other morning in the locker room shower. Now, he could take a closer look. "Tell me about this."

"It's the shield of Achilles, the one he used during his famous fight with Hector of Troy. Look," Nikos said, pointing to the centre ring. "This is the earth, surrounded by the sun and moon. The edge of this ring is the sea. The outer rings are filled with people. Here's a wedding. On the other side is an army attacking a city. This is a king, and here's a farmer. It represents the balance of civilization. Peace. War. Rich. Poor. For there to be good, there must also be bad. Achilles was always my favourite hero from the mythologies."

"Wasn't he a bloodthirsty killer?"

"It was ancient times. You either killed or were killed. And it was war! If it weren't for Achilles, the Greeks wouldn't have defeated the deceitful Trojans."

"I think the big wooden horse deserves some of the credit." Sebastien flashed him a cocky smile.

"Horse or no horse, Achilles would have found a way into the city."

"If you're Achilles, does that make me your legendary lover, Patroclus?"

Nikos pulled him closer until they could feel the rise and fall of each other's breathing. "You are my Patroclus."

"Hopefully I don't die so soon in battle like he did. Then you wouldn't have to avenge my death by killing Hector."

"In our version, I would rescue you. Hector would still die in the end, though."

"And what's your weakness — your Achilles heel?"

"You are," Nikos said, closing his eyes and resting his forehead against Sebastien's lips. "You're my weakness."

"And this can be our house." Sebastien looked up at the vaulted ceiling above them and realized for the first time it was painted like a starlit sky. "The House of the Heel."

NINE

Sirens

The island of Santorini is shaped like a crescent moon or a human fetus, depending on whom you ask. Nestled in the curve is a smaller island that slopes upward into a volcanic cone.

The island was whole, once. Some even say it was a flourishing nation that inspired the legend of Atlantis. When it erupted thousands of years ago, the centre collapsed into the sea. Only the eastern caldera and a scattering of fragments remain.

Today, Santorini is the picture of Greece sought after by every traveller. Villages of whitewashed walls and blue domes cling to the side of the caldera high above the water. Every patio is filled with dreamers and lovers as the sun sets fire to the sky before dipping behind the horizon.

It was here Sebastien took a sip of his coffee, bitter and foamy on top, and gazed out over the edge of the restaurant balcony to the endless sea. The *Glacier* looked like a toy boat in a bathtub, docked far below near the base of the caldera. Cruise ships sailed into the harbour throughout summer, each releasing its infestation of travellers on the island. They swarmed the winding streets, consuming everything in sight, before sailing away to the next victim. The cycle repeated itself until winter.

"It's been only two days since Athens, and it already feels like people are forgetting about Dominic." Diya wore round sunglasses and a sweater the colour of cilantro. She was always cold despite the heat. Sebastien and Ilya fanned themselves with paper menus as they roasted beneath the afternoon sun. "This can't just be the end of it, can it?"

Sebastien recalled what Rosa had said to him the day Dominic disembarked. "We didn't get what we wanted, but I think it made a difference. It woke people up."

"I've never seen Kostas like that before. It looked like his face was going to erupt." Diya looked troubled as she sipped tea from a white cup. "And the way Giorgos treated Contessa ..."

"What do you mean?" Sebastien asked. "There was so much going on, I wasn't paying attention to him."

"Right before the electricity was shut down, he went over and grabbed her by the arm. Hard. He tried pulling her to her feet, but she resisted. He looked furious. There was so much noise and chaos, I don't think a lot of people noticed. But I saw what happened." Diya leaned forward, wrapping her arms around herself. "She must have known she'd be in trouble for getting involved with the protest. I admire her. She just wanted to help. But I'm scared of what she might be facing behind closed doors."

A waiter arrived to deliver plates filled with sundried octopus and tzatziki drizzled with olive oil. Sebastien and Diya expected Ilya to dig in ravenously, but he just stared at the food. The normally sunny fitness trainer had had an absent look in his eyes since the morning.

"What's going on with you?" Sebastien asked.

"I've been wondering the same thing," Diya added. "You're acting like your brain has been hijacked by aliens."

Ilya's eyes darted between them as though he'd just woken up from a trance. "What? Oh. I'm fine." He forced a gravelly laugh, but it was clear Sebastien and Diya weren't convinced. With a deep breath, he sat back and let his arms hang over the side of his chair. "I just ... Something happened last night that's been bothering me."

"Go on," Sebastien said as he speared a tentacle with his fork.

"It was after my shift last night. I was in the crew bar with Cory. You know, my British dancer friend. It was quieter than usual, I guess, because the mood has been different since the Giorgos incident at the party. Most of the people there were *malákas*, and they were sailor-wasted. It was like a sad little party for insecure boys in white suits."

"I'm glad I wasn't there," Diya said. "The last thing I need right now is to be smothered by officers."

"They were being obnoxious, but we just ignored them. Cory and I were minding our business when two of them came up to us. One of them said, 'You two faggots. Nobody wants to see that. This isn't Mykonos.' Then they just laughed and walked away."

Diya was so shocked that she spilled her tea onto the plate in front of her. "Please tell me you're joking."

Ilya looked sombre. "I was too stunned to do anything. I wanted to speak, but no words came out. I wanted to bash in his teeth, but I couldn't move. My whole body froze, like those stupid statues on the ship. Cory and I just sat there, helpless. I thought I would never have to feel that way again when I moved to the *Glacier*. I thought I had left that feeling behind in Ukraine."

"How bad was it there?" Sebastien asked, unsure if he was prepared for the answer.

"Bad." There was something woeful in the way Ilya squinted his eyes as he looked beyond the balcony's edge. It was a quality Sebastien wasn't used to seeing in him. "I learned how to fit in, how to play the part so people would leave me alone, but that wasn't my best friend's style. He wasn't one to hide in the shadows.

"Misha believed in the good of people. He knew how to look past the hatred and the violence to see the fear underneath. 'They hate us because they fear us,' he used to say to me. 'They fear us because they don't know us. So, we make them know us.' He would always say that last line with a big stupid grin." Ilya smiled, but the sadness had settled across the rest of his face. "Misha had a way of making complicated things seem simple. He died four years ago."

"What happened?" Sebastien asked after a short silence.

"It was late in Kiev. We shared a flat back then, and we were walking home from our favourite club. I still remember exactly how he looked that night. His messy hair was tied back in a 'baby bun,' as he called it. He wore the yellow T-shirt I had given him for his birthday. It said 'Misha for Mayor' across the front. I spray-painted it myself.

"We were drunk and laughing when a group of men stopped us. I don't know how many there were. I only remember what one of them looked like. He had a shaved head, but his jaw was covered in a trimmed beard. He was ugly except for his eyes. They sparkled like blue gems. That man asked us if we were fags. The word came out of his mouth so easily, just like it did last night in the crew bar.

"Misha wasn't afraid of them. He had been through this before. He looked at the ugly man's face and said, 'Before you waste your time, you should know you're not my type.'" Ilya laughed at the memory, rubbing his eyes. "Misha was punched in the face. I was punched in the gut. Those men didn't want us dead. They just wanted to scare us. Perhaps it made them feel stronger than they really were. Misha fell, and the back of his head hit a brick wall. They ran when they saw the blood. They ran like frightened children."

Sebastien felt his skin go cold as he listened to Ilya's story. He could feel his heartbeat slow until it was barely detectable.

"Misha used to say, 'It's easier to hate someone when they don't have a face. We need to show the people our faces.' When I wanted to move as far away from Ukraine as I could get, he was the only reason I stayed. 'This country isn't going to change if people like us run away,' he said to me. 'We need to stay, and we need to fight.'

"I spent hours at the police station that night. I answered all their questions. I knew after ten minutes that they weren't going to do a thing. Justice wasn't meant for people like us.

"I didn't know what to do with myself as the months went by. Life was starting to return to something that resembled normal, until winter came. I was walking through the Old Town when something caught my eye through a window. It was a bearded man with a shaved head. Even from the other side of the window, I could see the blue in his eyes sparkle.

"I stood there, frozen, as the snow fell around me. The ugly man poured beer from behind the bar. I wanted so badly to step inside that room, but I resisted. 'Keep walking,' I could hear Misha say.

"But I found my way to that window the next evening, and the next. Every evening, the same glowing window, the same bearded man. I would stand outside for a few minutes before circling the block and returning. The routine would last an hour or two, but in the end I would go home.

"The night before Christmas Eve I stood and waited. I didn't even feel the cold. I watched as people left the bar until it was empty. The man was wiping down the counters. He waved goodbye to the waitress as she left for the night. He put on a coat and wrapped a scarf around his neck.

"I followed him down a narrow alley. He had no idea I was behind him. I waited until we reached a small court-yard where the snow on the ground was untouched. 'Merry Christmas,' I said. There was a lantern above us, and the light made the man's skin look yellow. He just looked at me, then he said, 'How's your friend?'"

Their grim faces contrasted with the bright Santorini setting around them. They could feel the chill of the Ukrainian winter, hear the buzz of the lantern above.

"I lost control," Ilya said. "I knocked him to the ground and couldn't stop punching. I remember tears freezing to my eyelashes as my fists lashed out, over and over and over again. I hated the look of his sick smile, so I hit his mouth until it was bloody and broken. I had him pinned against the floor. He was helpless. I could see he was trying to say something, so I stopped when my arms were tired. He couldn't speak properly by then, but I think he was trying to say they didn't mean to kill him."

Ilya buried his face in his hands. His body trembled.

"I wanted to end it so badly. My hands were itching to wrap around his throat, to watch the life fade from his eyes. I didn't feel guilty or scared. My mind was made. The only thing that stopped me was Misha. I knew he would have been so disappointed in me. He wouldn't have wanted that."

"You let him go?" Sebastien asked.

"I walked away and went straight home. Packed my bags. Took a train to Bratislava, then Vienna, then Zurich. I didn't know where I was going, but I knew I couldn't stop moving. I ended up in Copenhagen. Two months later I boarded the *Glacier*. It sailed the Baltic back then."

Sebastien and Diya moved their chairs to either side of Ilya. The other tables on the patio stole glances at the three of them as they held each other.

"I like to think that Misha's inside of me," Ilya went on. "That he instilled some of his goodness. I try to see the world the way Misha did. It felt easier to do on the ship. Everyone was allowed to be who they were, to love who they wanted. I didn't think I'd experience that kind of hatred again until last night in the crew bar."

"Don't let a couple *malákas* take anything away from you," Sebastien said, squeezing Ilya's shoulder. "You're stronger than that. The three of us together are even stronger."

Sebastien could see that Ilya wasn't convinced, despite the forced smile, and he understood. He wanted to feel reassured himself, but something had changed on board the *Glacier*. He couldn't quite place it, but it felt insidious.

The spray of the sea wet their faces as the tender ferried them away from the caldera. The *Glacier* loomed ahead like an island of its own.

Something felt amiss as soon as they stepped through the security gates. People were clustered together along Styx, looking intently at the walls. There were more posters, this time printed on dark red paper. They were posted along the corridor like emergency lights.

The message was in bold black letters.

Staff & Crew:
Due to recent misconduct, a new morality
code will take effect immediately.
The following improprieties are no longer
tolerated:
Drunkenness
Insubordination
Offensive sexual behaviour
Violations may lead to immediate dismissal.
Regards, Your Commanding Officers

❖

Sebastien was twenty-five when they met.

Jérôme St-Germain had just moved back to Petit Géant after several years in Montréal. The people in town remembered him being a bookish boy, peculiar and reserved. They were surprised to see him return as an attractive young man with easy charm and a confident style. The town was happy to welcome an eligible bachelor.

Sebastien was freelancing for the local newspaper at the time, mostly shooting fundraisers and hockey tournaments. Jérôme found him peering through the viewfinder of his camera while on assignment at the local college's graduation ceremony. The diplomas had been handed out, the mortarboards had been thrown. The young graduates now clustered together in optimistic groups.

"I hear you're the town's star photographer," Jérôme said with a smile. He appeared tidy and down-to-earth. His hair was a dense sweep of chestnut. Behind the thin frames of his glasses were two penetrating grey eyes tinged with blue like pools of rainwater.

"That is definitely an overstatement," Sebastien responded. "I'm just the only guy in town who knows what an aperture is."

The handsome stranger laughed. He crossed his arms and scanned the gymnasium, which was filled with electric blue gowns and bright faces. "I went to this school almost a decade ago. It hasn't changed a bit. They still haven't fixed that." His head nodded toward a domed lamp hanging from the ceiling that was dark, unlike the others.

"I used to go here, too. I remember you."

Jérôme turned to him, surprised. "Aren't you a few years younger?"

"You hosted an art show in the café to raise money for the class trip to Europe. You painted sea monsters. There was one that looked like a man with octopus tentacles instead of legs. I loved it."

"I'm glad someone appreciated it. The genteel denizens of Petit Géant seemed more disturbed than anything else. I suppose that's what I get for showcasing art in a cultural black hole." He looked at the floor with a nostalgic expression before his eyes shot up to Sebastien. "No offence!"

He laughed. "None taken. I have no attachment to this place. It's just a cage to me."

Jérôme adjusted his wool blazer and looked at Sebastien with his rainwater eyes. "I have an offer for you."

That afternoon, they went together to the same café that had hosted the art show so many years earlier. Jérôme laughed when he stepped through the door, amazed how little it had changed. Sebastien didn't know what to make of this man as they settled into a corner table, but he soon understood they shared something.

Jérôme explained that it hadn't been easy leaving Montréal. The bohemian bars filled with artists and students teemed with ideas aching to be explored and expanded. Jérôme had found a place that felt like home. When his father fell ill and his mother became distraught, he knew the occasional weekend visit to Petit Géant would no longer suffice. He told himself it would be temporary.

When it was clear his father's condition was only going to worsen before it got better, he accepted that his stay in town would be longer than he had hoped. He was a headstrong man, not one to sit on his hands. This was an opportunity for him to leave a positive imprint on his much-maligned hometown.

He decided to open a shop. Part gallery, part portrait studio, part camera store, it would be different from anything the town had ever seen. He wanted Sebastien's help.

Although Sebastien had no wealth to invest, Jérôme treated him like a business partner. From branding to merchandising, all decisions were made together. They decided to name the shop Camera Obscura.

By the time preparations for the grand opening were underway, they were spending nearly every morning, afternoon, and evening together. Their friendship was instantaneous. They shared a feeling of alienation — they were both outsiders in a town that enforced conformity — but Jérôme possessed an optimism that things could change.

It was late one night when they first kissed. It had been an exhausting day of painting the interior walls. Sheets of thick brown paper covered the front windows. Sebastien ran a paint roller down his friend's back, smearing him from neck to rear with the same mint colour as the newly painted walls. Jérôme retaliated, and it wasn't long before the two men were rolling across the newspaper-covered floor entangled in each other's limbs. It was his first taste of a man's lips, and he liked it. He let Jérôme do things with their bodies he had never done before.

"What got you into photography?" Jérôme asked as they lay on the floor beneath a blanket they had retrieved from the trunk of his car.

"My mother," Sebastien said, wondering if the answer sounded childish. "We used to have a cheap thirty-five-millimetre camera when I was a kid. We took pictures of everything over the years. There must be at least five big boxes full in her closet. Even now, she insists we print every shot to add to the collection."

"Life passes by so quickly. Photos give us a way to remember it."

Sebastien rolled onto his side and draped his arm across Jérôme's stomach. "I love how cameras can freeze time. The shutter opens and the moment solidifies into something that will remain long after we're gone."

Jérôme leaned into him until their foreheads touched. "Where did you come from, Sebastien Goh?" he said with a smile.

The grand opening of the shop was a success: people actually showed up. Ruby arrived in her favourite red cheongsam. Jérôme's mother pushed her husband's wheelchair. They stayed for only twenty minutes, but their son was happy to see them smile.

Half of the room was a gallery space displaying work from artists in the region, including several framed photographs by Sebastien. In the centre of one wall was Jérôme's adolescent painting of the octopus man, which he had gifted to his new friend. Servers holding trays of delicate hors d'oeuvres circulated, while a quartet of jazz musicians performed in a corner.

"How fabulous," Sophie said when she arrived with two friends. Sebastien kissed her on the cheek.

Sophie gushed about his new "project," as she called it, but behind the smile was worry. Sebastien seemed different. There was something in the way he held himself that hinted at newfound contentment. It was unexpected. The weeks leading up to their latest breakup months earlier had been especially rocky. He had been aimless and unfulfilled. She was sure he'd come back to her eventually.

Now, seeing the confident way he spoke to his guests and the smart clothes he wore, she felt the creep of uncertainty. Her eyes scanned the mint-coloured room and his new charismatic friend with suspicion.

Sophie found the photographs a month later. Sebastien had been careless. They were stored loosely in a desk drawer in the back room. He had asked her to watch the shop for thirty minutes while he and Jérôme picked up a set of new shelves. She wouldn't have found them had she not been snooping, but she sensed something was being hidden from her.

The black-and-white photographs printed on glossy paper displayed the nude bodies of two beautiful men. Sebastien was alone in some of them, a suggestive look in his eyes and hair tousled even more wildly than usual. Both men appeared in most of the images. Foreheads touched. Fingers intertwined. Mouths met skin. They looked happy and in love.

Sophie's hands shook as she reached for her phone. She didn't know why she felt the need to capture these images and send them to her closest friend, Chloe. She would say she wasn't thinking, that she just needed someone's opinion, but she must have known what Chloe would do.

By the time Sebastien and Jérôme returned to the shop, the images of their secret affair were rushing through town like the torrents of a flood.

⸭

"Offensive sexual behaviour," Ilya said, his eyes wide and agitated. He couldn't stop running his hands through his short sandy hair. "You know what that means, don't you? Anything they want. I'm sure me and Cory kissing in the crew bar would be considered offensive in their eyes. They won't spell it out, but they want us to know they have the power to get rid of us for any reason they see fit."

One of the red posters rested on the floor of Diya's cramped cabin. They looked at it as though it were diseased.

Sebastien rubbed his temples with his hands. All he could see was Jérôme's face from four years before. The colour of the posters was the same shade of red as the paint scrawled across the storefront of Camera Obscura.

"Hypocrisy is what this is," Diya said. Her face was flushed with anger. "What about the deck commander who's cheating on his wife with a younger woman? I'll bet they wouldn't consider that offensive. It doesn't count because he's one of them."

"Don't forget the officers who have loyalty cards at the brothels in every port," Ilya added. He sat on the bottom bunk, his arms hanging limply between his legs.

There's also the hotel commander who abandoned a woman and their unborn son in a foreign country like they were yesterday's trash, Sebastien wanted to say. He bit his bottom lip and swallowed the words before they could leave his mouth.

"I just don't get what's going through his head." Diya took a seat beside Ilya and hugged a pillow against her chest. "He knows this will cause more outrage than he already has. Why would he go to so much trouble to provoke us?"

"The commanders are trying to send us a message," Ilya said. "They want us to know they control us, that they can do whatever they want. They think we're powerless to stop them."

"They're testing us," Diya added. "They want to see if and how we respond so they know how much power they really have. We need to send them a message of our own. We need to fight back."

"They're distracting us." Sebastien had been quiet since they encountered the red posters in the corridor. Diya and Ilya looked at him with curiosity, waiting for him to elaborate. "When I met with Dominic the day before the protest, he told me he saw something he shouldn't have seen. That's why he was locked in his cabin and thrown off the ship. The fight with Giorgos was just a convenient excuse. He said Kostas and the officers are hiding something — something bad — in cabin A66."

"You're just telling us this now?" Ilya asked with an incredulous shake of the head.

"I'm sorry. There was just so much going on." Sebastien paused, bracing himself for the next revelation. "There's more. Something strange happened at the party in the crew bar, before the fight with Giorgos. I saw a young officer pour white powder into Dominic's drink. The powder was given to him by Kostas. It looked like an order from the commander."

Diya and Ilya stared at him from the bottom bunk. They wore identical expressions of incomprehension on their faces.

"I stopped Dominic from drinking it," Sebastien went on. "I was going to tell you, Ilya, but I was interrupted by Giorgos. Then everything exploded from there. Dominic thought the commanders were trying to drug him as an excuse to throw him off the ship — because of what he saw."

"What was it then?" Diya asked with impatience. "What was in cabin A66?"

"I don't know. He wouldn't tell me. I sent him a message after he disembarked in Athens. I just got a response today. He keeps saying I'm better off not knowing, and that he just wants to forget it ever happened. I think he's scared."

The room became silent except for the sound of Diya's bedside clock ticking away the seconds.

"You're both right." Sebastien reached out and took each of them by the hand. "We'll show them how powerless we are. But if we're not careful, they'll throw us off the ship like they did with Dominic. We'll send them a message. We'll fight back. And we'll find out what's in cabin A66."

❖

The *Glacier* docked at the hedonistic island of Mykonos the following day. Ilya spent the entire afternoon wearing a pink tank top that flaunted his sculpted shoulders and biceps. The words on the front said *Good boys go to heaven, bad boys go to Mykonos* in fluorescent green letters.

The ship's horn thundered across the bay as the *Glacier* set sail in the evening. Across all decks of the ship, staff and guests prepared for the festivities. They styled their hair and put on their finest clothes. The women slipped their feet into precipitous heels and sprayed perfume on their shoulders. The men tied silk bows around their necks with varying degrees of proficiency. It was black-tie night aboard the *Glacier*.

Their cabin felt more confined than usual. Sebastien and Ilya manoeuvred around each other as they showered and dressed. Besides the captain's cocktail party, black-tie night was the only event when staff weren't required to wear their evening uniform of turquoise blazers and white pants while off duty in guest areas. They were always eager to dress up for the occasion. Since crew members were permitted in the upper decks only while on duty, they couldn't partake in the festivities.

"How do I look?" Sebastien wore the black tuxedo Ilya had lent him. The shoulders were slightly loose and the pants a touch long, but he was a dashing figure nonetheless. He glanced at the framed photograph of his mother on the desk beside his bunk. He wished she could see him dressed so finely. She would have been proud.

"Cooler than James Bond." Ilya stepped out of the shower and dried his body with a towel. The mirror behind him revealed the scatter of circular white scars on his back.

Sebastien had been hesitant to ask Ilya about the scars, but they'd grown close enough to meet the people they were beneath the surface.

"How did you get those marks on your back?"

Ilya looked behind himself at his reflection. He had a curious look on his face, as though he'd forgotten about the scars. "They're cigarette burns. I got them in school. A bunch of older boys held me down. They wanted to see if I would cry. I didn't."

Sebastien's eyes fell to the floor. He was embarrassed for asking.

"It's okay," Ilya said as he adjusted Sebastien's bow tie. "I've been fighting against boys like them ever since. Maybe one day I'll win."

The two men looked like movie stars when they emerged from their cabin. Ilya's jacket was made of dark purple velvet.

Their patent leather shoes announced their arrival as they walked along the opulent decks of the guest quarters. They smiled at uniformed members of staff and crew as they passed. Bartenders, waiters, cleaners, casino dealers — they all smiled back with a look of solidarity.

Diya met them in the Agora lobby dressed in a form-fitting emerald gown that sparkled with reflected light. They could have passed as part of the privileged crowd that surrounded them if it weren't for the golden name badges that identified them as staff.

"Looking sharp, boys." She smiled, impressed, as they exchanged kisses on the cheek. "I'm the luckiest lady on board to have you two as my escorts."

"You look like Lady Luck herself," Sebastien said as Diya linked her arm through his.

The three of them climbed the grand staircase where Sebastien had tumbled down just one week earlier. Once again he tripped as his shoe caught the edge of a step, but this time his companions kept him from falling to his knees.

"You clumsy goat," Ilya said, holding him firmly by the elbow.

They sauntered toward the stern of Adriatic Deck until they arrived at a rotating glass door. A bouncer dressed in a tuxedo gave them a nod as they entered the dark hall on the other side. They were immediately greeted by the sounds of overly synthesized dance music. The bass vibrated along the floor.

Sirens was the ship's nightclub, lovingly referred to by staff as "the disco." It was a two-level chamber of neon lights and contorting bodies. The entrance gave onto a mezzanine that overlooked the action below. The dance floor was a checkerboard of square tiles lit up with erratic colours. A hypnotic sequence of light particles undulated across the video screens that wrapped the walls.

It was a mythical place for crew members. None of them had set foot inside except for the cleaners and bartenders who worked there. The crew would talk about the exclusive room as though it were Shangri-La, while the staff took the privilege for granted.

As with most black-tie nights at Sirens, the majority of the crowd consisted of staff laughing over cocktails and exchanging provocative glances. The mood was more subdued than usual, though. There was tension in the air as people clustered around tables and lingered in corners.

Sebastien, Diya, and Ilya greeted a group of spa therapists before making their way down the winding staircase that led to the main lounge. The risk level of these twisting steps correlated with the number of drinks consumed and the height of the heels worn. Many victims had been claimed over the years.

The dance floor was empty except for a few guests on the younger end of the spectrum. They moved to the beat of an electropop song that was a hit well over a decade ago. The commanding officers' favourite era was the excess that led to the global financial crisis, so the DJ was instructed to reflect those simpler, happier times through his set list.

Tinted mirrors lined the walls of the lounge underneath the mezzanine. Displayed throughout the area were sculptures of human torsos. The seductive shoulders, chests, stomachs, and pelvises stood in bold fluorescent colours, heads and limbs nowhere to be seen.

The room was crowded with sharply dressed staff. A pack of officers huddled together on lounge chairs and sofas, surveying the scene with drinks in hand. Their white uniforms were a bluish hue beneath the ultraviolet light.

When a couple from the entertainment staff distracted Diya and Ilya, Nikos walked over from the officers' corner and stood by Sebastien's side.

"Good evening, Patroclus." He had the slightest hint of a smile in the corners of his lips.

"Good evening to you, Achilles. Cause any destruction today?"

"Only to those who deserved it," Nikos responded. "You look very handsome."

"Ilya gets the credit. I'm wearing his suit."

"I don't care about the suit. It's what's underneath I want."

"I believe that may now be classified as 'offensive sexual behaviour.'" Sebastien turned to Nikos with darkness in his eyes.

Nikos looked away. "I know. It's messed up."

"What is Kostas thinking?"

"I have no idea."

"You work for him," Sebastien said, unconvinced. "He treats you like his favourite son."

Nikos shrugged and shoved his hands inside the pockets of his pants. "He was humiliated by the Dominic protest. This is part of the punishment. He thinks staff and crew have too much freedom, which leads to acts of insubordination. He sees the environment below decks — the sex, the drink — as corrupting."

"Do you know why, Nikos? It's because he thinks we're his slaves. He wants to tell us what we can and cannot do, who we can and cannot fuck."

"The rule isn't black and white."

"Exactly. The rule applies to anything they might find offensive. And you told me yourself. They're disgusted by people like us."

Nikos's face flushed with embarrassment.

As if on cue, Kostas descended the spiral staircase. Holding him by the hand was his elegant wife with the pointed nose. She wore a satin dress that hovered above her knees. It was white like her husband's uniform.

Sebastien watched as the crowd parted to make way for them. The prestigious couple held themselves proudly, gliding through the lounge to their exclusive corner of fellow officers. His stare was so intense that the woman looked startled as their eyes connected. He felt his throat go dry.

"It seems like you're upset with me," Nikos said, "so I'll go."

Sebastien pulled his gaze away from the couple in white. "What do you know about Kostas's wife?"

"Alexis? Not much. She isn't very talkative but seems like a good mother. Lives with the kids in a posh part of Athens. Comes on board for a sailing or two every few months. Why?"

"Just curious," Sebastien said, a distant quality in the tone of his voice. "I'm not upset with you. I'm just disturbed by what's happening. You should be, too."

Nikos was about to respond when someone called his name from the officers' corner. "I'll find you later," he said before forging through the crowd.

The young commander made his way to Kostas. Something wasn't quite right in that corner of the lounge. Amid the sea of white suits stood a woman in black whom Sebastien didn't recognize. She was young, with straight dark hair and eyes wide as an owl's. Kostas pulled Nikos close to him and said something into his ear. Nikos nodded, took the woman by the arm, and led her to the back of the room. She resisted at first, but his grip was firm. He pushed a panel in the wall to reveal a secret door leading to a brightly lit corridor out of bounds to guests. They stepped into the rectangle of light before the door closed behind them.

Sebastien was trying to make sense of what he had just seen when he was interrupted by loud cheers from the crowd around him. Storming the raised dance floor was the ship's cast of dancers, a flurry of fiery colours punctuated by fitted white shirts and slim black pants.

The line of athletic bodies parted in the middle to reveal Contessa Bloor. She stood apart from the others in a white dress that shimmered beneath the spotlights. A burst of flowers was tied into her hair.

Ilya returned to Sebastien's side. "So it begins," Ilya said.

"Welcome to black-tie night on the *Glacier!*" Contessa announced as the audience cheered around her. "Just sit back, relax, and let us take you to paradise."

The staccato rhythm of a Latin dance song blared over the speakers while Contessa's voice filled the disco. Her dancers twisted and spun behind her in a dazzling blur of salsa, rumba, sequins, and skin.

Sebastien eyed a tall man in a white uniform standing near the base of the winding staircase. It was Giorgos. His gaze was fixed on Contessa, clearly captivated.

A dignified woman in her forties stood rigidly beside him. She wore a sleek silver dress and a gold mesh necklace. She seemed less impressed by the entertainment.

Must be his wife, Sebastien thought. *The poor lady is going to regret falling for the uniform, if she doesn't already.* He looked at Contessa and saw she could pass as a younger, more hopeful version of the woman who stood beside Giorgos.

✦

Diya stood against the wall, several paces from Sebastien. Her attention was also captured by the proud woman beside

Giorgos. Diya knew her name was Elena and that they'd been married for several years, but everything else about her was a mystery. Did she love her husband? Was he kind to her? Gentle? Did she know about the affair? Did she care? These questions drifted through her mind as she tried to read what was behind the woman's impenetrable eyes.

Contessa whirled across the floor, her arms sweeping through the air in theatrical motions. Only one person in the audience noticed a faint purple blemish on the skin of Contessa's arm. Diya had no doubts about what it was. The combination of makeup and bruised skin was one she knew well. Anger and sadness wrestled within her belly. She watched the singer smile through the performance while Giorgos observed her like prey.

Suddenly a disorderly noise blasted through the speakers and resounded throughout the disco. The lights that swirled across the video screens on the walls were replaced with unsteady footage of the scene from B Deck four days earlier. Dozens of black-clad protestors huddled together on the steel floor of Styx. They shouted and held onto each other as security guards and officers attempted to pull them apart.

The hotel commander's face towered above the audience as it appeared on the walls, every muscle tense with contempt. "A right to protest?" The speakers amplified the undercurrent of madness in his voice. "What makes you think that?" The man's eyes blinked mechanically on the enormous screens. "This is my ship. You have no rights unless I say so. You are powerless."

That final line repeated three more times to drive the point home. Groans rippled through the crowd of spectators. Contessa and her dancers stared in awe at the performance that had eclipsed their own.

The footage of the protest was spliced with scenes that were almost pornographic. Anonymous legs wrapped around naked hips. Mouths kissed sweat-speckled skin. Every combination of man and woman and other took part in the indulgence of each other's bodies. They twisted across the walls in an uninhibited display of sexuality between fragments of the staff and crew's defiance.

A message materialized in stark white letters.

Don't light matches on paper ships.

The video faded to black, and a final message flashed on the screen.

Love, The Powerless

TEN

Little Rebellions

Those final words were a love letter scrawled across the walls of Sirens. An effusive roar rumbled throughout the crowd. Confetti rained onto the dance floor from the group of spa therapists standing on the mezzanine.

As if to drive the point home, two female dancers on stage held each other's faces as they shared a passionate kiss. Two male dancers turned to each other and did the same. Soon, everyone on stage was kissing as though it were a provocative New Year's Eve special.

A satisfied smile tickled Sebastien's lips as he saw Kostas. The man wasn't pleased. His mouth moved rapidly and his hands sliced through the air, though his words couldn't be heard above the noise. Nikos, who had returned from the hidden door in the wall, appeared anxious with his hands on his head. After an animated exchange with Kostas, he looked at two of his guards and pointed to the stage.

The applause quickly turned into jeers as the two blue-suited guards charged forward to remove the kissing dancers. They resisted. A guard tried to grab one of the women by the arm. She wrenched herself from his grip and screamed profanities at him. The other dancers swarmed, standing between the men and their targets like a human barricade.

The guards stood helplessly on the edge of the stage, the lights of the tiled floor dancing beneath their feet. They turned to their commander, eager for him to make their decisions for them.

Nikos exhaled loudly, visibly irritated, and his shoulders slumped. He recovered with the next inhale, expanding his chest until he resembled a figure of authority. He shot Sebastien a disapproving look as he stepped onto the stage. It was clear he knew who was to blame.

⚜

Two days after Sophie discovered the illicit photographs, Sebastien and Jérôme arrived at their shop to find the front windows covered in paint. The letters spelled *FAIRIES* in jagged strokes of red. They didn't say a word to each other as they unlocked the door, filled a bucket with soapy water, and went to work on the red.

The shame Sebastien felt during the previous two days had been crippling, his thoughts consumed by panic. But the feeling passed and was replaced with indifference. Nothing much had changed, really. The townspeople had always avoided eye contact with him. This wasn't an irreparable fall from grace because he'd never earned grace to begin with.

Now they knew he was queer, but he'd always been accused of that anyway.

Jérôme's reaction was different. He wanted to be accepted, and he had come close, but he wasn't prepared for how ugly the town could be. Red paint on windows. Snickers and sidelong glances. Mothers shielding their children as they passed on the street. Unlike Sebastien, he wasn't used to these everyday slights.

The effect on their relationship was immediate. There were no dramatic fights, no words of blame. It just felt different when they touched. There was hesitation when there hadn't been before, heavy silences when there used to be laughter. With the business now at risk, they agreed to focus on that instead. The bond between them never recovered.

"Are you gay?" Sophie had asked that day, confused and distressed. She nearly spat out the words, and it sounded like an accusation. Sebastien felt so guilty that he couldn't even be angry at her for her violation.

"I think I was destined to be queer. But I'm still attracted to women."

"So our relationship wasn't just a cover-up?"

"Of course not." He held her closely against his chest and rocked her back and forth. Sophie knew it had begun. Sebastien was returning to her.

Nearly half of the red paint was gone from the storefront when Ruby walked over. "What's wrong with being fairies?" she asked. "They're beautiful, magical creatures. It's like trying to insult someone by calling them a doctor. People here are stupid."

Jérôme laughed for the first time in days, pushing his glasses up the bridge of his nose. "I can't argue with you there, Ruby."

When he disappeared into the store to refill the bucket, Ruby sidled up to her son. "He's a good man."

Sebastien nodded.

"I'm no expert on love," Ruby said. "You know that. But I'll tell you this. When that man looks at you, he sees you. When Sophie Lamoureux looks at you, she sees who she wants you to be."

❖

Nobody in the Odeon had ever seen the ship's palatial theatre filled with staff and crew before, rather than the well-heeled guests who normally sat in the rows of plush seats. It was a strange sight, so many of them gathered somewhere other than the crew bar. They filed into the theatre, their uniforms demarcating social classes in streams of white, gold, turquoise, and grey.

Sebastien, Diya, and Ilya arrived together and found seats in the centre of the orchestra section. They felt the tension in the air, as heavy and substantial as the icicle chandelier that hung above their heads.

It was the day after black-tie night. The *Glacier* was docked at the island of Naxos, and most guests were enjoying the afternoon in port. Off-duty staff and crew would normally be doing the same except that Kostas had called a mandatory meeting in the Odeon. No one but the guests and shore excursion guides had been permitted to leave the ship.

"This is going to be interesting," Diya whispered.

"His move," Sebastien said. "Let's see what he does with it."

"I wonder what inspired their aesthetic," Ilya said, looking at the stage. It was empty except for a frosted-glass podium that stood in the middle. A black velvet curtain provided the backdrop. "Soviet Russia or the Empire from *Star Wars*?"

The hum of the audience became quiet as Kostas made his way down the richly carpeted aisle. He wore a jolly smile on his face, nodding at certain people as he passed. Sebastien recalled the look of rage from the previous night, the blood surging through the veins in his forehead as he hurled verbal abuse at Nikos. Much of the audience had seen it, too.

Smile all you want, Sebastien thought. *We know who you really are.*

The spotlight from above followed Kostas as he climbed the stairs and travelled across the stage. The golden stripes on his shoulders shone under the beam. By the time he stood in front of the glass podium, there was silence.

"My beloved staff and crew of the *Glacier*," he said, hands sweeping outward in a dramatic gesture of inclusion. "I consider every single one of you my friend. Better yet, my family. I treat you as I treat my own children."

Diya and Ilya shifted in their seats and passed each other the subtlest of glances.

"I want to guide you. I want to protect you. I want to give you the best life possible." Kostas's head nodded along as if agreeing with itself. "But there is a disease on board this ship. Something toxic. It kills gratitude and spawns entitlement. It feeds on respect and vomits contempt. It replaces dignity with immorality."

His gaze drifted upward. Sebastien turned in his seat to see that the balcony was filled with the white-and-gold suits of the officers. They hovered above the sea of staff and crew in an overt display of power. Nikos's eyes met his. He was seated in the front row beside Giorgos, the polished gold buttons of their uniforms shining in the light.

On stage, the smile faded from Kostas's face.

"I find the recent spate of misconduct very troubling. It's one thing to disrupt order in the lower decks, but the disgusting display in the disco last night was unacceptable. This is not your ship. You are here because we allow you to be. That is the arrangement. If you don't like it, you leave. It's that simple."

Sebastien's temperature rose a degree with every word that came out Kostas's mouth. His hands gripped the velvet armrest on either side of him.

"I received this letter today." Kostas unfolded a sheet of paper with theatrical flair and cleared his throat. "'We, The Powerless, as you like to think of us, condemn the recent morality code as an attack on our human rights and freedom.' Blah, blah, blah. Oh! Here's the good part: 'We propose a council made up of elected representatives from staff and crew to aid in governance of all affairs that affect us. We also call for the removal of the divisive class distinctions between staff and crew, including the associated privileges, so that all employees may enjoy the same decency and respect.'"

He looked up at the audience, comical astonishment on his face, before laughing so heartily that his entire body convulsed. The laughter stopped as suddenly as it had started. With a swift closing of his fist, the letter was crushed and dropped to the stage.

"Acts of insubordination will not be tolerated. I don't take demands from anonymous cowards. Four dancers were evicted today for their involvement in last night's fiasco. Do you want to be next?" A few boos were shouted from the entertainment staff seated behind Sebastien.

"Settle down, settle down," Kostas said, his palms held out to the crowd. "They broke the rules. They defied authority in open view of guests and their commanding officers. It was a stupid thing to do. Now, I know not all of you have been infected by this disease. Most of you, even, are probably innocent. There is a small band of provocateurs stirring up trouble. They are ruining things for all of you.

"So here's what I'm going to do. I will reward one thousand euros to anyone who comes forward with legitimate information about who is leading these little rebellions. Until then, staff privileges will be suspended. That means staff will be no different from crew. No gallivanting around guest areas unless on duty, no more captain's cocktail party, no more black-tie night, no disco, no spa, nothing. You want class distinctions removed? Well, now you have it."

The tension that once filled the immense space turned to anger as shouts echoed across the near-perfect acoustics of the theatre. Diya turned to face Sebastien and Ilya. "He's trying to divide us."

"We are also implementing a curfew for all staff and crew," Kostas went on. "Unless you are on duty, you must be in your cabins before midnight. These rules will be strictly enforced by Nikos and his security team. Violations will result in immediate eviction. That includes the morality code."

Sebastien's chest contracted and expanded as breath heaved out his nostrils. He felt the rage seeping out of his lungs. It was so pure, white like his father's uniform. He wanted to let go, like he'd done before, but he fought it. He couldn't afford the risk of being evicted. There was still so much that needed to be done.

"Remember," Kostas said as the shouts died down. "These latest rules only apply until we've identified those responsible for spreading this corruption. Help us find them."

❖

Sex with Nikos felt like an act of rebellion. Their bodies came together at the altar of the House of the Heel, their secret temple. This little room with the starlit sky painted above them was designed to be a place of worship, yet the two men used it to worship each other instead of god. They bowed their heads and confessed sins in each other's ears. The purity of the white curtains spread out from under them.

This rebellion was against man, not god. Only man could hate something as pure as sex.

They wrapped themselves in the sheets and each other's bodies. "I've never met anyone like you." Nikos ran his fingertips along Sebastien's cheek.

"How so?"

"I can't be angry with you. All I want to do is hold you and put my lips on you."

"But you wish you could be angry with me?" He tried to read the mystery in Nikos's eyes.

"Sometimes. I wanted to be angry last night. That was a risky stunt you pulled in the disco. I know it was you."

Sebastien pulled away ever so slightly. "That wasn't a stunt, Nikos. It was a message. It came with its consequences, but it was received loud and clear."

"What did it achieve? You won't accomplish anything with these little acts of defiance. There will just be more punishment until this ship is miserable."

"Do you know why Diya Sharma left India to live here?" Sebastien's tone sharpened. "Because she was being beaten by her husband. Do you know why Ilya Tereshchenko fled Ukraine? His friend was killed for being gay. Everyone on this ship has a story like theirs. This place isn't just a job. It's our refuge from the things we ran away from. Now that oppression is happening here. We can't keep running."

Nikos tightened his hold on Sebastien's body. "There's injustice everywhere. You can't escape it. It has existed since the beginning of the human race, and it will persist until we're wiped out." His tone was soft like a gentle breeze despite the brittle words.

"But we can fight. Everyone on this ship knows that now. That's what we've achieved. When we're discriminated against, and abused, and punished, and forced into submission, forced to be quiet, we can choose to fight back."

"That stunt last night wasn't fighting back. It was provocation."

"No. It was a warning."

Nikos was silent as he studied the face before him. It was his turn to decode the mystery in Sebastien's eyes.

"I can only do so much to protect you," Nikos said.

"I know." Sebastien leaned forward and kissed him softly on the lips. "Who was that woman you escorted out of Sirens last night?"

He felt the muscles tighten slightly in Nikos's body. There was a hesitation. "What woman?"

"The young woman with the long dark hair. I saw Kostas order you to take her away. Then you pulled her through a hidden door in the wall. Who was she?"

"I don't know. I'd never seen her before. He told me to take her to A Deck. Some of the officers have family on board. I guess she's with one of them."

"Where on A Deck?"

"Sebastien, why are you so interested in this?"

"Where exactly on A Deck did you take her?"

Nikos took a deep breath, the blinking of his eyes more rapid than normal. "Just to the officers' quarters. She told me she had a cabin key and could find her way." His skin became warmer under Sebastien's touch. He chose his words more carefully. "There are things that happen below decks that are better left behind closed doors. Even the security cameras down there don't work. There are blind spots everywhere. I try to mind my own business. I'm discreet. We wouldn't want everyone knowing about what we do here, would we?"

"Why not?"

Nikos wasn't prepared for the challenge. Sebastien enjoyed watching him fumble for an answer.

"Because it's between you and me. It's private. Nobody's business but ours. I don't want anyone disturbing what we have together."

"Just like Achilles and Patroclus," Sebastien said. "People can speculate, but nobody will ever know the truth."

"Exactly." He smiled, relieved.

It wasn't long until Nikos was curled up, asleep. His stomach rose and fell like he was a Greek god made mortal. Sebastien held him, unsure of what was hidden behind the soft skin and hardened armour. He felt the urge to hurt this man who thought of himself as invincible while being so eager to submit. The feeling was faint yet distinct, this power to inflict pain on someone vulnerable.

He was careful as he reached for the officer's pants beside him. Attached to a ring that held Nikos's cards was the rectangle of black plastic he was looking for — the skeleton key.

ELEVEN

Backstage

A calm would settle over the ship during the hour leading up to dinner. Guests were in their cabins getting ready for the evening. Staff and crew slipped out for cigarette breaks and micro-naps. It often felt like they were preparing for a battle to begin. They put on their armour and preserved energy to brace themselves for the impending onslaught.

The casino was empty except for a few glassy-eyed passengers on the slot machines. Diya ducked into the Odeon and walked along the carpeted aisle toward the stage. Everything was muted in the still theatre. The plush turquoise velvet absorbed the sound of her footsteps.

It was a peaceful sanctuary compared to the volatile scene that had played out earlier in the day. Kostas had exited the stage with a self-satisfied grin on his face. He must have felt the hostility emanating from the audience, but Diya knew he didn't care. He probably expected they would soon turn on each other like a pack of hungry rats.

She wanted him to continue thinking he was invincible, though. She knew it would turn out to be his greatest weakness.

Behind the curtain of the stage was a world of trap doors and pulleys, machinery and painted landscapes. The things found here could make a mortal man fly and a goddess vanish into the sea. Diya had seen a few of the productions, wishing she could be a part of them. She imagined herself as a dancer in an elaborate costume, on a stage that would transform itself in the time it took for the curtain to close and open.

She passed a bank of counters and mirrors where the cast would prepare for each show. They would apply finishing touches and scan their reflections one last time before shedding their individuality to become one tile of a brilliant mosaic.

Diya entered a narrow hall. She was searching for their star.

Light spilled out the partly open door of one room. Inside was an old-fashioned dressing table with curved legs and ornate drawers. Bright round bulbs lined the edges of the mirror. The woman sitting there wore a plain cotton top as she swiped concealer underneath her eyes. Her hair was tied back into a sleek ponytail. Diya could see her reflection.

Contessa Bloor's body went rigid, then relaxed. "Diya," she said with a soft laugh. "You startled me." She smiled, covering the look of surprise on her face. "Come in. I'm just getting ready for tonight. Cocktail hour in the Agora. I'm going to do this bluesy rendition of an old Killers' song. Not sure if it'll be the right crowd, but we'll see how it goes."

Diya pulled up a seat beside her. "I'll get right to the point. I've been wanting to talk to you about something. Forgive me. It's none of my business. But I know what it's like having to plan what to wear, to find the right shade of concealer that won't rub off, to keep track of the excuses to avoid repeating the same one twice — just to hide the evidence."

Diya looked at Contessa's bare arm. It was covered in a thick layer of bronze makeup, but the purple underneath appeared angrier than it had the previous night. Contessa's eyes darted to her hands on the surface of the table.

"You can tell me that you bumped into a door frame," Diya went on. "You can say you fell. I won't question you. But I saw how Giorgos grabbed you at the protest. I saw how he looked at you. I know this much: any man who treats a woman like that in public will do much worse in private."

Contessa sat stiffly in her chair. She had wanted someone to confront her for months, to force the truth out of her so she could confront it herself. She had wished for someone to see through her makeup and her costumes. Now that it was finally happening, she found herself wanting to push it away, to reject the help, to deny it all.

Diya shifted closer. "My husband, Rajan, seemed so kind when we met. He used to sing to me. He had a terrible voice, and he would always get the words mixed up, but it was sweet.

"I was surprised the first time he hit me. It must have been an accident, I told myself, even though my face stung so badly I had tears in my eyes. After the second time, I told myself I must have done something wrong. It was my fault for anger-ing him, even though he wasn't the one left with bruises for days. I was so confused. How could this man who hurt me be the same man who used to sing to me?"

Contessa's body crumpled, her strong posture wilting like a flower. Her face remained composed, but now tears clung to her long black lashes. She reached for a porcelain teacup beside a bottle of brandy and took a long sip.

"Giorgos was angry." The confession spilled out of Contessa like water from a broken vase. "He said I shouldn't have been involved in the protest. The same thing happened last night in his cabin after Sirens. He thought I had something to do with it. I denied it, of course. He didn't care." She paused and looked into the mirror, the teacup clutched in her hands. "He's never hit me, though. He just grabs me, shakes me by the arms. Sometimes he pins me to the floor. He's so strong. I don't think he realizes how much it hurts."

"You're wrong," Diya said. "He knows. He does it to hurt you, to dominate you."

"I don't know what to do." Contessa looked at Diya's reflection in the mirror. She placed the teacup on the table. Her hands hovered above her chest, paralyzed and helpless.

"Leave him. Why are you still with him?"

She shook her head. Her gaze drifted past the mirror to something distant. "It felt like a romance novel in the beginning. The dashing officer and his mistress. We stole kisses when nobody was looking. He'd sneak me into his cabin in the commanders' wing. I felt desired." Youthfulness washed over her face as she spoke, as though youth were an emotion rather than an age. "Now I know I'm a fool. What used to be forbidden and exciting just feels desperate." The last word blew past her lips like cigarette smoke. "I'm thirty-seven. I have no family of my own, no companion. I share a bed with another woman's husband, but is it better to be alone?"

"I left Rajan knowing no other man in my country would look at me again," Diya said. "I would be marked. I knew my family and friends would turn their backs on me. It didn't matter. What mattered was never having to wake up being afraid. So, yes, it's better to be alone than to be someone's possession."

Contessa took another long draw from her teacup. "I'm not strong like you," she said, her voice quiet. "Sometimes I wonder who I am. The shining star that everyone sees in the spotlight? Or the weak woman hiding backstage? Maybe I'm neither, or both. I can't tell anymore." She let out a mocking laugh. "I was never like this before Giorgos. He makes me feel small. It's like I'm in a crowded room with a locked door whenever I'm with him. He tells me how old I'm beginning to look, that nobody would want me anymore. He tells me how much he loves his wife. He wants me to remember that I'm nobody to him — just here to keep him amused while he's at sea." There was a note of surrender in her sigh as she looked at her hands. "I don't have a say in the matter. Giorgos is a powerful man. He said once he would kill me if I tried to leave him. At the very least I'd be terrorized. What can I do?"

Diya could feel Rajan's hands around her neck. They trembled, itching to squeeze tighter until they crushed what they held. Maybe then he would be free, his anger released into the wind now that he'd killed what he hated.

She faced Contessa and leaned in close. "You make the fucker pay."

TWELVE

Family Portrait

"Smile!"

Click.

Preview.

"Come back in an hour."

It hadn't taken long for the work to become monotonous. After a tiring shift at Sebastien's photo station in the atrium, the passengers of the *Glacier* began to look like carbon copies of each other.

"Smile!" he would say, remembering to smile himself. His cheeks would hurt by the end of the day.

Click. The camera would flash. Their faces would be frozen in whatever stiff pose they had chosen, often with their eyes opened unnaturally wide.

Preview. They would always want to see how they looked.

He calculated that six of every ten shots would be unsatisfactory and retaken. Roughly one third of those would have to be reshot yet again. The people in this category would often blame him, offering unhelpful tips to improve his photographic competence.

"Come back in an hour," he would tell them once they were happy with the final shot. "It'll be ready for purchase in the portrait gallery."

Sebastien was used to uninspiring photography assignments. After all, he had taken portraits of almost every family in Petit Géant's upper crust while working at Camera Obscura. He knew how to capture them looking as happy as they wished they were. He would imagine how he'd want his own family to look, then replicate it with his clients. Sometimes his imagination would insert himself in the picture, often standing beside the father or kneeling in front with the brother.

Jérôme would usually be in the shop with him, stifling laughs as Sebastien shot him coded glances, and that would make the work easy to enjoy.

"Come back in an hour," he said to a British couple who looked like brother and sister. "It'll be ready for purchase in the portrait gallery."

"Mr. Goh!"

Blood surged through his arteries as he looked up to see Kostas. He was dressed for the evening in his finest white uniform. His wife stood beside him. Her hair was pulled tightly around her head, curling up at the top like a conch shell. She was elegant, as always, in a simple black gown that pooled at her ankles. Her nose pointed at him like an arrow.

The daughter's mind was somewhere distant, judging by her crossed arms and floating gaze.

The boy was more present. Kristo smiled easily, revealing dimples in his cheeks and one missing tooth. His wild hair was weighed down by shiny wax. The little navy-blue suit he wore was a perfect fit.

"Kostas, sir," he said. "I see you brought the whole family."

Do they know about your other one?

"Yes, yes," he said with a laugh. "This is my lovely wife, Alexis. The beautiful young lady beside her is Katerina. And this little devil is Kristo. He's going to run this ship one day."

"I could do it now," the boy said with a flippant shrug of the shoulders.

I'm sure you'd run it to the ground, just like our father.

"You're eleven! What's the hurry?" Kostas shook his head as though Kristo were exceptional in some way that wasn't obvious to Sebastien.

"It's nice to meet the family. He doesn't talk about you much."

Kostas crinkled his forehead. "We're here to get our annual family portrait, Mr. Goh. These two will be taller than their father soon, so let's catch them before that happens."

Unlike most guests, they chose the atrium as their backdrop. Sebastien arranged them so that husband and wife were flanked by their two darling children. It was the same order they usually stood in their photos. He had studied them for hours over the years. He knew every distinguishing feature, read the looks in their eyes. Kristo had a little brown mole on the left slope of his nose. Katerina's head always tilted to the right, toward her mother. He knew this family intimately. He was almost part of it himself.

"Smile!"

Alexis peered at Sebastien, and he knew she remembered him from Sirens the other night and the elevator on embarkation day. She wouldn't forget those eyes.

He couldn't imagine a woman less like his mother. Alexis held herself like she expected only the best out of life, though her face implied she didn't care for any of it. She had a family she had chosen, but Sebastien knew it wasn't good enough for her. The way she sighed whenever anybody looked at her, the way her lips tightened at the sound of her husband's voice. She had floated through life, accumulating things that other people had to fight for. She wouldn't know how it felt to be abandoned and unwanted.

She offered Sebastien a tight-lipped smile as they parted ways. He watched the Kourakis family hurry off together toward the dining hall. There was so much pride contained between these four people. It wasn't fair.

"Kostas!"

His father turned around to face Sebastien with an expectant expression.

What makes them good enough?

"Come back in an hour. It'll be ready for purchase in the portrait gallery."

❈

Sebastien's life started to look promising right before it began to crumble. Wasn't that always the way? Things went up before they went down, like a cosmic rollercoaster, the universe rebalancing itself with little regard for those who got crushed along the way.

This was before he and Sophie would officially become the most controversial young couple in Petit Géant, and many years before Jérôme would return to town. Before the black-and-white photographs. Before the red paint.

It was Sebastien's nineteenth birthday. In a few weeks he would graduate, near the top of his class. In a few months he would move three hundred kilometres away to attend university in Québec City, bringing his mother along with him. At least, that was the plan at the time.

He would never have been able to afford it himself, but he had applied for every scholarship he could find. The fatherless child with the wild hair had grown up to be an intelligent young man, a formidable lacrosse player, and a student hellbent on making the most of himself. The people in town still avoided him but they took notice, not that he ever wasted a brain cell worrying about what they thought.

"Happy birthday, son." Ruby leaned across their kitchen table and held his hand. The smoke from the blown-out candles meandered through the air like snakes from a charmer's basket. "I'm so proud of you."

Sebastien was proud, too. It hadn't been easy. He had feared something would go wrong — that the work wouldn't pay off, that the scholarship would be withdrawn, every school application rejected — but it looked like he was going to pull it off.

They removed the candles, sucking the frosting off the bottoms just as they had done every birthday before. Ruby had made his favourite cake: white confetti from the box with cream cheese frosting. Below the sugary handwritten message of *Happy 19th Birthday Son* was a plastic toy boat floating in an ocean of bright blue glaze.

Sebastien served each of them a large wedge of cake. They devoured it, staining their lips and teeth blue.

"I have a surprise for you." She gave him a mischievous smile and skipped into her bedroom before returning seconds later with a package in her hands. It was a gift. Little red-suited Santas covered the box, on cheap paper left over from Christmas.

"You hid this from me?"

"I didn't want you peeking."

Sebastien was surprised to feel the weight of the gift. He unwrapped the paper gingerly so they could reuse it. Ruby clasped her hands in her lap, tense with anticipation. He only needed to open one corner to know what it was.

"Mama, what were you thinking? You can't afford this!"

It was a camera. The school's art faculty had loaned one of theirs to Sebastien, but he would have to return it when he graduated. It had been attached to his eye for most of the year. His neck felt naked without the nylon strap against his skin. Ruby had spent days researching cameras to find the right one.

"Don't tell me what I can and can't afford," she said, giving him a playful slap on the shoulder.

"I'm serious. I can't accept this. These things cost hundreds of dollars."

"Just pretend I stole it."

"Very funny. I'm going to take photography in second year. I might be able to use my scholarship money to get a camera then."

"That's over a year from now!" Ruby shot him that don't-argue-with-me look she loved, and he knew he wasn't going to win. "What will you do until then? How will you remember your first year of university? When the time comes, you can buy a better camera. But I want you to have this one now. Because it's from me, and you deserve it."

He couldn't fight the tears that pooled in his eyes. His fingers picked at the rest of the cellophane tape that clung to the paper. "Thank you."

Ruby put her arms around him and rested her head on his shoulder. "You can take lots of photos of me in front of all the old buildings in the city. And the water! We'll take photos by the water."

The table vibrated as Ruby's cell phone buzzed. Her hand snatched it before Sebastien could see the number on the screen. She flashed him a cautious look, then smiled apologetically. "I need to take this. It'll just be a minute." Her bedroom door closed behind her.

Sebastien sat in the silent kitchen, staring at the half-eaten cake in front of him, and listened to the muffled sounds of his mother's hushed voice. He couldn't hear what she was saying, but she had been wearing a cloak of secrecy during the past few months that never used to exist. There were mysterious phone calls and vague answers to questions about her whereabouts. He tried not to let it worry him, but he had begun to realize he didn't know his mother as well as he once thought.

It wasn't difficult finding where the Kourakis family was staying on board the *Glacier*. Ilya's tank-like laptop was a portal to the ship's less heavily guarded systems. It had given them easy access to the audiovisual network of Sirens. It took only a few minutes to infiltrate the entire guest directory. "I wasn't always Mr. Fitness," Ilya said the first day they met. "Everyone on board has a past life. For me, computer engineering paid the bills."

Now Sebastien stalked along the familiar hallway of seafoam carpet and scallop-shell lamps toward cabin 1450 on Riviera Deck, the same level as the House of the Heel. The late seating in the dining hall was complete. The guests, including the Kourakis family, would be in the Odeon enjoying the evening's performance — a modern retelling of Jason's voyage on the *Argo*, complete with harpies dressed like Japanese manga characters and Contessa as a steampunk Medea. He knew the terrible show had another hour before the curtain fell.

He had taken Nikos's skeleton key yesterday with the intention of slipping into the commanders' wing that night and uncovering what, if anything, was hidden in cabin A66. Finding what Dominic had seen there was pressing, but he changed his mind after meeting the Kourakis family earlier. They called to him like a siren's song. He couldn't resist.

Cabin 1450 was on the opposite end of Riviera Deck from the secret temple he shared with Nikos. He scanned the hall and confirmed it was deserted. Wearing a borrowed grey suit from cabin service that was a size too small, he pulled the little bellboy cap farther down his face. The rectangle of black plastic in his fingers felt so flimsy for something so powerful. He inserted it in the thin slot of the door. A green dot flashed beside the handle.

The first thing he noticed when he entered the dark room was the perfume. It smelled expensive and overpowering, more floral than a flower and spicier than black pepper. He remembered inhaling whiffs of the scent as Alexis passed him earlier.

He switched on the lights to reveal a luxurious sitting room. The hardwood floors were carpeted with rich wool. Lounge chairs were upholstered in muted colours and covered in ornamental cushions. The walls displayed abstract paintings of geometric shapes in overly saturated tones. A statue of a Greek god dominated one corner, covered in the same blue glaze as the others that stood guard throughout the ship. Windows lined the far wall. A pair of glass doors opened onto a balcony. The curtains were drawn back, and the Mediterranean Sea blurred into the sky.

Sebastien pictured the narrow cabin that he and Ilya shared. It was so dark at night with just three walls and a door. The sitting room in Alexis's suite was at least eight times the size.

He stepped through a door to his right. There were two queen-sized beds at opposing ends of the room. The sheets and duvets were expertly arranged, no doubt by the housekeeping staff. It was clear which bed belonged to Kristo and which to Katerina. The reserved girl kept a glossy magazine and several loose pieces of jewellery on her bedside table. A few articles of boys' clothing had been thrown on Kristo's bed, including a mariner's sweater with thick white-and-blue stripes. Part of the bedding was still damp from a pair of green swim trunks.

Sebastien stood over the boy's nightstand. Underneath a handful of rocks and a pair of binoculars was a notebook. He picked it up and flipped through the pages. He couldn't read the Greek words written in the curves of the boy's handwriting, but it looked like it could be poetry. The lines of text scattered across the centre of the pages in lonely islands and wandering rivers.

He closed the book and gripped it in his hands. The discovery agitated him. Kristo couldn't be a poet.

The air was dense with perfume as he walked across the sitting room and stepped through the door on the far wall. Light washed over the room from lamps suspended from the ceiling like floating orbs. It looked like Alexis had moved into her bedroom indefinitely. The dresser was covered with her things: a hairbrush with an ivory handle, several vials of perfume, a leather box with various compartments, a little bronze tree where she hung necklaces and earrings.

She had even brought a photograph from home. It stood beside a vase of fresh flowers in a frame made of bevelled glass. The same image hung proudly in Kostas's office. The four of them stood on the deck of a yacht with the wind in their hair. It was a strange thing to do, to bring this photo on holiday, but nothing this family did could surprise Sebastien. He wasn't equipped to understand these people.

The closet doors slid open to reveal an entirely separate little room. Shelves displayed several pairs of shoes arranged as meticulously as a museum exhibit. Sebastien flipped through the dresses and sweaters that hung from wooden hangers along the rods. Each item must have cost more than what his mother had earned in a week. He could tell just by how the fabric felt against his fingertips. He couldn't comprehend this kind of excess.

He was about to step out of the closet when something caught his eye. He pushed aside the other clothes with both hands. Hanging there was a slim dress. It was black, edged with red piping. A golden web of flowers and smoke was embroidered across the dress — a Chinese cheongsam. Unlike his mother's favourite cheap red replica, this cheongsam was made to measure from the finest silk. Alexis Kourakis deserved only the finest. She expected it.

Sebastien felt it coming, and there was nothing he could have done to stop the surge. His vision blurred and refocused as the blood rushed to his head. His lungs tightened, the rage pushing its way up his throat. Every muscle in his body flexed in protest, but it was no use.

His hands pulled the dress off the hanger. It tore easily. He shook as he ripped it from collar to hem. Hands lashed out, grabbing gowns and cashmere cardigans. A growl rumbled from the back of his mouth as he tore everything apart. Buttons flew into the air. Silk floated to the floor like strips of skin.

He stumbled out the closet doors and into the bedroom. A sweep of the arms and the floor was covered in cosmetics and jewels. He grabbed the vase of flowers and threw it against the headboard of the bed. It shattered like an egg, spilling water and petals across the walls and duvet.

The Kourakis family portrait watched him from its bevelled frame. Their smiles hinted suppressed laughter. Sebastien held the frame in his hand, trying to decipher what was behind their eyes.

It was pity.

A sound escaped him like the roar of a wounded animal. He hurled the frame at the mirror that spanned the length of the dresser. It exploded into a thousand pieces. He could see his reflection in every jagged shard as it fell to the carpeted floor. The panic in his eyes. His mouth stretched open in an irregular shape.

His head jerked toward a sound at the door. The breath caught in his throat as he looked into a pair of deep green eyes. The boy stared back at him. They stood there, frozen and silent, seeing something both familiar and incomprehensible.

He could see Kristo was going to scream before the sound burst out his mouth. The boy turned to run away, but it was too late. Sebastien leapt across the room and tackled him to the ground. Kristo wriggled free and ran to the table in the middle of the sitting room. A barrage of books and magazines pelted Sebastien, knocking the cap off his head, but he couldn't feel a thing. Within seconds, Kristo was locked in his arms.

"Sssh," Sebastien hissed, his hand clamped over the boy's mouth. "I'm not going to hurt you."

Kristo could barely move despite how hard he struggled. His screams were completely muted.

"Listen to me. I'm going to let you go. You're going to stay quiet. You'll forget you ever saw me. You returned to your cabin and nobody was here. You didn't see anything. Do you understand?"

Kristo's eyes were wild as he fought harder. Sebastien was impressed. He tightened his grip and looked down at the frightened face. He knew this face so well. He had watched it take shape over the years, studied it from the other side of a screen. Now it was right in front of him. Flesh and bone. He wouldn't hurt this boy, would he?

"If you tell anyone you saw me here, I will kill your mother."

He looked into the boy's eyes and knew their secret was safe. They were brothers, after all.

THIRTEEN

The Weakest of Men

The sky was a soothing shade of blue as the *Glacier* pulled into port that morning. The city of Limassol on the island of Cyprus kissed the water with its tree-lined shore and seaside boulevard. Buildings old and new the colour of sun-bleached bone sprawled across the rolling hills in the distance.

Kostas's ban on off-duty appearances in guest areas proved easy to manoeuvre around. Staff could simply wear their uniforms and act like they were working to gain access to the upper decks. Every corner of the ship was linked by a network of crew corridors and stairways hidden behind the decorative walls of the guest areas. Unseen, Diya and Contessa were making their way through these passageways.

An incident had occurred the previous night on Riviera Deck. They'd been told the entire floor was teeming with security like hounds on a fox hunt. Some sort of investigation was underway. Kostas was seen early in the morning, looking disturbed.

The two women stepped through the heavy metal door that led to the seafoam-carpeted hallway. The door on this side was painted the same pale rose colour as the wall. The hounds were mostly clustered on the starboard side of the deck. The hall where the two women stood was clear. They wore matching grey uniforms, complete with pale pink aprons, borrowed from the housekeeping staff. Diya had never seen Contessa's face void of makeup. Her beauty was natural, but she looked like a different woman — more vulnerable, perhaps, but less hidden.

They knew deck commander Giorgos was on duty on Olympus, the name everyone used for the navigation bridge, covering for the captain who liked to sleep in. They would have plenty of time to do what they needed to do, uninterrupted.

Contessa hesitated as they stood in front of the door to cabin 1423. She took a deep, silent breath. "I don't know if I can do this," she said, turning to her newfound ally.

"I know you can," Diya said. "This is how you get your power back."

Contessa nodded, convincing herself she agreed. Her fist shot up and knocked firmly against the door. The two of them stopped breathing in the silence that followed.

The door opened to reveal a classic Greek woman, statuesque in the way she held herself. Elena was proud long before she married a commanding officer, but the fire within her had diminished over the years. Yet even as she stood there in a simple cotton robe with her dark hair tied back and no embellishment on her bare skin, there was something fierce behind her clear, cool eyes.

"Elena." Contessa's voice was soft and sincere. There was no hint of the theatrical flair she often imbued her speech with. "May we come in?"

Elena's eyes scanned them from their flat-heeled shoes to the ruffled headpieces pinned into their hair. She knew they weren't ordinary housekeepers. Her face was difficult to read as she nodded, stepping aside.

The sitting room was almost identical to the suite around the corner belonging to Alexis Kourakis, although it was smaller. The paintings on the walls were different, more oblong than sharp-edged. The dry hills of Cyprus simmered beneath the sun outside the windows. A breeze drifted from the open balcony doors, permeating the air with the subtle scent of jasmine.

"Please, take a seat." Elena's voice was deep and assured. She gestured to the cushioned sofa as she placed herself within an armchair. "Shall I order some tea?"

Contessa could have used a cup of brandy, but she declined with an uncertain smile.

Ever since the first kiss she shared with Giorgos two long years ago, his mysterious wife had haunted her. She would imagine Elena being a sad, helpless woman who had given up on life. As the affair progressed and her guilt intensified, her vision of Elena evolved as well to become spiteful and possessive. *I'm liberating Giorgos from an unhappy marriage*, she would tell herself.

She had always known that none of this was true. Giorgos loved his wife. He would often remind her of that. Still, she let herself be comforted by her vision of the woman.

Whenever Elena visited for a sailing, the married couple would pass freely through the Agora or sit in the audience during a performance. They didn't have to hide behind locked doors. There was always more tension when the wife was on board. Contessa would see Giorgos less frequently during these weeks, but their lovemaking would be far more intense than usual.

This was her first time meeting Elena face to face. Now that she could see the woman apart from the man, she saw they weren't so different.

Diya sat silently by Contessa's side on the pale blue sofa. She was there for support. This wasn't her conversation to have.

"I need to tell you something." There was no waver in Contessa's voice. Diya was proud of her.

"Go on."

"It's about your husband."

Elena's face was solid as stone. She waited patiently to hear what Contessa had to say, legs crossed and palms placed in her lap.

"We've been having an affair for the past two years."

Elena blinked but kept her eyes fixed on the woman in front of her.

"I'm not here to confront you," Contessa went on, the features on her face softening. "I know what I did was wrong, and I take responsibility. I want it to end. I'm going to walk away from Giorgos, and you'll never have to see me again. But I thought you should know." She swallowed hard and tucked a few loose strands of hair behind her ear. "If I were you, I would want to know."

A strange silence settled across the room. Something unseen and unspoken bound the three women together. It was neither hostile nor comforting. They simply shared the things that had been taken from them.

"I know who you are," Elena said, breaking the silence. "You have a beautiful voice." She sighed, glancing down at her hands. "Giorgos is away at sea for months at a time. I'm no longer naive enough to think he stays faithful. He's always been a weak man." She laughed gently as if to herself. Her eyes wandered back up to Contessa. "I used to worry. I couldn't stop myself from imagining the things he would do on this ship, the people he would do them with. It consumed me. But then one day I stopped worrying. It was out of my control. What was I to do? I couldn't cage him like a bird."

"I'm sorry," Contessa said, surprised, "but you're going to let him get away with cheating?"

"Sometimes I miss the days when I worried. At least then I knew I loved him. I could feel it. That's what love is — doubt and dependence. It's not that I don't care anymore. I suppose I've just accepted the way things are." Elena was calm. There was sadness in the creases of her face, but even it was worn proudly. "You're still young. You have much more life to live. You'll find someone new and forget about Giorgos, but you will remember me and avoid the mistakes I made. Then, when you're my age, you won't have this conversation with someone younger and more hopeful than yourself."

"You can do it, too." Contessa's tone sharpened as she leaned forward. "You've given him so much of your life; don't let him take any more."

Elena offered a soft smile. "I turn fifty soon. I wouldn't know what to do with myself. My husband keeps his secrets while I fade away, but is it better to be alone?"

"Yes." The word came out of Contessa's mouth instantly. With a quick glance at Diya, she went on. "It's better to be alone than to wake up being afraid."

Uncertainty flashed across Elena's face. "I'm not sure what you mean."

Contessa took a deep breath. "Does he ever hit you?"

"Never." Elena was surprised by the question. They could see she was telling the truth. Her eyes spotted the faint purple marks, and she understood. Getting up from her chair, she kneeled in front of Contessa and touched her gently on the arms. Her lips trembled. "Who did this to you?"

Neither woman needed the name to be spoken.

❖

It was that period in the evening when the distant sun painted everything gold. The *Glacier* was scheduled to set sail for Crete in an hour when Elena stepped off the gangplank. She wore a simple black dress and fashionable heels as she pulled her suitcase along the concrete pier. She was dressed for mourning, but that wasn't how she felt.

Contessa was right. It was better to be alone — than watching the days float by from an empty house, than never knowing what could have been, than sharing a life with a violent man. That's what she told Giorgos before making her exit. As she walked across the pier, away from him, she felt there was still so much life to live.

❖

"I'll just be five minutes!" Diya shouted at the security guards before running down the gangplank. "Contessa! Wait!"

The singer was halfway across the pier when she turned around. The wind tossed the hair about her face as she stood in the spotlight cast by the dying sun, her shadow stretching along the concrete behind her. One hand clutched an oversized suitcase that held almost everything she owned.

"Where are you going?" Diya asked when she caught up to her. News had travelled quickly about Contessa's sudden departure. Throngs of staff and crew crowded along the edge of the bow above. They waved their hands and called her name.

"I'm going to find another home." She smiled as tears formed in her eyes. "Maybe even back to Minnesota for a while."

"Why?"

"Giorgos will be a part of my life as long as I stay here. He's searching for me as we speak." She looked up at the steel behemoth that towered above them. It felt surreal to be walking away from this place she had called home for so long. "I'm ready. Elena was right. There's more life to be lived. I have so many mistakes to make still, but I won't make the same ones."

The two women wrapped their arms around each other. "Thank you, Diya. You gave me one drop of your strength, and it was enough."

The city of Limassol was a blanket of twinkling lights as the *Glacier* drifted away thirty minutes later. Giorgos was locked in his cabin, alone. His humourless face was streaked with tears as his mind replayed every scenario of what he could have done differently to have avoided this outcome. He never imagined having to face consequences for his actions. Had he known he'd lose the greatest thing in his life, he would never have taken the risk. He had wanted to follow Elena earlier, to make a grand gesture of his love, but he couldn't do that. He was deck commander. The ship needed him. The only thing that had brought him comfort was knowing there was still a woman on board he could turn to. Now he'd lost her, too.

The island of Cyprus shrank from his window. He imagined what Elena and Contessa were doing at that moment, on that island, left behind, and he shuddered with regret.

He was interrupted by a knock. "Hold on," he shouted in his deepest voice. He wiped the tears from his face and glanced in the mirror before opening the cabin door.

Standing there in the carpeted hallway of the commanders' quarters was a round woman in a grey uniform and pink apron. He looked at the golden badge pinned on her bosom. She was Rosa from the Philippines.

"Room service," she said cheerfully. He had forgotten that some of the cabin-service crew had access to this elite wing of A Deck.

"Room service? I didn't order anything."

"Yes, you did. This is for you, deck commander Giorgos." She gave him a wide smile and placed the cardboard box in his hands. He didn't know what else to do but to accept it.

Once the door was shut, he opened the box. The square cake was encased in a firm shell of white frosting. Flakes of gold covered the sides. Hardened swirls of caramel sat in abstract shapes in one corner.

He didn't notice any of this. All he saw was the message written on the surface of the cake in elegant, looping letters.

Cheaters & Beaters Are the Weakest of Men

A little paper card was attached to the box. He shook as he read the message inside.

Love, The Powerless

The suite that belonged to Alexis Kourakis had been filled with security guards and officers since the previous night. They scoured every inch of every room to find clues as to who would be bold enough to target the hotel commander's family in such a violent way.

"It was those damn rebels!" Kostas shouted. "This time they've gone too far." Nikos had never seen him so enraged. The man's entire body vibrated like an engine as he paced across the carpet of the crime scene.

Little Kristo, normally impossible to shut up, sat still in a chair looking vacant and stunned. "I didn't see anything" was all he said when Nikos asked him what had happened. Something about the boy's answer wasn't quite right. It sounded rehearsed.

It was clear Alexis was deeply disturbed. Her bedroom had borne the brunt of the damage. "This feels personal," she said, combing through the shreds of clothing scattered on the floor. Nikos couldn't disagree as he picked up the framed portrait that had been used to shatter the mirror.

Now that the Kourakis family had been relocated to a different suite guarded around the clock by Nikos's men, cabin 1450 on Riviera Deck was peaceful again. The island of Cyprus disappeared in the distance. Nikos sat on the edge of Alexis's bed, which had been stripped of its sheets, and stared at his reflection in the jagged fragments that remained of the mirror. His face appeared even more serious than usual. His eyes were bloodshot. A darkening layer of stubble ran along his jaw.

He looked down at the little metal stud in his hand. It was round and black, just like the one Sebastien wore in his left ear. He knew it was the same one as soon as his finger touched its smooth, cold surface. It had been embedded in the fibres of the wool carpet underneath the sofa.

Kostas was right. Sebastien had gone too far this time. Nikos couldn't rationalize what Sebastien could have been thinking, but he knew he wouldn't be able to betray him.

You really are my weakness, he thought to himself. *My Achilles heel.*

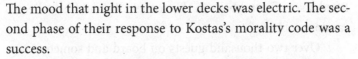

The mood that night in the lower decks was electric. The second phase of their response to Kostas's morality code was a success.

The once-untouchable deck commander had fallen from his pedestal. Giorgos had been seen striding through the corridors earlier that evening, frantically searching for his mistress, a panicked look on his face. It was the most emotion they'd ever witnessed from him.

Shortly afterward, dozens of photos and videos were leaked online to every email address and social media account in the employee directory. They exposed officers in various compromising positions: creeping in and out of brothels in Mykonos, getting extra friendly with women who weren't their wives, being invited into guest cabins very late at night. A battalion of staff and crew armed with cameras had spent the last four days documenting every possible offence committed against sexual morality by the ship's ruling class of officers.

To top it off, the video footage of the protest against Dominic's eviction was posted in numerous online forums, sharing the *Glacier*'s corruption with the world beyond the sea.

A celebration was underway in the crew bar while many officers braced themselves for the repercussions. The hypocrisy

was undeniable, though nobody could find anything incrimi-
nating against the prime target, Kostas Kourakis.

In Sebastien and Ilya's cabin on B Deck, the leaders of
The Powerless felt less victorious. They knew the fight was far
from over.

"This attack on Kostas's family worries me," Diya said.
She sat on the edge of the desk, her hands clutched around
a steaming mug. "That wasn't part of the plan. They're
innocent."

"Maybe it had nothing to do with us," Ilya grunted as he
lifted a set of dumbbells in the corner. "It could have been a
random robbery."

"Over two thousand guests on board and someone ran-
domly breaks into that exact cabin?" Diya took a sip of her
tea. "No way. This has The Powerless written all over it. And
we should be concerned. What if we've started something we
can't control?"

"What did Nikos have to say?" Ilya looked at the silent
Sebastien as he curled and uncurled his arms. "Your boy toy
must know something."

The mention of Nikos's name stung. "I haven't seen him
since it happened."

"Maybe it was one of them," Diya said. "One of the
malákas. They could be trying to pin the blame on us."

"You're right," Ilya said. "They have access to all the cabins. Maybe they're trying to pour gasoline on the fire."

"It was me." Sebastien's eyes darted between them. They
didn't say a word as the confession hung in the air. Ilya
dropped the dumbbells to the floor. "I need to tell you both
something," he continued, standing up from the bottom bunk
and grabbing his hair in his hands. "You're not going to be
happy."

"What is it?" Diya and Ilya said in near-perfect unison.

"Kostas is my father."

The three friends stared at each other from different corners of the little cabin. Sebastien took a long breath and continued. "I'd never met him until I came on board the *Glacier*. He abandoned my mother when she was carrying me. I don't know why he left. All I know is my mother met him in Singapore and boarded the cargo ship he worked on back then. She claims they fell in love and that he promised to take her to France. They didn't make it. He left us in Québec."

Sebastien paced around the cabin in tiny clockwise loops. His tone was manic. He felt his heart thudding against his ribs like a hammer on piano keys.

"Is this her?" Diya picked up the framed photograph that stood on the desk. Ruby's eyes were alive behind the glass.

Sebastien nodded.

"She looks fierce."

"It doesn't seem right, though," he went on. "I used to assume he got scared off by the pregnancy, so he ran off like a coward. It happens all the time, right? But the more I think about it, the less sense it makes."

"Why are you really here, then?" Ilya's expression was a hybrid of concern and disillusionment.

"I needed to meet him." He stopped pacing and stood before them as though testifying in front of a jury. "My mother died a few months ago. I blamed him. I blamed him for everything we had to go through. I needed to find out why he did what he did. I wanted revenge."

"So this entire rebellion isn't about us?" Diya asked. "It's about revenge?"

"No," Sebastien said, frantically grasping for how to explain himself. "I didn't know what he would be like, but I never imagined it to be this bad. He's trying to strip us of the power we have over our lives, just like he did to me and my mother. We're fighting for our home. For each other. Kostas is just —"

He couldn't finish the thought. His body quivered. He was cornered. Somehow he had alienated the people closest to him. Ilya put his arms around Sebastien and held him closely against his chest. Diya wrapped her arms around them, too.

"It's okay," Ilya said. "We are in this together. We all have our own story of what brought us here. Now we know yours." He held Sebastien's face in his hands. The calming effect was immediate. "The only difference is most of us are running away from something. You are running toward it."

The moment was interrupted by three sharp knocks on the cabin door. Diya was the first to reach it. Standing in the corridor was a grave-faced officer in a blinding white uniform. Every muscle was held to project authority. They were surprised to see it was Nikos Antonopolous.

"Sebastien," he said, peering inside. "Kostas wants a word with you."

FOURTEEN

A Gift

The steel corridors of Hades were alive with drunken shouts and music spilling from parties that couldn't be contained within cabins. Everyone went quiet as Nikos passed, but they applauded Sebastien with their eyes. Despite the severity of Kostas's punishments, as well as the cash reward, the staff and crew hadn't turned on one another. Tonight more than ever they were united in their cause, even though the strictly enforced midnight curfew was only an hour away.

"How goes the night for Achilles?" Sebastien watched him from the corners of his eyes as they walked down the main thoroughfare of Styx.

"I've had better."

It wasn't clear whether or not Nikos's coldness was part of the act. He was a different man in public, but they would normally pass each other hints of intimacy through whispers and glances. Tonight seemed different.

"Is everything okay?" he asked as they climbed a set of stairs to the officers' realm of A Deck.

Nikos reached inside his jacket. He held out his hand. Sitting in his palm was the little black stud Sebastien had lost the previous night.

"I believe this is yours."

"Where did you find that?" Sebastien asked, tucking the stud into the pocket of his pants. He knew what the answer would be.

"Riviera Deck. Cabin 1450." Their eyes met as they arrived at the door to Kostas's office. "Good luck," Nikos said. There was no chance to respond before he spun on his heel and marched away.

Sebastien hesitated before opening the door. He didn't think Nikos would turn him in, but he knew a line had been crossed.

Kostas was sitting at his desk when Sebastien walked inside. The wall of Kourakis family memories unfolded behind him. The scene was almost identical to their first encounter here except for one thing. The hotel commander's smug demeanor no longer consumed the air in the room. Nervous electricity hissed along every surface. He was rattled.

"Mr. Goh!" There was friction between his eyes and the smile on his face. "Please, sit down."

"You wanted to see me?"

Kostas leaned forward with his elbows on the desk. His officer's jacket was hung on the back of his chair. He wore a short-sleeved collared shirt that was perfectly pressed, revealing strong forearms covered in hair like a carpet of moss. A gaudy gold watch wrapped around one wrist.

"It has been an interesting day," he said, clasping his thick hands together. "You've heard about what happened?"

"Yes, I'm shocked to hear about your wife's cabin." He crinkled his eyebrows to show concern. It was time to convince his father how compassionate Sebastien Goh could be. "It must have been terribly frightening for your family. Everyone's okay, though?

"Yes, yes. They're fine. Alarmed, inconvenienced, but fine." He stared intently into Sebastien's eyes, attempting to read what was behind the surface. "I think this attack on my family was orchestrated by the same deviants who hijacked Sirens the other night. You agree they've gone too far, Mr. Goh?"

"Of course." He held his father's gaze, careful not to look away.

"Do you know anything about these recent troubling incidents?"

He pretended to be caught off guard by the question. "No, sir. I mean, I was there at Sirens that night. I heard about what happened to Giorgos today. But I have no idea who's behind all this."

The little muscles in Kostas's face twitched with the subtlest of movements, as though he were a machine processing the veracity of Sebastien's comments. His unruly hair was slicked back, and the crooked scar above his right ear appeared redder in colour than usual.

"You were very vocal about the Dominic situation," he said. "I know you were part of the protest, along with much of my staff and crew. I thought maybe you might have heard or witnessed something that could lead to identifying these cowards."

"I wish I could help," Sebastien said. It was harder now to hold his mask of compassion. "All of this is getting out of hand."

"Yes!" Kostas said, nodding vigorously. "Yes, this is getting out of hand." His face relaxed as he sat back in his chair. Finally, a conclusion had been reached. "You're a passionate young man, Mr. Goh. You proved that the last time we spoke here in this room. It's a quality I respect. You remind me of myself when I was your age. You have spirit."

Sebastien forced a smile as his lungs filled with heat. "Thank you."

I'm nothing like you. I'll never be you.

"I don't have the easiest job," Kostas said, crossing his hairy arms over his chest. "I make the rules, so I must punish those who break them. It's so easy to paint me as the villain. But underneath this uniform, I'm just an ordinary man. I have a family to protect, to provide for. I have a job to perform, a staff and crew to take care of. I make mistakes. But I'm not the enemy."

Sebastien realized he had forgotten to remove his smile as Kostas spoke. He quickly switched his expression to empathetic, narrowing his eyes and relaxing his jaw.

"I never used to have all of this, you know." Kostas didn't seem to notice the mechanical shifting of emotions on Sebastien. "I grew up poor. My mother had me very young. She made a mistake with a boy from the village, and that was that. No marriage. No respect. I never knew my father."

Sebastien's body stiffened. A shadow of gloom fell over Kostas's face as he stared vacantly at the hands on his lap. It was an unexpected confession for them both. For a moment, they felt like family.

"I wasn't raised on ideals and dreams," he went on. "Only the very privileged can afford that. I grew up learning how to work hard, how to struggle and sweat, how to pull myself up in the world. I used to spend every day on the water catching fish, then every evening selling it. Joyless work, but it's what I had to do to survive. I did that for years before I found a job on board a cargo ship." He leaned forward, placing his palms flat on the surface of the desk. "This is why I'm here today. I started at the bottom, but I fought for it. I don't believe in treating everyone the same because we are not all the same. Only the most entitled would think that. You get what you deserve. That's how it works in the real world, and that's how I run my ship."

Sebastien perked up in his chair. Perhaps Kostas wasn't as immovable as he seemed. Here was a chance to influence him.

"I think your staff and crew just want to have some power over their lives," Sebastien said, the expression on his face now sincere. "This ship is our home. These latest restrictions tell us we have no control, no autonomy. Please, sir, retract these rules and give us some of our humanity back."

Kostas seemed to roll Sebastien's words around in his head. Finally, his eyes darted across the desk.

"Not everyone can be trusted with power," he said, delivering his verdict with a sigh. "That's why the powerless will never possess it."

Sebastien looked away. It felt like he'd been tricked into lowering his defences.

Nice move.

"It's getting late," Sebastien said. "If it's all right with you, I'd like to head back to my cabin before the curfew."

"Of course," he said with a smile. "Thank you for your time, Mr. Goh. Come see me if you hear anything that can help the investigation. You'd be rewarded generously for your co-operation."

Sebastien stood up and remembered what was clutched in his hand. It was the photograph he had taken of the Kourakis family in the atrium the previous night. They hadn't come to retrieve it. The portrait was displayed in a shimmering silver frame. He held it out to his father across the desk.

"I brought this for you," he said. "A gift."

❖

The following day would be spent at sea as the *Glacier* sailed toward the island of Crete. For several crew members, it would also be their last full day on board.

While everyone was sleeping off the effects of the night's revelry, a pack of security guards was unleashed throughout the lower decks of Hades. They knocked on cabin doors and escorted groggy crew members to the medical clinic on B Deck, all the while crossing names off a list. The targets had been identified as participating in "suspicious conduct" the previous night and were required to undergo mandatory drug and alcohol testing. By six in the morning, a line of irate and confused crew members displaying various degrees of intoxication snaked out the medical clinic's doors and along the main passageway of Styx.

Within two hours, letters of immediate eviction had been handed out to nine servers, eight housekeepers, six cabin-service attendants, six cooks, and three deck cleaners. Members of the more privileged class of staff escaped the witch hunt except for two male musicians — one bassist from the jazz quartet and the pianist who had often accompanied Contessa's solo performances. They had been seen violating the sexual morality code in creative ways in a dark corner of the crew bar.

Thirty-four employees were dismissed in total, the largest cull of the ship's staff and crew in years. The official reason for most of the evictions was failure to pass the mandatory drug and alcohol testing. Despite the fact that alcohol was generously and encouragingly served to staff and crew, being intoxicated was officially forbidden. Drunken sailors weren't of much use in times of nautical emergency. This rule was generally ignored, but it proved to be a convenient way for the commanding officers to eliminate people who were problematic.

Kostas's revenge had begun.

Sebastien spent most of the night staring up at the bottom of Ilya's bunk above him. His nerves felt frayed, crackling with electricity. Diya could have been right. Maybe they'd started something they could no longer control. Perhaps Kostas was right, too. Had he gone too far?

He replayed scenes from the previous two nights over and over in the projection room of his mind. Diya calming herself with a mug of hot tea. The reassuring feeling of Ilya's hands on his face. The little black stud in the middle of Nikos's palm. Kostas accepting Sebastien's gift, arm outstretched with a gracious smile.

The end of the reel was always the same — little Kristo's eyes staring up at him, wide, fearful, shining with hatred.

That hadn't been part of the plan, but there was nothing he could have done to stop it. He knew that violence lived in everyone, but he was scared by his inability to control his own.

Sebastien imagined the checkerboard he and his mother had made with cardboard and felt pen when he was a child. Ruby would always be calm as she played, while he would often fidget with anxiety, worried about making the wrong move. "You have to think three steps ahead," she would say. "And while your opponent thinks he has the upper hand, you better make sure your next move counts."

They're here.

Ilya sent the signal to Sebastien through the messaging app used by most staff and crew on their phones.

"Good morning!" he said even more cheerfully than usual. The lights reflected off the mirrored walls of the fitness studio as his next class entered. They were a strange sight in their gym outfits. In soccer shorts and cotton T-shirts, they were mere mortals without the power of their imposing white uniforms. Kostas and Giorgos could pass as harmless dads fighting off the greying, sagging effects of age. Most of the other officers were younger, but even they looked weathered now, standing in the same room as the sunny Ukrainian.

"Wake up, boys! You know the drill. I want to see you move like you mean it." Ilya led the elite group of officers through the same kickboxing class every Thursday and Sunday morning. They never missed a class. He was surprised to see Giorgos come out of hiding, looking like he had plenty of sweat and aggression to release.

"Take it easy on us, Mr. Tereshchenko," Kostas said. "We've had a long night."

"What do I say to that, everyone?" Ilya asked, stretching his muscular arms above his head.

"Accept no excuses," the group of officers responded in a chorus of limp voices.

"That's right!" Ilya flashed his signature smile. "Make it count or you might as well go back to bed."

Several levels below the fitness studio, Sebastien climbed up the stairwell to the officers' quarters on A Deck. He tucked his phone with Ilya's all-clear message into his pocket and pushed open the door.

Other than the offices of Kostas and Nikos, the entire deck was unfamiliar territory. He walked along the main corridor toward the stern of the ship where the commanding officers lived. He knew this elite wing was where he would find cabin A66.

Dressed in the borrowed grey uniform he had worn the other night on Riviera Deck, he hoped to be ignored as a cabin-service attendant by any officers he might encounter along the way. He had even practised holding the shiny tray and cloche in his hand in front of the mirror. Even though Ilya had confirmed it all looked convincing, he could feel the sweat forming underneath his matted hair and bellboy cap.

He walked past an officer he recognized as one of Nikos's friends. Keeping his eyes fixed ahead, he sensed the man slow down with suspicion. He braced himself for being identified, but the young officer walked on without a word.

The locked door that required key-card access appeared at the end of the corridor. He had tested the skeleton key on a few random doors earlier that morning and was relieved to find it still worked. Nikos either hadn't discovered it was missing or couldn't deactivate it.

He glanced around before inserting the cold rectangle of black plastic into the slot above the handle of the door. His breath caught in his throat as he waited for entry to be granted or denied. A gush of air escaped his mouth when the green dot of light appeared. He steadied himself, nearly dropping the silver tray in his hand.

The hallway on the other side of the door was far less utilitarian than any other corridor below decks. As Ilya had claimed on the day they first met, the entire wing was covered in plush carpet the colour of Concord grapes. The decorative wallpaper mimicked dark-green panels of wainscotting.

The wing was deserted. Most of the commanding officers were either at work on the navigation bridge or attending Ilya's kickboxing class, but there was always the chance of someone popping in or out of a cabin. He had to move quickly.

As he crept down the hall, he realized he had never seen Nikos's cabin. The opposite had also been true until the previous night, when Nikos appeared at his door unannounced to escort him to Kostas's office. The only place they were allowed to be themselves was the House of the Heel. It had to be hidden away, kept secret like the one he was about to uncover.

He found his destination as he turned a corner at the end of the hall. As with the other cabins, the address was engraved on a bronze plaque affixed to the front of the door: A66.

He hesitated as he stood in the corridor with the skeleton key pressed between his fingertips. Something bad was behind this door, according to Dominic. Something he wasn't supposed to see. Something his father was hiding.

With a deep breath and a determined shake of the head, he inserted the key and pushed open the door.

FIFTEEN

Six Little Circles

The cabin was simple and modestly furnished, yet larger and more comfortable than those the staff and crew called home. A bed sat in the far corner to the right, its sheets twisted together like a braid. A chest of drawers and a desk were anchored against the wall to the left. The sea churned outside a rectangular window with rounded corners and large hexagonal bolts holding its thick frame.

Sebastien scanned the quiet cabin and almost didn't notice the young woman sitting in the corner with her back against the wall. Her long hair fell over her shoulders like the mane of an ebony horse. She had rich Mediterranean skin. Her eyes were wide as she clutched a pillow against her chest.

He recognized her immediately. She was the woman Nikos had led out of Sirens through a hidden door in the wall the night they sailed away from Mykonos. Her clothing was similar to what she wore that night, jeans and a T-shirt, black from head to toe.

"I'm sorry." They were the first words that came to mind. "I didn't know there was anyone in here."

The startled look on her face dissolved into panic. "Help me." Her voice was hoarse as it caught in her throat. It rang out across the room more clearly the second time. "Help me."

"Who are you?" Sebastien inched toward her with his hands held up to show he wasn't a threat. "It's okay. I'm a friend."

"We need to get out of here." The pitch of her voice heightened. "They'll be back soon."

"Who?" He kneeled in front of the young woman. She was frightened. The classical features of her face and the contralto of her words hinted she was Greek.

"The men in the white suits."

"Are you trapped here?"

She nodded.

"Why?"

Her eyes shot to the floor as she tightened her grip on the pillow. "I borrowed money from them I can't pay back. They told me I could work off the debt in three months at a clothing factory in France. They told me I would just have to sew." Her body started to shake, her words distressed. "They're liars. They haven't let me out of this room since I came on board in Athens. I don't know where I'm going or what they'll do with me once I get there. You need to help me."

There was desperation in her eyes.

"Did you say you boarded the ship in Athens?"

She nodded.

"That means you would've been here just about a week."

"I think so," she said, unsure.

Dominic had been escorted off the ship the same day she came on board, which meant he couldn't have seen this young woman. Whatever he stumbled upon here happened days before they docked in Athens. He must have seen something else — or someone else.

Another woman. The thought echoed through his mind like a whisper. *There was another woman here.*

"We need to go." Sebastien sprang to his feet and held out his hand. She hesitated before grabbing hold.

"The door locks automatically from the outside," she said, tossing the pillow onto the bed. "We won't be able to get out."

"I have a key." Clothes spilled out of the woman's suitcase at the bottom of the closet. He rummaged through the contents before holding up a cap and hooded sweatshirt. "Tie your hair back and put these on."

She did as she was instructed while Sebastien paced across the floor with his hands in his hair, straining to formulate a plan.

"Where are we going?" she asked as she pulled the bill of the cap over her eyes. He surveyed her with approval. She looked less memorable.

"I know a place. To get there, we need to cross the officers' deck where someone might recognize you. It'll draw attention if we go together. I'll walk ten paces in front of you. Just follow me."

She nodded, the fear returning to her eyes.

"If anyone tries to talk to you, just keep walking. Ignore them. Are you ready?"

"Yes." She tilted her chin down and pursed her lips. Her hands were balled into fists.

Sebastien inserted the skeleton key into the door and exhaled in relief as the green light appeared. After poking his head out to scan the empty hallway, he motioned for her to follow.

He hurried along the carpeted corridor with the woman trailing behind. He braced himself for one of the cabin doors to fling open, but they remained closed like sleeping eyes, keeping their secrets safe within. The exit at the end of the hall seemed impossibly far until the door finally materialized in front of him. The metal handle felt cold as he balanced the shiny tray in his other hand. He turned to look at the woman who stood exactly ten paces behind him.

"This leads to the officers' deck," he whispered. "Remember what I said. And if anyone stops me, just keep walking."

She tilted her chin forward in a stealthy nod.

Sebastien pushed open the door and stepped onto the grey metallic floor. There were a couple of white suits in the distance, but the deck was mostly clear. If they could make it to the stairwell that led to B Deck below, they'd be able to use the network of hidden stairs and passageways that snaked throughout the ship's interior.

The woman's footsteps could be heard behind him as they marched past Nikos's office. The door was closed.

A young officer with close-cropped hair and a faint goatee turned a corner and passed Sebastien, his pace unhurried.

"Are you lost, beautiful?" His voice was boyish and suggestive. The woman's footsteps continued on without missing a beat. "I asked you a question," the officer called out after her. He muttered something under his breath as he walked away in defeat.

Sebastien quickened his pace when he saw the white door that led to the staircase. His lungs released a sigh as he stepped onto the landing. The woman appeared seconds later.

He had learned how to traverse the ship through the hidden passageways. Staff and crew used these tunnels and stairwells to reach all corners of the *Glacier* without being seen by guests. It didn't take long for them to climb several levels above to Riviera Deck.

Sebastien guided the woman by the hand as they stepped through the doorway and onto the familiar seafoam carpet. "It's just at the end of the hall," he said, flashing her an encouraging glance.

With the skeleton key in his fingers, he opened the double doors and pulled the woman inside the sanctuary. It looked untouched since the last time he had been there. Piles of white sheets were laid across the floor of the raised stage. The glass panels along the walls cast a warm glow throughout the egg-shaped room.

"Where are we?" She shook her hair out of the cap and wiped the sweat that glistened across her forehead.

"You're safe here," he said. "This is the House of the Heel."

❖

The day after Sebastien's nineteenth birthday, Sophie baked him a cake. He told her it wasn't necessary, that his mother had already baked him one the previous night, but she didn't listen. She had a way of turning everything into a production. "Birthdays are important," she said.

She held the cake in front of her ceremoniously as she sang, taking careful steps toward him. Nine candles were blue and ten were white. They flickered softly, casting shadows on her face. She placed the cake in front of him on the Lamoureux family dining table.

"Make a wish," she said with a self-satisfied smile.

He paused, then blew. Every candle flickered out except for one. She took a seat beside him at the table fit for ten.

"What did you wish for?"

He knew she was going to ask that exact question.

"A baby goat."

Sophie giggled and slapped him playfully on the shoulder. "Be serious."

"Seriously. I want a baby goat. And a time machine, but I guess I only get one wish."

"Then you're going to be very disappointed in the gift I have for you." Sophie climbed onto his lap and straddled his waist. Her mouth tasted like icing sugar. His body flooded with warmth as she ran her fingers through his hair. This was all very new to him still. Ever since she had shown him the things he could do with his body a few months earlier, he craved her like nicotine. Their parents didn't approve, but that was tinder to the fire. They would be ridiculed as a couple, so they kept their friendship private. Come September, they would part ways for different schools in different cities where they would become different people and begin different lives, but until then they found home in each other's bodies.

Sophie's dress was halfway over her head when they heard the front door open, echoing across the high ceiling of the foyer. She pulled her clothes back on and slid off Sebastien's lap in one seamless motion.

Her father appeared at the dining room entrance a second later. He was large and intimidating, dressed in a wool suit. The knot of his red tie hung loosely against his wrinkled shirt. A black leather briefcase was clenched in his fist.

"Daddy," she said, trying to sound nonchalant while straightening her hair. "You're back from work early."

"What's he doing here?" His eyes shot from the burned-out candles on the cake to Sebastien's tousled hair.

"It's his birthday," Sophie explained.

Sebastien stood up. "I was just heading home, sir."

Marcel Lamoureux grunted before disappearing up the stairs.

The afternoon air was chillier than usual for that time of year as Sebastien walked down the peaceful streets of Petit Géant. He was remembering the smell of Sophie's skin as he wandered past the brightly lit windows of shops and houses.

The apartment he shared with his mother was quiet. Ruby's purse was on the kitchen table. "Mama?" he called out as he set down the box containing the remains of Sophie's cake.

He knocked on her bedroom door, but there was no answer.

"Mama, you in there?"

Silence. Worried and curious, he turned the unlocked doorknob.

His mother was wrapped in her favourite robe of blue satin and a pattern of cherry blossoms. She stood in front of a tall oval mirror she had purchased at a garage sale many years earlier. Her back was turned to Sebastien, but he caught a glimpse of deep purple skin before she pulled the robe tightly around her thin body.

"What happened to your shoulder?"

"It's nothing," she said with an embarrassed smile. "I had a fall. That's all."

"You fell on your shoulder?"

"I'm fine!" she cried, waving her hands at him to signal she didn't want to make a fuss about it. "Your mama can handle a little tumble."

Sebastien studied her face but couldn't read it. She put her hand on his cheek as though she knew he didn't believe her. "I'm fine," she said. "It's all going to be fine."

The young woman with the dark hair was in the same position when Sebastien returned, sitting on a heap of cushions with a white sheet wrapped around her shoulders. He placed the tray in front of her and lifted the shiny cloche, revealing a shallow bowl filled with thick ribbons of pasta swimming in a blood-red sauce. The plate beside it was piled high with focaccia bread.

"Eat up," he said as he took a seat on the floor. She smiled shyly, the first time since he found her, and proceeded with stabbing and twirling the noodles with her fork.

"My name is Sebastien. What's yours?"

"Athena." The woman wiped her lips with the cloth napkin on her lap. "Athena Vissi."

"It's nice to meet you, Athena." He offered a comforting smile, but her eyes darted to the bowl in front of her. "You told me earlier that you're being taken to France to pay off a debt. Is that right?"

She nodded, eyes cast downward.

"Tell me more."

Athena put down her fork and knife. She took a sip of water and wrapped the sheet more tightly around her shoulders.

"Those men are dangerous," she said at last. Her gaze drifted slowly to meet Sebastien's. She examined his face, as if wanting to trust him, to believe he wasn't like the others.

"How do you know those men?"

"I don't know who they are. All I know is they are powerful. A friend — someone I thought was a friend — connected me with them." She looked away, ashamed for having been fooled.

"Tell me more," Sebastien said, urging her to go on in his softest tone.

She hesitated, the words clinging to her lips before spilling over the edge.

"My family owned a shop in Athens. Nothing special. Liquor. Cigarettes. Sweets. The economy collapsed and the business went with it. We survived off our savings while my brother and I worked whatever jobs we could find. The money dried up a few years later. Our wages were enough to feed us but not enough to pay for our father's medication. Without it, he would get very sick."

Her voice was low and solemn. She spoke slowly as she held a cushion against her chest. This story wasn't going to end happily.

"He got worse every month he went without the pills. We were desperate. I told a friend about our situation. I didn't want anything from him except someone to talk to, but he said he could help. I knew they were criminals. I'm not stupid. I needed the money and didn't care where it came from." She paused as she grabbed a square of bread and bit into it. "Father died less than a year later. It had nothing to do with the pills. His heart just failed him. He was a good man."

She stared at the floor, her face blank. The crying had ended long ago. There were no tears left.

"All of a sudden we didn't need the money anymore," she went on. "No medication, no need for money. I figured I'd have more time to find a better job and start paying off the debt. Easy, right? Not for those snakes. They told me I had to pay everything at once. I couldn't do that. No way. Then the men said they had an idea."

Athena couldn't stop shaking her head. It was painful to recount the series of events that had led her to the *Glacier*. Looking back, she saw the many things she could have done differently to avoid falling into the trap that was laid for her.

"They told me they had a factory in France. All I had to do was work off my debt. It would be paid in three months. They would even take me there on this beautiful ship. It would be like a holiday." An empty smile spread across her face to emphasize the absurdity. "I believed them. But even if I hadn't, what else could I have done? I was trapped."

"What happened when you boarded in Athens?"

"They took me to that room and locked me inside. Even then, I didn't realize how much trouble I was in. It only started to become clear when they sent a man to mark me." The composure she had maintained began to slip as her shoulders shook and her breathing became heavy.

"What do you mean?" Sebastien was scared to hear the answer.

She paused, mustering courage. With a laboured breath, Athena turned to face the wall and swept her dark hair to one side. Carved into the delicate skin on the back of her neck were smooth black lines of ink. Six little circles intersected each other to form a round web of petals. The skin around it was red and raw.

"It's Aphrodite's flower," she said. "They told me all their girls are marked with one. I used to hear stories about these people, about this symbol, when I was very young. That's when I knew I was their property."

Silence hovered above them in the dim sanctuary. Sebastien didn't know what to say. The symbol confirmed what he had always suspected to be true. His father was a monster.

"It's my fault," she said. "I should never have trusted that man who introduced me to them. I was blinded by his kindness. I thought he was my friend. He would call me Pallas Athena, after the ancient goddess, and we would drink mastika and talk about books. I was a fool."

The stillness was interrupted by the hum of Sebastien's phone as it vibrated in his pocket. He almost forgot about the message he had sent Nikos. "I'm here" said the words on the screen.

"I'm going to get you off this ship," he said. There was fierceness in his eyes, and he could see that she believed him. "Stay here for a few minutes. I just need to meet a friend. I'll be back, and we'll figure out a plan."

The hallway of Riviera Deck felt unusually cold as he closed the doors behind him. He ran through the empty corridor until he reached the balcony that overlooked the atrium. The sounds of music and laughter drifted through the air from the lobby far below. Nikos stood beside a pillar with his arms crossed over his chest.

"What's going on?" Nikos kept his voice low, but it sounded interrogative. "Why can't we meet in our usual spot? And why are you wearing that?"

Sebastien was still dressed in the grey cabin-service uniform that was a size too small. The pastille-shaped buttons strained against the fabric across his chest. Curls of hair fell from beneath the stiff bellboy cap.

"Listen to me. There's something awful happening on board this ship. But before I say anything else, I need you to answer me. Can I trust you?"

His eyes blinked rapidly as he processed the question. "Of course."

"Convince me that I can trust you."

"You can trust me. You're my Patroclus."

Despite the stern lines of the officer's face, there was always softness in his eyes like warm honey.

"I think Kostas is involved in a trafficking ring." The words sounded ridiculous as they hung in the air. Nikos's face was blank as he tried to make sense of them.

"What?"

"I found a girl locked in cabin A66 in the commanders' wing. She told me she's being taken to France to pay off a debt. She's being held captive. Nikos, do you know what I'm saying? This is human trafficking. She's being sold as a slave."

Nikos's expression contorted into a puzzled frown. He shook his head. "You did what?"

"I rescued her. She's hiding in the House of the Heel."

"Oh god." Nikos stumbled to the edge of the balcony with his head hanging over his chest. "Please tell me you're joking."

"Do you know anything about this?" It was Sebastien's turn to interrogate.

Nikos turned around, the sunlit atrium unfolding behind him. "That's Kostas's niece. She's not well."

"That can't be true."

"She has a history of delusions. She was kept in that cabin for her own safety. She can be dangerous — to herself and to others."

Sebastien felt nauseous as he weighed the possibility of this being true against everything he had witnessed that day. Nikos stepped toward him until their faces almost touched.

"You shouldn't have taken her. That was a terrible thing to do. But it's okay. I'm going to help you." His voice was gentle as he held Sebastien by the arms. "We just need to bring her back before Kostas realizes she's missing."

"She seems so convinced," he said as he rested his face on Nikos's shoulder. "I believed every word she said."

"She believes them, too. She's not well."

Sebastien looked into his eyes and pulled away. His entire body felt stiff, like he had gazed upon Medusa and was turning to stone.

"She's the woman I saw at Sirens." He took another step backward. "You escorted her out through a door in the wall. You told me you didn't know who she was, that you took her down to A Deck and she found her way back to her cabin."

Nikos let out an exasperated sigh and fumbled for the right words. "I didn't know who she was until later. Kostas asked me to take her below decks, so that's what I did."

The atrium that surrounded them crystallized into perfect clarity. Sebastien could see every reflection in the tinted glass, every vein in the leaves that draped over the edges, every thread on the upholstered cushions.

"How did she get back to her cabin without a key?"

"This is ridiculous," Nikos said with an incredulous grin. "I took her back to the cabin myself."

"That's not what you told me. Why would you lie?"

Nikos's mouth hung open, searching for the words. His hands were held in front of him, pleading. "I ... I don't ... I must have been mixed up." A helpless laugh slipped past his lips.

"What are you hiding from me?"

"Wait," he said as a shadow fell across his face. "How did you get past the door? How did you get into the commanders' wing in the first place?"

Sebastien reached into his pocket and held up the rectangle of black plastic.

"You stole the skull key?"

"Skeleton key."

"You took that from me?" The muscles in his face tightened. His shoulders hunched up against his neck.

"Don't try to change the subject."

"Do you know what could have happened if someone found out I lost that key?" Nikos's eyes were wide with betrayal. Sebastien couldn't ignore the tendrils of guilt that wrapped around his lungs.

"You're trying to avoid —"

"I could have lost my rank, Sebastien! Everything I've worked for, years of training and proving myself, could have been wiped out because you took advantage of my love."

The words stung. Sebastien stood there, turned to stone now, no defence to offer. Nikos looked more sad than angry, the air deflating from his proud chest. Neither man knew what to say.

"Sebastien?"

The voice rang out across the atrium, striking the silence like the chime of a bell. He thought it must have been an illusion at first, the woman standing there with skin that smelled like warm butter and lips the colour of cranberries. He knew every atom of her so intimately that perhaps his mind had moulded her out of the air, breathed life into this apparition.

Standing there on the balcony was Sophie Lamoureux.

SIXTEEN

The Beginning of Something Else

Sebastien graduated college three weeks after his nineteenth birthday. The sky was clear and the sun was out — perfect weather for a day that would alter his life in ways he could never have predicted.

The school system in Québec was different from what was depicted in the American movies he watched. High school ended sooner, then two to three years of publicly funded college were required to apply for university. The local college was thirty minutes away by bus, far enough to give him a taste of life outside Petit Géant, even though all the same faces were there.

It was a funny feeling to be both proud and embarrassed. The embarrassment had nothing to do with the silly gown and tasselled cap he wore. It came from how proud he actually felt. He sat between Heather Gagnon and Etienne Guérin as he waited for his name to be called. He would walk across the stage, retrieve his diploma, and know it would be the beginning of the end of his stay in this vicious little town. His legs twitched with nervous excitement.

The students sat in rows of collapsible chairs arranged across the field beside the school, their beaming parents in the bleachers behind them. It was a warm spring day. Sebastien's cap wouldn't stay put on his dense tangle of hair, so he used it to fan himself as the sun beat down on them.

Sophie's voice sparkled as she announced his name into the microphone. Being the class valedictorian, she had the privilege of calling every graduate to the stage. Her smile was radiant as he climbed the stairs. The applause was scattered, and there might have been a few heckles, but he paid no attention. All he saw was Sophie and the rest of his life unfurled behind her.

"I am the proudest woman in the world!" Ruby said after the ceremony. She threw her arms around his shoulders and let herself be lifted up by her handsome son. "My boy, college graduate, soon-to-be university scholar. You'll be famous one day. Just watch. You are destined for big things."

Her arm was linked with his as they crossed the field and entered the cold brick building that was the athletics wing. Flimsy wooden tables covered in trays of store-bought cheese and crackers were arranged throughout the blemished surface of the gymnasium floor. Domed lamps that dangled from the ceiling illuminated the vast room in stark light, except for one rebel that remained dark. Students in their electric blue gowns clustered together in various tribes, none of which included Sebastien.

"I don't need to be famous." He looked at the grey cardstock folder that hid his diploma, its power heavy in his hand.

"I just want to get far away from this place. Start over. Build a home where we belong. Just you and me, Mama."

Ruby rested her head against his arm. It sounded lovely. "How about France?"

"France would do." He smiled down at her and kissed the side of her head.

Sophie spotted them from across the room and hurried in their direction, slicing through huddles of students and families. Her heels announced her approach as they poked at the floor.

"I'll leave you with your pretty lady," Ruby said with a knowing look in her eyes. "I need to use the washroom, anyway." She raced away before Sophie reached them.

"If I didn't know any better, I would think you were a pompous intellectual," Sophie said with a girlish giggle, her hair cascading from beneath her cap in elaborate waves.

"If anyone would know better, it would be you." He hesitated before placing a soft kiss on her right cheek.

"I guess this is it," she said, looking around the room with a theatrical flourish in her movements.

He laughed. "We have the entire summer before we say our melodramatic goodbyes."

"This feels big, though, doesn't it? This moment?" She held the grey folder against her stomach as her eyelashes fluttered. "It's the end of one thing, and the beginning of something else."

He took a step closer until he could smell her buttery skin. "We have an entire lifetime of beginnings and ends ahead of us," he said, taking a mental photograph of Sophie's face in that moment, so much hope and promise.

Twenty minutes passed, and Ruby hadn't returned. Chloe Villeneuve slithered over and insisted on taking Sophie with her. Sebastien stood in the middle of the floor, alone, before deciding to find his mother. He lingered outside the ladies' room until someone exited. The heavyset woman shook her head when asked if there was anyone inside.

The halls around the gymnasium were a maze of corners and closets, the walls lined with bins filled with rubber spheres and mesh jerseys. Pale light drifted from the metal dishes that dangled from the ceiling. He was about to walk through the exit to the field when he heard a noise.

He knew the voice, deep like a bassoon. The tone was hushed but tinged with aggression. It tickled the hairs on Sebastien's arms. Then came a voice he would recognize underwater. It was soft, but he heard the fear as if she were screaming.

Sebastien ran down the hall toward the sounds. He turned a corner and came up against a dead end with racks of lacrosse sticks. Standing there were his mother and Marcel Lamoureux — Sophie's father.

⸎

The noises that echoed across the *Glacier's* atrium seemed to go silent. Sebastien stared at the woman in front of him, a ghost from a past life.

"Sophie?"

The dagger-like heels of her shoes sank into the carpet as she rushed to Sebastien and hooked her arms around his neck. He felt drunk on the past, breathing in the unforgotten scent of her hair and skin and perfume. It took a few seconds for his frozen arms to reanimate themselves. He held her as she clung to him.

"How did you find me?" His voice came out like a whisper.

"It doesn't matter." She put her hands on his face and looked into his eyes. "I arrived in Crete last night and boarded this morning. I'm here now."

"You talked to Jérôme," he said, his eyebrows crinkling in surprise. "He was the only one who knew where I was."

She paused, brushing the hair from his forehead. "I was desperate."

"You shouldn't have come here."

She let go of his face and pulled away. "Why did you leave? You just ran away in the middle of dinner with no warning, no explanation."

"I left a note." He regretted the words as soon as they slipped out of his mouth.

She threw her manicured hands in the air. "That was so very considerate of you."

"I just couldn't stay in that town another minute," he said, feeling suddenly silly for being dressed the way he was. He removed the bellboy cap from his head and ran his fingers through his hair.

"I know you blame that town for every shitty thing that's happened in your life, but one day you'll have to face the truth."

"And what truth is that?" His glare challenged her to put into words what he knew she had always thought. It felt like he was back in that place, standing on the side of the street, feeling small and powerless.

"You can't keep believing it's everyone's fault but your own." Sophie paused as her face softened. "You own some of the blame."

The clamour of the atrium returned as they stood across from each other. They were familiar faces in foreign circumstances, two people so far removed from their context they might as well have been strangers.

Sophie took a step back as Sebastien spun his body around the balcony. He'd just remembered something critical.

"Where's Nikos?"

"Who?"

He grabbed her by the hand and led her down the carpeted hall toward the front of the ship. She ran alongside him despite her hazardous heels, not bothering to ask where they were going. They reached the double doors at the end of the hall. With a flick of the wrist, the door was unlocked and opened.

"Athena!" His voice slid along the curved walls of the still room. The House of the Heel was empty.

"Who's Athena?" Sophie let go of his hand and examined the strange room draped in white sheets and soft light.

"Nikos," he said, shaking his head and clenching his fists. "He took her."

At his feet was a silver tray. The bowl was empty except for a few curled noodles and streaks of red sauce. The napkin and silverware lay on the sheet Athena had been sitting on. If it weren't for the evidence, he might have thought she had never been there to begin with.

⌘

For over a thousand years, the city of Heraklion on the island of Crete was coveted and conquered by whomever had the power to decide it was theirs. The Arabs called it rabd al-handaq and made it the capital of their far-flung island emirate, where pirates took refuge between attacks at sea. The Byzantines watched it burn, along with everyone in it, before building a new city on the ashes they called Chandax. The Venetians brought the enlightenment of the Renaissance to their newly christened city of Candia. It took twenty-one years of siege for the Ottomans to breach the fortified walls and conquer the city, killing tens of thousands and calling it Kandiye. Eventually it was reclaimed by the Greeks, who gave the city its present name after the symbol of strength and masculinity that was Zeus's son — Heracles.

It's not enough for men to take something away from another. They must make it their own. Brand it for themselves. Leave their mark.

The city of Heraklion was several shades of rust from outside the large windows of Sophie's cabin on Riviera Deck. Just beyond her balcony were the stone battlements and parapets of the fortress of Koules. It stood watch over the harbour as it had done since the Venetians built it centuries ago.

Diya and Ilya sat on the sofa like captivated schoolchildren as Sebastien filled them in on everything that had transpired that day: what he found in cabin A66, Athena's story of abduction, Nikos's claim about her identity, and the unexpected reunion with Sophie. The three of them were dressed in their evening uniforms. They would be on duty in their respective corners of the *Glacier* as soon as they set sail from Crete.

"Do you trust this man? This Nikos?" Sophie leaned against a pillar beside the sofa, her arms crossed in front of her.

Diya and Ilya turned to face him with impressive synchronicity. They wondered the same thing.

"I thought I did." Sebastien could hear the strain and uncertainty in his own voice. "He's been on my side up to this point. He could have turned me in when he found the ear stud I left in Alexis's cabin. He didn't."

"He lied about escorting Athena down to her cabin on black-tie night," Diya said, clearly skeptical. "Why lie about that if she were just Kostas's niece?"

"I don't know." Sebastien reclined in the cushioned arm-chair with his arms hanging over the sides. "He said he got mixed up."

"And if she really is Kostas's niece, why doesn't anyone know about her?" Diya scanned the room like a prosecutor seducing a jury. "Nobody's seen her anywhere except in Sirens, and it was clear she wasn't welcome there. It sure sounds like she's being hidden to me."

Ilya leaned forward, his arms flexing underneath the fitted polo shirt. "She came on board the same day Dominic disem-barked, right? So she couldn't have been what he saw in that cabin. It was something else. If Athena is Kostas's delusional niece, what are the chances of her being put in the same cabin where Dominic saw something he shouldn't have seen? Her story lines up. She says she's being hidden away in the same cabin where Dominic saw something that was supposed to be hidden."

Sophie placed her hands on her temples as she strug-gled to follow along. "Wait a sec. This Dominic person saw something in that cabin he shouldn't have seen, right? But it couldn't have been Athena because she hadn't boarded the ship yet. So if it wasn't Athena, what did he see?"

All eyes turned to Sebastien.

"Another woman." He said it quietly as if to himself. "That was my first thought. Athena is one of many. Dominic saw another woman trapped in that cabin on her way somewhere terrible. They get coaxed or coerced on board, then they're transported — trafficked — somewhere along the ship's route. Athena says she's being taken to France. Maybe the woman Dominic saw was removed in Athens."

"It makes sense." Ilya had a fearful look in his eyes.

"This is fucking bad," Diya said, wrapping her arms around herself.

Sophie shook her head in disbelief. "Sebastien, what did you get yourself into?"

"This is what we've been fighting for," he said. "How can we stand for justice, then sit back and do nothing when this is happening right in front of us? We need to stop it."

Ilya leaned back on the sofa with a sigh. "You're right. But how do we do it?"

"We arrive in Cannes in a week," Sebastien said. "That means one week before Athena is taken away. We need a plan. This is no longer a little rebellion. This is war."

"Smile!"

The smiles remained on the faces of the elderly Norwegian couple a few seconds longer than necessary as they were blinded by the light from the camera's flash.

"Come back in an hour," Sebastien said in his sweetest voice. "It'll be ready for purchase in the portrait gallery."

The massive horn bellowed across the harbour from several decks above. The sound was muted from within the ship, but it reverberated through the glass and marble of the central atrium. It signalled their departure from the island of Crete. The upcoming voyage would be thirty-six hours at sea before their next port of call: the ancient city of Palermo on the island of Sicily.

The photo station on Adriatic Deck was quiet. Sebastien leaned over the edge of the balcony to view the Agora below. The evening was coming to life with the arrival of passengers in tasteful gowns and summer suits. Contessa's replacement, a Scottish singer who had boarded that morning, began her first performance from a small, oval stage. She crooned into

the microphone, matching her predecessor's technical prowess but lacking the special something that made Contessa
a star. The pianist accompanying her was also new, a slight
young man with brilliant orange hair.

Sebastien watched the staff and crew put on a performance of their own. Bartenders stood guard behind their
countertops, mixing and shaking their potions. Waiters
and waitresses carried trays with poise, handing out glasses
and dishes with flirtatious charm. The attendants at the
guest services desk answered questions as if they were ani-
matronic. Everyone's smiles were convincing, their movements perfectly timed. A passenger would never guess these
charming members of the underclass were in the throes of
rebellion below decks in Hades — a fight between the rulers
and the ruled.

The Kourakis family, minus the patriarch, stepped gingerly down the marble staircase that led from Adriatic Deck
to the Agora below. Alexis was less ostentatious than usual
in a simple black dress and her hair pulled back in a ponytail. Katerina trailed two paces behind while Kristo held his
mother's hand protectively. They were followed farther back
by one of Nikos's blue-shirted guards.

Little Kristo's eyes widened when he noticed Sebastien
staring at them from across the atrium. His body went stiff.
Sebastien gave him a discreet little wave. He looked away and
urged his mother down the stairs.

Where's father?

Seeing Kristo brought Sophie's musical voice into the
chamber of his mind.

You can't keep believing it's everyone's fault but your own.

"You own some of the blame." He repeated her words
under his breath.

His thoughts were interrupted by the chirp of another woman's voice. "Sebastien?" He turned around to see his manager, Claudette, standing in front of him. She forced a smile but there was an unusual quality in the way she held herself. "Nikos here wants a word with you."

Sure enough, the brooding officer stood beside her.

"Come with me, please." He spoke with his most authoritative tone, deep and firm. His voice softened as they walked away from Claudette, side by side. "I'm supposed to bring you to Kostas."

Sebastien sensed a hint of unease. "What's going on?"

"I'm not sure," Nikos said, "but he wants to see you immediately."

They walked along the arcade of shops selling everything from Baltic amber to Greek loukoumi. Recorded classical music was piped into the hall.

"Does this have anything to do with Athena?"

"I don't think he knows she was taken to begin with, unless she told him."

"Why did you take her back down there?" The words sounded more like an accusation than he had intended.

"I did that for you," Nikos said, shooting him a cautionary glance. "You'd be packing your bags, or worse, if Kostas had found out what you did. I got her back below decks just in time."

They stepped into an empty elevator at the end of the hall. The walls were mirrored with shiny gold trim. Sebastien looked at Nikos's reflection and noticed how striking he was. It was funny how some things could be seen more clearly in a reflection than in reality. He looked at himself and saw the strain around his eyes and his untidier-than-usual hair.

"How do you know she's Kostas's niece?"

"It's what he told me." He turned to face Sebastien and something flickered between them that could have resulted in a kiss. It lasted only a moment as the elevator made its way skyward.

Sebastien didn't move, but he felt a tickle of relief. Nikos might still be innocent, might be trusting enough to be deceived by Kostas's lies.

"Does Achilles believe everything he hears?"

"Achilles knows when it's in his best interest to not question what he's told." The slightest suggestion of a smile danced in the corners of Nikos's lips. "It's something his dear Patroclus could afford to learn."

The elevator doors opened to a rush of salted Mediterranean air. The expanse of the sea spread outward from their view on Sunset Deck. The sun was a fiery disc in the distance, casting flames along the waves. Guests gathered by the edges of the deck to watch the *Glacier* sail away from the storied island of Crete, now nothing more than a bald, featureless mound of rock.

Nikos led him through a pair of glass doors to a lounge at the stern of the ship. Tables and chairs were neatly arranged on the teakwood deck. Past the railing was the enormous wake left by the *Glacier*. It snaked across the rippling sea like the tail of a dragon.

"I'll leave you here," Nikos said under his breath. "Don't do or say anything stupid."

Sebastien stepped into the lounge as his hair was tossed in the wind. Sitting alone at a table by the railing was his father.

❖

Ruby Goh and Marcel Lamoureux stood frozen in the dim corner of the athletics wing. The startled look in Marcel's eyes would have been comical if it weren't for his hand gripped tightly around her arm. Or the blushing of freshly struck skin on her cheek. Or the fearful, defensive splay of her fingers. Her veil of long black hair fell across her face.

"Mama?" Sebastien's voice trickled out like water from a loose faucet. "What ..."

"Go back to the party," she said. The words were meant to be firm, but they came out shaky. He saw that Ruby's red lipstick was smeared around her lips.

"What's going on?"

"You heard her." Marcel's hand remained fixed around her arm. "Get back to the party."

That feeling Sebastien feared pressed against his lungs. Warmth spread across his chest like fire. "Let go of her."

Ruby winced as the man's grip tightened, but then something flickered behind his eyes. He exhaled loudly, then released Ruby's arm. "Get out of my sight," he said with a flick of the chin. "Both of you."

Without a moment's hesitation, Ruby turned to Sebastien and took him by the wrist, pulling him toward the exit. She pulled harder when she realized he wouldn't move. "Let's go," she said, her voice frayed at the edges.

She continued to tug at Sebastien's wrist in desperation, but his legs were stiff as stone. All he could feel was the burn and smoulder as it pushed its way up his throat. He could barely hear himself when he said, "Did you hit her?" The words sounded quiet and composed, even though a dangerous frequency hummed along his skin.

Marcel hesitated, his eyes darting between mother and son, as if deciding whether to offer a damning truth or an unbelievable lie. As the features of his face tightened, it seemed as though he'd choose denial. But the creases around his eyes softened at the last second, and Sebastien knew he'd be given the truth. Marcel Lamoureux was too proud a man to play pretend for someone like Sebastien.

"What if I did?" Marcel took a step toward him. His tone was unthreatening, but he was four inches taller and thirty pounds heavier. The buttons of his crisp white shirt strained against the heaving of his chest. "Your mother's no saint. Everyone knows it but you. Maybe it's time you learned."

"Be quiet," Ruby said, her voice sharp.

"Tell the boy the truth," Marcel said, challenging her. "Doesn't he deserve to know?"

"What's he talking about?" Sebastien's teeth ground in his mouth as he fought the violence pounding against his ribs. Every nerve flared with electricity.

His mother whimpered as her shoulders collapsed forward, closing like a clam shell.

"Every time she came looking for me, luring me, I gave her what she wanted." Marcel's breath smelled like chalky mint and cigarette tar. "I always knew she was trouble, but how could I resist? I'm only a man. Now she wants to leave, just like that. Move to the city with her worthless son. What gives her the right to do that? So sure, maybe I lost my cool, but someone had to teach her."

It flooded his arteries, pure and white. He could barely see Marcel's face in front of him. The world was blinding.

"But I'm glad you know," Marcel went on, a hint of a smile gathering in the corners of his lips. "You should know the kind of woman she really is."

Ruby screamed as she lunged forward, clawing at the side of his head, leaving jagged lines of red across the skin of his neck. The sound was deafening, like a rock through a window, as the back of his hand connected with her face.

Sebastien didn't recognize the noises that growled from his throat. He grabbed a lacrosse stick from the rack on the wall. It sliced through the air onto Marcel's back like an axe against timber. The man buckled against the blow before being tackled to the floor. Sebastien pinned him, and his fists pummelled downward. Splatters of red redecorated his robe.

Marcel's hands grasped for anything he could defend himself with until his fingers wrapped around a helmet on the floor. It crashed against Sebastien's skull with a dull thud. Sebastien fell backward as a fist found his gut.

Marcel got to his feet and stumbled down the hall. Ruby grabbed him by the arm, but a shove sent her colliding with the brick wall. Sebastien watched as he made his way toward a sliver of light before pushing through the double doors.

The sunshine was glorious as Marcel staggered across the grassy field. Blood gushed down his face from his newly broken nose, leaving trails of gore down his white shirt. His mouth was a gaping red wound. The expensive suit he wore was torn at both shoulders.

A crowd of students and their families were standing paralyzed on the lawn. Marcel seemed unaware of Sebastien chasing him from behind with a lacrosse stick in his hand. Everyone else on the field saw, though.

They watched as Sebastien Goh swung the wooden stick again and again until Marcel Lamoureux lay in a heap on the ground. It took three men to pull Sebastien off of him. Every witness interviewed later that day said the same thing. The boy was consumed by rage.

SEVENTEEN

The Calm or the Storm

The sun's dying light and the hum of voices dimmed as Sebastien stepped toward the back of the deck. Kostas sat at a table for two set with linen napkins and polished silverware, a good distance apart from the other diners. The shallow bowl in front of him displayed the vibrant red of ripe tomatoes and distilled gold of olive oil. Two of Nikos's blue-suited guards stood against the railing about two metres from him on either side. A feeling of unease rumbled from the bottom of Sebastien's stomach.

"Mr. Goh!" Kostas wiped his lips with a napkin and smiled warmly. He shook Sebastien's hand and didn't seem to have any intention of releasing it, gripping firmly as their eyes connected. The smile didn't leave his face. Finally, he let go and they settled into their seats.

"Nikos said you wanted to see me." He shifted in his chair, trying to find a position that felt natural.

"Yes, yes." Kostas stabbed a tomato with his fork and inserted it into his mouth. His hair was slicked back in the usual rigid waves, revealing a portion of the white scar above his ear. The skin along his jaw and neck looked angry, as though he had shaved in a hurry. The evening sun exposed three tiny red cuts near his lips. "Do you know why I want to speak with you, Mr. Goh?"

He shook his head slowly. "I can't think of a reason."

Kostas chuckled quietly as he chewed before taking a sip from his glass of wine. "I was young once, just like you. I had so much passion. It burned inside me like a bonfire. Sometimes people would get singed by it, but it's what kept me alive. Without it, I would still be trapped in my village, selling dried fish in the market." He let out a soft sigh. "I thought I was invincible when I first started living at sea. Tell me, Mr. Goh. Do you think you are invincible?"

The disquieting feeling spread throughout Sebastien's gut. He clasped his hands together and held them against his stomach. His most charming smile spread across his face. "No, sir. No one's invincible."

Kostas's shoulders bounced as he laughed. "You're right! No one is invincible. We are men, not gods, yet our actions don't always prove we understand this simple truth. Sometimes we do things that are irrational. Stupid."

The smile vanished from Kostas's face as though it had never been there. The warmth chilled into something venomous. "I know who you are, Mr. Goh."

Every muscle in Sebastien's body stiffened. His breathing stopped. The anxiety that had danced along his nerves went cold.

"Who am I, sir?"

Say it. I'm your son. I'm the boy you abandoned.

"I must admit, you remind me of my younger self," Kostas went on. "Fearless, but reckless. Daring, but damaged. More bold than smart."

I'm not a coward like you.

"Tell me, Mr. Goh. What did you hope to accomplish with this little rebellion?" He leaned across the table. Their deep green eyes were locked like they were staring into a mirror.

"I don't know what you're talking about." The words came out convincingly, but they didn't match the icy expression. There was no use in putting on a mask. Kostas was staring into his own face.

"You're the leader of this uprising." Kostas's tone was more matter-of-fact than menacing. "I've suspected as much for some time, but now I have proof. Someone turned you in — someone you might even consider a friend."

"I don't know what you're talking about." The repeated words were mechanical this time. Warmth tickled his lungs. The heat rose steadily like a furnace, but he knew soon it would smoulder throughout his body.

"It doesn't matter what you say." Kostas leaned back in his chair. "You're fired. You will disembark in Palermo and never set foot on the *Glacier* again. Until then, you will not be permitted outside your cabin. Consider yourself lucky. I have plenty more punishment in store for your friends. I'll wear them down until there's nothing left."

"You will lose." The words spat out of his mouth.

Kostas laughed so loudly that the guests seated around them turned their heads. He sat back and looked at Sebastien as though he were an adorable, stupid child.

"You've already lost," he said with a superior smile. "And what did you accomplish? A few childish pranks? The only thing you've done is make life harder for the people who work on this ship."

"It won't matter that I'm gone. We've started something here, and it will only get stronger. Now everyone knows they can fight back against your oppression."

"Fight back?" Kostas said with a sympathetic look. "They are powerless. They have less freedom than they had before you came along. Nearly forty people have lost their jobs because of you. What will they do now, where will they go? Was this fight worth it for them?"

Sebastien's chest was on fire now. The rage crawled up his throat. His skin felt like it was melting.

"It's better than doing nothing," he said, his tone less steady.

He kept his eyes fixed on his father, but he could sense the other people seated around them. Only someone like Kostas would choose to have this conversation in such a public place. This boldness could only belong to someone so arrogant he had no fear of the repercussions. He was protected from them.

It brought Sebastien back to the gymnasium's dim hallway ten years earlier. Only someone like Marcel Lamoureux could feel so shielded from the consequences that he would assault a woman at her son's graduation. People like Sebastien and Ruby could never afford to be so brazen, while it was second nature to Kostas and Marcel.

"You didn't do nothing," Kostas said. "I'll give you that much. That's why you remind me of myself. You have spirit. But you know what else I see?"

Sebastien didn't say a word as he dug his fingernails into his knees.

"Anger." Kostas nodded, agreeing with himself. "Hatred. Violence. I see it in your eyes."

They're your eyes, asshole.

I'm your son.

Why wasn't I good enough?

Why wasn't my mother good enough?

Why did you leave her? Us?

I hate you. I hope you die violently.

I hope you find your wife fucking a better man.

I hope your children grow up to despise you, to be ashamed of you.

I know about Athena. I know where you're taking her.

I know what you do.

You enslave people.

You treat them like animals to make yourself feel powerful.

You're a weak, sick, pathetic man.

I see you.

I know who you are.

The rage scorched him from inside. He could feel himself start to shake, feel his breath feeding the fire in his lungs. His thoughts pushed against the inside of his mouth, forcing the dam to burst. At least Kostas would know there was one man who could see him for what he was, naked and exposed.

He held back with all his strength. Knowledge was his only power now.

"I have a soft spot for you," Kostas said, his tone patronizing. "You fight because it's all you've ever known. You think the whole world is against you. You blame everyone else for the hatred you feel." He shook his head. "Perhaps your parents didn't show you enough love."

Sebastien's vision blurred into brilliant white light. His hands sprang from beneath the table and he threw it to one side. Startled cries pierced the air. Glasses and dishes shattered against the floor while silverware ricocheted off surrounding tables. He couldn't control himself as he lunged forward, grabbing the front of Kostas's stiff white shirt. His other fist shot up in the air, angled toward his father like a lightning bolt from the hands of Zeus. He looked into the face in front of him and all he could see was pain.

Deep red paint streaked across walls and windows.

His mother's hands raw from cleaning.

Belittling words spat in his direction.

Bruised skin the colour of wine.

He froze, one fist clutching his father's shirt, the other suspended in the air. Kostas didn't move. The two guards by the railing didn't move. They stood there, ready to pounce, but didn't try to stop him. Kostas wanted to be hit in front of all these people. This was a trap, and he'd walked right into it.

As soon as he dropped his hands, he felt someone take hold of his arms protectively from behind. He could tell by the scent of his skin it was Nikos.

Kostas sat back in his chair and crossed one leg over the other. "You prove my point. Nikos, escort Mr. Goh back to his cabin. Be sure he doesn't leave until he disembarks in Palermo."

Sebastien didn't struggle as Nikos guided him by the arm away from the overturned table and broken glass. The lounge was so quiet he could hear his muted footsteps against the teakwood floor, but he felt molested by the stares, eyes having their way with his image, inventing stories and passing judgment.

"One more thing," Kostas said from behind. Sebastien turned to face him with Nikos's hand still on his arm. "Thank you again for the gift, Mr. Goh. It's my new favourite family portrait. But if you come near my family again, you will wish we had never met."

◈

Nikos loosened his grip as they exited the lounge. There were fewer people crowding the sides of Sunset Deck than before. The sun was almost touching the horizon, painting the sky a peaceful shade of orange. The silence simmered between them.

They stepped inside the mirrored elevator and watched the doors close. They were alone.

"You can't lock me in my cabin, Nikos."

"I can. I must." He was in full security commander mode, staring at the reflection of his own expressionless face.

"You have a choice, you know?" Sebastien looked into the eyes of the reflection beside him, but Nikos resisted the urge to soften his restraint. "You can let everyone make your decisions for you, or you can choose yourself. You can choose to let me go. You can choose to be honest with yourself, and everyone else, instead of hiding behind locked doors and hidden rooms."

The subtlest crack formed in Nikos's carefully constructed facade. "You don't leave me any choice. I don't know what you would do if I let you go. First, you destroy Alexis's cabin. Then, you abduct a woman. Now, you assault the hotel commander in front of dozens of people. I know it couldn't have been easy hearing him speak to you like that, but you went too far. I'm worried about you."

"I lost control back there." A warm current of shame passed through him. "It was a stupid thing to do. I know that. But Kostas was playing me. He wanted me to hit him."

"Not to mention that you stole from me. Me! What does that say about us?"

"I needed to find out what was hidden in cabin A66. I didn't want to ask you to take the risk of helping me, and I knew you wouldn't have done it, anyway."

"I've deactivated the skull key, by the way, so don't bother trying to use it."

"Skeleton key."

He shook his head with impatience.

"You can believe Kostas when he claims Athena's mentally ill, but I know it's not true," Sebastien said in a quiet voice. "There's something far more sinister happening here. You can choose to ignore it, but remember that it's a choice."

"As much as it will hurt to see you go in Palermo, I think it might be for the best." Nikos turned away from his reflection and looked into Sebastien's eyes. "Life at sea isn't for everyone. It's isolating. People lose touch with reality, with themselves. I can't just stand down and watch you lose control. That's why I'm going to do what Kostas instructed. I'm taking you to your cabin."

Sebastien leaned forward and put his hands on Nikos's face. They inhaled the scent of each other as their lips met seconds before the elevator doors opened.

"I guess that will be the last time we do that." Sebastien pulled away, watching the conflict on the face in front of him.

Nikos was overcome with emotion, but he fought it as he had trained himself to do. He knew how to harden his face, but he couldn't hide behind the transparency of his eyes and the twitch of his lips.

"Goodbye, Achilles," Sebastien said. "Take me to my cell, Nikos."

The only sound in the cabin that night was the gentle ticking of the little round clock with the white face that sat on the desk. Sebastien lay in the bottom bunk, staring up at the metal slats that held the empty mattress above. He would have given anything to speak to Ilya, but his friend had been relocated to another cabin. He was carrying a stuffed duffel bag when they passed in the corridor. Ilya flashed him a silent look to show he wasn't giving up just yet.

Sebastien was to be kept in isolation for the next thirty hours until they reached Palermo. One of Nikos's guards was stationed outside his door — the Dominic treatment. The only human contact he'd enjoyed since returning to his cabin was when the guard passed him a tray of cold lasagna and slices of bland tomato. *It must be Italian night in the cafeteria,* he thought as he picked at the food.

Sleep wasn't going to come easily. Every time he closed his eyes, he could see the blinding light, feel the inferno in his lungs, as he turned over the table and grabbed Kostas by the shirt. It was the same feeling ten years earlier when he attacked Marcel Lamoureux. The same feeling in Alexis Kourakis's bedroom. Complete and utter surrender to the rage that burned inside him. He felt himself drift a little further each time it happened. It frightened him. He would question who he truly was — the calm or the storm.

Maybe Kostas was right about what he could see in Sebastien's eyes. Anger. Hatred. Violence.

The aftermath of graduation day ten years earlier had been immediate and crushing. All he could hear were screams as he lay on the warm grass, restrained by hands and knees. His vision returned in full cinematic resolution, disorienting him with light and colour. He saw Sophie and her mother claw their way through the crowd to get to the wreckage in the centre. Panic was carved into their faces.

Two men held Ruby back as her arms flailed in the wind. Her voice sounded like the siren of an ambulance as she cried his name. Soon, her voice was overpowered by the real sirens.

Sebastien didn't struggle. He submitted to whatever needed to happen to him. He was carried away, guided into a vehicle, taken to an ugly room in an ugly building, asked questions. His answers were plain and honest.

The town had never been on his side, but they turned on him and his mother like a tsunami. What were once whispered insults became cries of condemnation. Ruby lost all of her housecleaning clients. Their neighbours chose either to vilify them or to shut them out entirely.

This would have been bearable had they been able to move to Québec City in the fall, as planned. Sebastien learned the hard way, however, that scholarships and acceptance letters could be taken away far more easily than they were handed out. Apparently, these honours were only available to young men unsullied by criminal charges with scary names like "aggravated assault."

Even if he were permitted to attend class in September, it would have been difficult focusing on anything other than hearings and trials. It made no difference that he wasn't sentenced to prison in the end. He was destined to receive court-ordered counselling rather than study fine arts in a university classroom. It was an outcome he learned to accept.

The following year was no more kind to Marcel Lamoureux. He was brought to the hospital badly broken, but they pieced him back together, more or less, although he was left with a permanent limp. He was exposed as the adulterer

and batterer that he was, and though nothing was more painful for Ruby than having to reveal the most shameful details
of her life, her story was convincing and she had the bruises
to prove it.

Even so, Marcel was a man, and a respected one at that.
Men like him were accustomed to getting away with crimes,
unpunished. He might have succeeded in eliciting the town's
sympathy while casting the wicked Gohs as the villains had it
not been for one person — Marie Lamoureux.

One look at Ruby's bruises and his wife was determined
to make Marcel pay for what he had done. He didn't spend a
minute in custody, but within a year he lost his marriage, the
support of his son and daughter, his family home, most of his
wealth, and the respect of the not-so-forgetful citizens of Petit
Géant. He packed his bags and moved to Vietnam.

The unexpected dishing-out of justice might have comforted Sebastien had he not lost everything himself. He often
found himself caught in a dark tempest of shame and guilt
and regret. He would lie in bed, fearful of who he was becoming, or who he had always been.

He had no power over the rage. What if this was simply
a part of him? Something inherited? He would wonder if his
father suffered from the same disease.

Now, many years after he learned the true magnitude
of this defect and how destructive it could be, he lay in the
bottom bunk of his cabin and drowned in the same swell of
helplessness. There was power in his anger he was unable to
control. It conflicted with the image of himself he worked so
hard to cultivate, irrefutable evidence that his entire identity
was a hoax. He wasn't the kind, intelligent champion of the
underprivileged with the effortless smile and compassionate
eyes but an embittered man with hatred stored inside him.

He wasn't the calm. He was the storm.

Ruby stared at him from her spot on the desk. Her eyes were forgiving behind the glass of the picture frame. "You did it for me," he could hear her say, her voice muted as though she were speaking from behind a velvet curtain. "All of the violence was to protect me."

A few days ago he might have considered this enough to exonerate him of his past and present crimes — he did whatever was needed to protect his mother, and he'd do the same for those being oppressed on board the *Glacier* — but now he could feel the flaw in the logic. Not everything true was also right.

He saw the look of fear in Kristo's face, the boy's screams stifled behind his hand. He heard the tearing of silk puncture the silence in Alexis's closet. He tasted the blood from his bitten lip as he held Kostas's shirt in his shaking fist. All of this was evidence he hadn't changed at all.

And what about Ruby? He had spent years defending his mother in his own mind. She was a victim, but that didn't mean her hands were clean. Her affair with Sophie's father proved that he hadn't known his mother as well as he'd thought. It was a truth he liked to dismiss.

It was easier to go on remembering Ruby Goh as innocent rather than a woman with the agency to make her own poor decisions.

It was easier to blame the men in her life for everything that went terribly, tragically wrong.

He looked at the portrait of Ruby beside his bunk. She knew the truth. That was evident in her cautious eyes and the hint of regret behind her smile. The truth would have been clear to him, too, if he had only known his mother better.

EIGHTEEN

Real Smoke

The young man on guard outside Sebastien's cabin could feel his eyelids get heavier with every exhale. Straightening his posture in the hard plastic chair, he glanced at the black-banded watch his ex-wife had given him for their first wedding anniversary. The time was 7:21 a.m. His shift had started at midnight.

The sound of approaching footsteps rang clearly throughout the quiet corridors. He couldn't see who was coming, but he heard the *clink-clink-clink* of heel against metal zigzag its way closer to him.

He anticipated someone turning the corner almost on the exact second it happened, but he didn't expect the person to look like the woman who stood before him. She was clearly a "cone," the term of endearment and derision the crew often used for guests. Her red-and-white candy-striped dress hugged her torso before bursting around her waist like an upside-down tulip. She was in her late twenties, with skin that looked pure as milk. Auburn hair fell onto her shoulders in loose ringlets.

"I'm so sorry," she said with an apologetic look on her pretty face. "Maybe you can help me. I'm looking for the jewellery shop, but I must have taken a wrong turn."

"You bet you did," said the guard with a warm smile. He was grateful for such a sweet distraction. "You've really lost your way. You're in the staff quarters."

"Oh my!" The woman put her hand to her mouth with an embarrassed giggle. "Silly me. I have no idea how I ended up here. You'll help?" Her innocent eyes coaxed him softly.

"Of course," he said, brushing the front of his pants with his hands as he stood up. "Let me take you."

⌘

Ilya hid around the corner, listening to Sophie lure the guard away from his post. The manipulation came naturally to her. He waited until their footsteps and voices diminished down the hall before he crept over to the door. He inserted his key card and held his breath, hoping it hadn't been deactivated. The green light appeared. With a sigh of relief, he stepped into the dark space.

Sebastien looked like a corpse in his bunk, arms and legs outstretched and a peaceful expression settled on his face. He still had on the turquoise uniform he had worn the previous night. His hair was a halo of dark curls.

"Wake up," Ilya whispered as he shook the body in the bunk.

Sebastien's limbs jolted back to life. His eyes shot open, wide and alert. They stared up at Ilya, processing his identity, determining whether he was real or imagined.

"Ilya, is that you? What's going on?"

"I'm breaking you out of here."

"How?" Sebastien sat up in his bunk. Memories of what happened the evening before trickled back to him. "Where's the guard outside?"

"Sophie dealt with it." Ilya reached into the duffel bag slung around his shoulder. He pulled out a grey sweatshirt and a golf cap. "Put these on. We don't have much time."

He did as he was told, stuffing his hair beneath the cap. Ilya covered two pillows with a sheet so they could pass as a person in the bunk. "I feel like I'm sneaking out of my parents' house in a bad teen movie," Sebastien said.

"Everything we know comes from the movies."

Ilya poked his head into the corridor and waved Sebastien toward him. They walked briskly through the halls. Every member of staff and crew they passed gave them a resolute nod or a subtle salute. The escape was underway.

They breathed more easily after stepping through the door that led to the network of tunnels and stairways that snaked throughout the ship.

"Am I hiding out in Sophie's cabin?"

"Too risky," Ilya said. "Nikos knows about Sophie. I have another place in mind."

"You really don't trust Nikos, do you?" It sounded more like a statement than a question.

Ilya turned to face him in the middle of the stairway. "I trust him like a wolf in a top hat."

They climbed higher, stopping only once to catch their breath. Each landing was a solid strip of perforated steel painted white. Corridors branched outward as more stairs led to the sky. Sebastien peered over the edge of the railing to see the stairs wind their way down to the bottom deck several levels below.

"We're almost there," Ilya said, urging him on. Sebastien followed as Ilya diverted from the stairs and took a tunnel that ran along the starboard side of the ship. They reached a door with a sign that proclaimed its location.

LIDO DECK
SPA OF THE ORACLE

The doorway was a portal between different worlds. They left the stark white passageway behind them and stepped into a refuge of calm. The spa was softly lit by cloud-shaped lamps that hung from the ceiling. Water cascaded down the length of a curved wall made of slabs of basalt, filling the air with its soothing sound.

Ilya led him down a peaceful hall protected by a canopy of broad, waxy leaves. Near the end was a door. "We're here," he whispered as he guided Sebastien inside.

The room was circular, and roughly the size of the apartment he once shared with his mother. The walls were punctuated by marble columns equally spaced apart. The centre of the room sank into a round pool, its bottom covered in a mosaic of blue and green tiles. Instead of holding water, it was lined with white cushions and sheets. Directly above the pool was a glass dome that stared up at the morning sky.

"Welcome to your hideout," Ilya said with a dramatic sweep of the arms. "This room was used for thalassotherapy treatments, but the filtration system in the pool broke a few days ago. Someone's coming on board in Cannes to fix it, which means you'll be safe here for the next week."

"That bed is fit for a king." Sebastien eyed the jumble of linen that filled the bottom of the empty pool.

"Only the best for you," Ilya said. A smile spread across his face for the first time that day. Sebastien had missed seeing it.

"What now?" He walked around the perimeter of the pool and gazed at the domed skylight above. "I'm thankful you broke me out, but what good does it do to hide here?"

"You won't just be hiding. We're going to rescue Athena. We need you."

Sebastien took a seat on the floor with his legs dangling over the edge of the pool. "I don't know, Ilya."

"What do you mean, you don't know?"

"I'm not sure about anything anymore." He took off the golf cap and ran his fingers through his matted hair. "Everything has escalated so quickly. I thought I knew what I was doing, what our purpose was, but now ..." The words trailed off. "I attacked Kostas in front of all those people. It was the same thing a few days ago in Alexis's bedroom. I just lost control. This has happened before, and it doesn't end well. I don't know if I can trust myself."

Ilya sat by his side and placed an arm around his shoulders. "Do you know how it felt when I found the man who killed my closest friend? Of course you do. You've felt it, too. The burning, blinding anger. It doesn't just come from nowhere. It's forced out of us when there's no other form of justice. I had Misha's killer in my hands. I could have made him pay. That would have been justice, no? But it wouldn't have brought Misha back, and it would have destroyed my life. This anger doesn't have to be a bad thing. It fuels our fight. It can be used for good, but only if we're smart."

"I just don't know how much fight I have left in me." Sebastien's shoulders slouched forward as he leaned into the hollow beneath Ilya's arm.

"This isn't about you. Not anymore. You started something that's bigger than us. Now people are paying attention. We're doing this for Dominic. For Misha. For your mother.

And most of all, for Athena. This is what we've been fighting for all along. What Athena is facing is evil. We can't sit back and let it happen."

Doubt brewed in the green pools of Sebastien's eyes. "What if Kostas is telling the truth? That she's delusional?"

"He's full of shit." Ilya spat the words out like venom. "I looked into that tattoo you saw on the back of her neck. Aphrodite's flower, right? Six connected little circles. It's the symbol of a trafficking ring based in Greece. They're part of a network of gangs, really bad people who traffic anything profitable and illegal. Drugs. Weapons. And yes, humans. They brand their girls with that exact symbol."

"I knew it," Sebastien said, biting his bottom lip. "There are others."

"Lots of others. But there are more rumours than facts. These criminals have been around for decades. They're well-connected. I wouldn't be surprised if they have tentacles in the government."

Sebastien sat upright. "Did you say decades?"

"Yes. If we have a chance at saving Athena, then we have no choice but to try. Imagine the scandal that would be. This utopian playground for the wealthy hiding such an evil secret. We probably couldn't take them all down, but exposing Kostas and the *Glacier* would be the first domino to fall. It could help expose the rest of these fuckers and the institutions that protect them."

Sebastien felt lightheaded, but he nodded in agreement. "You're right. But how do we do it?"

Ilya flashed him his devilish grin. "It's my turn to have a plan."

While Sebastien and Ilya made their escape upward to the Spa of the Oracle, Diya wandered through the depths of Hades. Everything felt dimmer and narrower down in the labyrinthine crew corridors of C Deck. She waded through a fog of cigarette smoke toward her destination.

The Filipino Mafia were a friendly, noisy bunch, not at all intimidating, unless they were crossed. They spent much of their off-duty time arranging secret gambling parties, selling haircuts, breakdancing in the halls, and running a black market that peddled everything from burner phones and bootlegged films to drugs of all flavours.

"Diya, my lucky lady!" A plump woman with an affable face greeted her with open arms and a kiss on the cheek. It was Rosa, the housekeeper who had helped them deliver the revenge cake to Giorgos the evening Elena and Contessa had disembarked. She once told Sebastien he had friends in the crew, and she had meant it.

"I'm so happy to see you, Rosa. This place is a maze. I have no idea where I'm going."

Rosa took Diya by the hand and led her through the winding passageways. Crew members loitered throughout the halls, swapping stories over cigarettes and laughing at each other's jokes. Some were dressed in grey uniforms, taking a break between shifts, while others wore soccer shorts and T-shirts. Rosa shouted greetings at all of them as she passed.

"We see your friends down here many times these days," she said to Diya. "Those handsome boys, so nice."

They reached a door with a poster of a beautiful woman wearing a beaded red gown and a sparkling tiara shaped like peacock feathers. Rosa knocked and shouted a few words in Tagalog. A wiry man with a short goatee appeared seconds later, music blaring behind him. He wore a loose black tracksuit. His fingers were covered in orange dust as he picked at a foil bag filled with triangular chips.

After a snappy exchange with Rosa, the man turned to Diya. "Hello, baby girl."

"I'm not your baby," she said with a scowl. "And I haven't been a girl for years."

The man put up his palms in surrender. "Sorry, sorry. How may I be of service, mademoiselle?"

"I'm looking for smoke," Diya said, "and I don't mean cigarettes. I'm talking about real smoke, and lots of it. Enough to cover half of Adriatic Deck."

The man looked at the fiery woman from her little black shoes to the bundle of curls on her head. He smiled deviously and licked the orange dust from his fingertips. "I have just what you need."

⚹

A gentle madness often settled over the *Glacier* during a full day at sea. Multiple activities would be scheduled every hour to keep the guests entertained: art auctions in the Agora, dance lessons in the Odeon, ice-carving competitions on Lido Deck, wellness seminars in the spa. Despite the manic distractions, everyone on board would float through the day in a state of malaise, not entirely sure what to do with themselves as they drifted in the middle of the sea.

It was no different that evening as the *Glacier* charged toward the island of Sicily. Adriatic Deck was packed with guests looking for something to do in the hour between dinner and the evening's show in the Odeon.

Nikos Antonopolous looked important in his crisp white uniform as he stood on the balcony looking over the crowded Agora lobby below. His dark hair was combed neatly to the side, and there was no sign of stubble along his angular jaw.

He noticed deck commander Giorgos standing beside an ornate marble pillar by the grand staircase. The man's hands were tucked into his pockets. There was no sign of sentience on his face. It was a closed door. The officers had never witnessed such emotion in Giorgos as the evening that Elena and Contessa disembarked in Cyprus. The loss of these two women had shaken the usually dignified man in devastating ways. Now, though, there was only emptiness.

Nikos frowned. He felt sorry for the broken man, but he was also disgusted by the sight of him.

"Smile!"

The bright voice rang across the atrium. A camera flashed, blinding the family of four standing in front of a canvas backdrop of the Amalfi Coast. The new photographer stationed there had been relocated from his usual post outside the dining hall. He was nothing like Sebastien. His short blond hair was almost white, and he didn't look old enough to drive a vehicle, let alone travel across the sea unsupervised.

Nikos's frown deepened. His chest felt hollow as he pictured Sebastien locked in a cabin three decks below. It was hard to fight the urge to run there and wrap himself around Sebastien's body, to inhale the earthy scent of his skin.

"Come back in an hour," said the too-young boy with the too-blond hair. "It'll be ready for purchase in the portrait gallery."

The radio attached to Nikos's belt hummed alive. He held the transceiver to his mouth. "What's going on?"

"Code orange in the casino," said the agitated voice on the radio. "We need you here, sir."

The boyish photographer eyed the handsome officer as he marched around the balcony. Nikos quickened his pace when he approached the casino, sensing something peculiar in the air. The colours and scents around him had been altered in some vague way. Shouts and cries overpowered the *ding-ding-ding* sounds of the slot machines. He could see why as soon as he stepped inside.

The entire room was choked in smoke. It fumed from several points throughout the casino in plumes of saturated colours — red, blue, green, purple, orange — that created a thick grey fog.

Nikos covered his mouth with the lapel of his jacket as he squinted to see through the haze. The entire casino had erupted into chaos as people took advantage of the sudden anonymity. Hands reached across the gaming tables to snatch up piles of chips. The green-suited dealers had frantic looks on their faces as they guarded their tables, swatting at hands that grabbed at them and shouting at people to back down. Several guests in evening wear crawled on the carpeted floor to scavenge for chips that had fallen in the fray.

Nikos was knocked to the ground as a heavyset man in a tuxedo ran into his shoulder. "*Gamóto!*" he cursed, pulling himself to his knees.

Looking up, he saw a dense tangle of dark hair walking away through the smoke. He knew who must have been behind this as soon as he had stepped inside. "Sebastien, stop right there!" he shouted, running up to the dark-haired man before gripping him by the shoulder. "I'm sorry," Nikos stammered to the unfamiliar face staring at him with bewildered eyes. "I thought you were someone else."

Nikos didn't feel the nimble little hand slip into the pocket of his pants. Diya's fingers wrapped around the ring of plastic cards exactly where Sebastien had told her she would find it. She walked away from the confused security commander and flipped through the cards. At the bottom of the stack was a rectangle of black plastic — the new skeleton key. Her movements were quick as she removed it from the silver ring and tucked it into her pocket. She replaced it with the identical key card that Sebastien had stolen several days earlier, the one that was now deactivated.

Nikos was shouting in Greek to two security guards when Diya circled the casino and made her way back to him. She slipped the ring of keys into his pocket as easily as she had plucked them. The entire operation took thirty seconds and was no more difficult than dealing a hand of blackjack.

The smoke grenades supplied by the Filipino Mafia were the perfect decoy. The coloured plumes subsided, but the haze remained heavy over the gaming tables and slot machines. Diya could still hear Nikos delivering commands in his overtly masculine voice as she strolled out of the casino toward the elevators.

Ilya, Sebastien, and Sophie were huddled together around the empty pool of the thalassotherapy room when Diya walked in. "This thing really does work," she said, holding up the black skeleton key with a triumphant smile.

Cheers resounded throughout the round room. "You're a legend," Sebastien said, wrapping his arms around her petite shoulders. He was already dressed in his grey cabin-service uniform with his wild hair gathered beneath the bellboy cap.

"What's it like downstairs?" Ilya asked, slapping his palm against hers.

"Madness," Diya said. "I'd wager the casino has already lost tens of thousands of euros. Even the rich can be complete animals if given the chance."

"They'll feel the pain now that we've hit 'em where it hurts," Sebastien said. "In the accounting department."

"Well, what are you waiting for?" Diya asked, shoving the skeleton key into Sebastien's palm. "Athena awaits in cabin A66. You need to go."

"There's been a change of plans," Ilya said, "but it might help us in the end. Rosa and the Filipino Mafia have been staking out A Deck all day. They saw Athena get escorted out this afternoon. They know we're coming."

"Where did they take her?"

"They're hiding her on Riviera Deck," Sebastien said. "It's a secret room at the end of the hall. It used to be a temple, but Nikos and I know it as the House of the Heel."

"That's only one deck below us," Diya said. "She's so close."

"I walked past earlier today," Sophie said, speaking for the first time since Diya arrived. She heard the tentative tone in her own voice, then cleared her throat to sound more confident. "A security guard was stationed outside the door. I passed it again ten minutes ago, and there was no one there. We need to go while it's unguarded."

"You're right," Sebastien said, adjusting his cap. "It's time."

Riviera Deck was quiet except for the faraway sounds of revelry that echoed across the atrium. The carpeted floor and papered walls absorbed the sounds of their footsteps. Sophie trailed behind Sebastien by several paces. Wearing a cobalt-blue cocktail dress and magenta heels, she would reprise her role as the innocent decoy if the double doors at the end of the hall were guarded. Once inside, Athena would recognize Sebastien as the man who had attempted to rescue her. They would escape through the hidden passageways behind the walls to their hideout in the spa. They estimated the operation would take less than eight minutes.

Sebastien halted mid-stride in the middle of the hall at the sound of voices around the corner. He recognized the sharp, excitable pitch of Kristo's voice. Alexis's deep purr could be heard more loudly as it came nearer.

Sebastien turned to Sophie with panic in his eyes. He put his finger to his lips and gestured for her to turn around. Sophie's cabin door was within sight, but they wouldn't have made it there in time before the Kourakis family turned the corner.

The voices were near when Sophie pushed Sebastien against the wall. He was partially hidden behind a statue of a frozen Greek god. He could smell her buttery skin as their lips pressed together. His hands found the familiar ridges of her hips. He was pinned against the wall by every curve of her body.

He barely noticed the voices pass, though he detected a girlish giggle. He peered at them from the corners of his eyes. Alexis held her son's hand as they walked farther down the hall while Katerina trailed behind. Kristo craned his head around to get a better view of the two lovers. The impish smile on his face vanished when he saw who was hiding behind the statue.

Sophie pulled herself away once the Kourakis family was no longer in sight, wiping her lips with the base of her palm before adjusting her dress.

"It's been a while since we've done that," he whispered with a sly smile. She flashed him an impatient look and urged him on with a wave of the hands.

They prowled down the hall and were relieved to see that the double doors at the end were unguarded. *We fooled them,*

Sebastien thought. *They're either dealing with the casino mayhem or waiting for us on A Deck.*

"Let me do the talking," he said to Sophie. "I think she trusts me."

He pulled the black skeleton key from his pocket. They slid past the doors and were bathed in the soft light that emanated from the glass panels on the walls. Sophie knew there was something wrong as soon as they stepped into the room, but it took a moment for Sebastien to understand what he was seeing among the white sheets. It looked like a ghost.

Sebastien stepped forward, shielding Sophie behind him. His voice came out like a growl. "What did you do with her?"

Palermo
to
Cannes

NINETEEN

Hotel Memoria

Nikos stood in the middle of the room surrounded by vast sheets of fabric. He was almost camouflaged, though his uniform was a more lucid shade of white. His arms hung at his sides, a casual stance, but Sebastien sensed turbulence beneath the calm exterior.

"I'm disappointed in you," Nikos said. His voice was a gentle caress compared to the cold slap of Sebastien's accusation.

"Answer me. What did you do with her?"

Nikos exhaled loudly, emphasizing his disappointment. "Did you really think I was stupid enough to move her here in the middle of the day? In front of all those people?" He cocked his head to the side and scratched his eyebrow. "Apparently yes, you did."

"It was a trap," Sophie said, holding her hands against her stomach.

"You don't get to speak," Nikos said sharply without even a glance in her direction.

Sophie opened her mouth to respond, but she read the look that Sebastien flashed her.

"Are you proud of yourself?" He stepped toward Nikos, his voice rough as gravel. "You fooled us. Now what? I get thrown off the ship tomorrow. Athena becomes someone's possession. And you? You help them get away with it, again. Is that what you want?"

Nikos shook his head as he adjusted the cuffs of his jacket. The superfluous movement betrayed his discomfort. "You really do think the world is against you."

"What are you talking about?"

"That's what Kostas said yesterday on Sunset Deck. You blame everyone else for the hate inside you." There was genuine sadness in the officer's eyes, though it was unclear whether it was for Sebastien or himself. "He was right. You only see people as victims or villains. Right or wrong. Good or evil. It's not that easy."

Sebastien could feel a tremor begin in his chest. It spread across his body until his fists trembled at the ends of his arms. "It's true," he said. "Athena is a victim. Kostas is the villain. That part's easy. But what does that make you?"

"She's a troubled girl. Kostas is her imperfect but harmless uncle. I'm just a man trying to protect someone I care very deeply about."

"I suppose you're talking about me."

"I am," he said with an intensity in his eyes. "You can convince yourself I'm the bad guy, but I'm doing this to help you. Do you realize what could have happened if you had pulled off this stunt of yours? Kostas could have pressed charges. You'd have been in serious trouble."

"How do you explain the tattoo on the back of her neck?" Sebastien's mouth felt dry as a desert. "Aphrodite's flower. It's the symbol of a trafficking ring. They brand their girls with it."

Nikos stared at him, silent. It looked like he would explode with laughter for a second, but he simply lowered his forehead. "Listen to yourself," he said. "You aren't making sense. I don't know about this Aphrodite's flower, but lots of people have tattoos. Even I have one, remember?"

Sebastien pictured the elaborate black design behind the white uniform. The shield of Achilles. He found himself aching to run his fingers along the skin. "Kostas is lying."

Nikos stepped toward him until their faces were inches apart. "I know you want to believe that. I don't blame you." Nikos held him gently by the arms, tentatively at first, not knowing what the reaction would be to his touch. "You have so many reasons to hate Kostas. It's easy to cast him as the enemy, especially when Pallas is so convincing."

Sebastien's eyes sharpened. "What did you call her?"

Nikos crinkled his brow, his mouth slightly open but silent.

I was blinded by his kindness. Athena's voice whispered the words into Sebastien's ears.

"Pallas. That's what you called Athena just now."

I thought he was my friend.

"I don't understand."

"You were the friend," Sebastien said, taking a step backward. "A man brought her to the criminals when she needed money. She thought this man was her friend, that he was trying to help. He called her Pallas Athena, after the ancient goddess. It was you."

A forced laugh escaped Nikos, reverberating along the curved walls of the House of the Heel. "Now I'm really worried about you. You sound unhinged."

"You called her Pallas." Every part of Sebastien shook. "Tell me, why would you call her that if you weren't that same man?"

Nikos was about to laugh again, but nothing came out his mouth. He threw his hands up in the air. "Everybody calls her that," he said, sweeping his gaze across the ceiling. "It's a common nickname for anyone with that name. It means 'young woman,' what the ancients called the goddess Athena."

"I don't believe you," Sebastien said. "Only someone obsessed with the ancient myths would call her that. Don't you agree, Achilles?"

"Careful."

"It was you all along."

"I'm trying to help, and you throw accusations at me."

"You sold her like a wild dog. Tell me, what did they give you in return?"

"You're not well."

Sebastien's lungs smouldered as he reached out and grabbed Nikos by the jacket, clutching the stiff fabric in his uneasy fists. His breath rushed past his lips like a humid wind.

"What are you going to do?" Nikos's voice was soft, almost tender. "Hit me? Or kiss me?"

Sebastien didn't know the answer. He stood there, frozen, the jacket clenched in his hands.

A melodic voice punctured the silence. "Break it up, you two," Sophie said. She stepped between them, placing one palm against each man's chest. Nikos pushed her away the moment they touched. The thrust of his arm was so forceful that she fell backward over a bench, tangling herself in the white sheet that covered it.

Sebastien ran to her side. "Are you okay?" he asked, holding her hand. She pulled herself upright and gave him a dazed nod.

His eyes shot up at Nikos. "Why did you do that?"

"I told her. She doesn't get to speak."

With a snarl, Sebastien charged forward and tackled Nikos to the floor. Their hands clawed at each other, grasping clothes and limbs as they rolled across the ground in a barrel of bodies. They knocked against the furniture, white sheets draped around them like angel wings.

Nikos was stronger. He held Sebastien against the floor, straddling his groin. It was a familiar position in unfamiliar circumstances. He leaned down until Sebastien could smell the sweat on his skin.

"I don't want to hurt you," he said, his voice unsteady between heavy breaths. "You forced me to do this, you know. You gave me no choice."

"You always have a choice." Sebastien could barely breathe with the weight of the man on top of him. He relaxed his muscles and let his resistance slip away. "You don't owe Kostas anything. You think he saved you from your miserable life, but that doesn't mean he owns you."

"You don't know anything." The words fell out of his mouth like raindrops.

"I know who you are now," Sebastien said. His vision drifted to the vaulted ceiling above them. The constellations looked different than they did their first night in this room. So much was different now.

Nikos heard the faintest creak of floorboards from behind. He turned around to see Sophie holding a ceramic vase above her head. She yelped as he bolted to his feet and pushed the vase from her hands. It shattered loudly, scattering fragments across the floor.

His two-way radio hummed alive as he held the transceiver to his mouth. "I need backup in the abandoned temple, forward portside Riviera Deck. I have two violent perps that must be detained."

Sebastien remained still as he stared up at the painted sky. There was no use in moving or resisting. He had already surrendered.

⁂

It was an unseasonably hot spring in Petit Géant the year after Sebastien Goh assaulted Marcel Lamoureux. Most of the spectators that day had gone on to university, far from the spiteful town that was now an obscure memory to them. Even the victim of the beating had fled to begin a new life in the emerald hills of Vietnam. It was a different story for Sebastien.

The heat in his bedroom was stifling. Warm air streamed toward him from the old electric fan that oscillated on its post of chipped metal. He lay glued to his mattress, wearing nothing but a pair of paper-thin running shorts.

The year had been unkind. One lapse of control on a grassy field had snuffed out all hope of pulling himself out of the pit where he had been born. Perhaps he was foolish to think he could amount to anything above his station. That wasn't how society worked. It was designed to keep the top at the top and the bottom at the bottom.

His actions on graduation day the previous year were meant to protect his mother. He had recited the story so many times — to the police, to lawyers, to reporters — he began to believe the heroism implied more confidently in each retelling. When it was over, when there was no one else to persuade, he could no longer deny the truth. Hidden inside him was violence and rage and hatred.

The familiar knock of his mother's bony knuckles against his bedroom door pulled him out of his stupor. "Come in," he said in a creaky voice, barely audible.

Ruby's face appeared in the crack of the open door. The lines in her face had become more defined over recent months. What were once gentle trails had eroded into ridges. A permanent crease had been carved above her eyebrows. Her skin had taken on a slightly deeper tone.

But her hair remained as black as the night sky, flowing behind her.

"You have a visitor," she said, lingering at the door to see his reaction.

He crinkled his face. "A visitor?"

She forced an uncertain smile before stepping aside.

A different hand knocked on the door, the sound more tentative than the one before. Sebastien rolled onto his side, peeling his skin from the sweat-drenched bedsheet. He knew exactly who it was by the scent of her skin.

"Sophie?"

The young woman stepped into the room and closed the door quietly behind her. The sweet, frivolous nature that Sebastien had once loved about her had hardened into an abrupt maturity. The giggles and playful spontaneity that used to flow freely were now contained within a well. She wore blue linen shorts and a simple crepe blouse the colour of almond milk. A cardboard box was held in her hands.

"What are you doing here?" he asked, genuinely surprised.

Their clumsy exploration of love and lust had ended the afternoon he attacked her father. The days that followed had been baffling for Sophie. She hadn't known what to believe about the two dearest men in her life. She didn't know who to hate and who to love. Eventually she felt hate and love for them both. As the people of Petit Géant argued about who was victim and who was villain, she knew they were all wrong. The truth was Sebastien and Marcel were neither victim nor villain. They were simply men — imperfect, impulsive, helpless men. That didn't mean they deserved to be pardoned, though.

Her mother had insisted that Sophie attend university in Montréal in the fall, as planned, despite her objections. "I'll be fine," her mother had said. "I'm a strong woman, like you." Sophie threw herself into her studies, finding refuge in textbooks, searching for peace in the aisles of the library. She needed logic to overcome the emotion.

"I wanted to bring you something," she said, taking a seat on Sebastien's bed. He sat upright, suddenly aware of his appearance. He ran his fingers through his unwashed hair.

"You haven't spoken to me in months," he said. There was so much he wanted to say.

"I wasn't ready." She pursed her lips and looked down at the ragged nails of her fingers. "I saw you at the courthouse last week."

"I was surprised you were there," he said, his chin lowered against his bare chest.

"The timing worked out. It was the day after my last exam." She paused. "I think the verdict was fair."

"I guess a psychiatrist's office should be more comfortable than a cell." He attempted a weak laugh. "At least, I'll find out soon enough."

Sophie looked around the humid room. It was less tidy than it used to be. Wrinkled clothes spilled out of the hamper.

Loose papers and torn envelopes littered the surface of his desk.
"I'm so sorry." The words burst out of Sebastien's mouth.
His eyes were glassy. "I'm sorry for what I did."

Sophie moved closer, putting her arms around his shoulders. He nestled his head into the curve of her neck. "I forgive you," she said, her tone decisive.

He pulled back to see her face. "How can you forgive me?"

"We're all human. Illogical beings. We make mistakes. But we can also make our own decisions. I can choose to hate you, or to be afraid of you, or I can choose to forgive."

Sebastien found no words. He felt more awake than he had in a long time.

"You also have a choice, you know." Sophie's face was calm and cool. There wasn't sympathy in her eyes, but something more powerful. "You can choose to lock yourself in your bedroom, hating yourself, replaying everything you could have done differently, knowing it won't make a difference. Or you can choose to get on with life." She picked up the cube-shaped box beside her and placed it on her lap. "You can surrender, or you can eat cake with me."

She opened the box. It wasn't a perfectly iced dessert fit for the cover of a magazine, like the ones Sophie liked to create. On her lap was Sebastien's favourite, the cheap kind made from a mix from the supermarket.

"Happy twentieth birthday, Sebastien Goh."

❧

The waves of the Tyrrhenian Sea were coloured like ink when the *Glacier* rounded the western tip of Sicily in the early morning. The sun was just beginning to peek over the mountains surrounding Palermo as the ship pulled into the narrow harbour. Mount Pellegrino stood watch over the sleeping city like an enormous citadel, its stone walls and jagged battlements impossible to breach. The clifftops were cloaked in a tapestry of green.

The staff and crew of the *Glacier* would have to admire it from the docked ship. Posters throughout Hades announced that the security checkpoints would be closed for the entire day. Nobody would be disembarking in Palermo besides guests and officers. Exceptions would be made for permanent departures, of course.

Sebastien and Sophie were escorted through the main thoroughfare of B Deck as soon as the anchor was dropped. There was a security guard on either side of them. It seemed the guards had been instructed to make as little verbal and visual contact as possible. All of Sebastien's belongings had been mindlessly stuffed into his hiking backpack. Sophie pulled a cream-coloured suitcase on wheels with a magenta scarf tied around the retractable handle.

The silence on B Deck was disturbed by shouts of their names. Turning around, they saw Ilya and Diya running toward them. They wore the sleepless night on their faces. Diya's hair flowed behind her in a cloud of curls while Ilya's eyes were tinted pink. Their footsteps clanged heavily against the steel floor.

The two security guards prevented them from coming closer. "Stop right there," one of them said in a voice that was consciously deep. "You're not permitted here."

"This is our deck," Diya cried, exasperated. "We live here."

"At least let us say goodbye." Ilya's eyes pleaded, but he knew Nikos had given his orders.

"You already have," the guard said. "There's no need to get any closer."

"It's okay." Sebastien looked at his two friends from the other side of the corridor, his face displaying gratitude and exhaustion. "I'll miss you both."

"This isn't over." Diya's voice rang across the steel walls. It was resolute, as always, but now strained with desperation.

"It is over," Sebastien said, unable to hide the defeat that had settled inside. "We've lost."

"For now." Ilya held his chin high.

Sophie and Sebastien were led down the gangplank while the indecisive wind whipped their hair around their faces. It felt consequential when their feet landed on the concrete pier. As Sophie had once said many years earlier, it felt like the end of one thing and the beginning of something else, except this time they weren't quite ready for a new start.

The buildings of Palermo pressed against the port in a colourful collection of Norman palaces, gothic bell towers, Phoenician walls, and modern hotels. The guards stood at the end of the gangplank and watched their retreat.

They were near the gates of the port when they heard a clamour from above. The *Glacier* towered over them, an imposing wall of white steel and blue-tinted glass. There must have been hundreds of people crowded along the edge of the bow. Sebastien spotted the grey and pink uniforms of the cabin-service crew, as well as the bright turquoise jackets with the gold buttons of the staff. They shouted and chanted, hands waving in the air. He scanned the crowd for one brooding officer in particular but didn't see the brilliant white uniform.

A cheer resounded along the bow as a black banner was released over the edge. It flapped in the wind as it unfurled, spanning the height of three decks. The message was painted in bold white letters against the dark cloth.

WE
ARE
ALL
POWERLESS

"They really love you," Sophie said, peeking at Sebastien from the corners of her eyes.

A wistful smile appeared on his lips. Creases gathered around his eyes as he squinted. "There's a woman up there named Rosa," he said, drawing the energy to speak. "She told me once that she had never seen the crew and staff so united. We give each other power when we work together. It wasn't enough. It may never be enough. But it made a difference to Rosa."

They checked into the first hotel they could find. It was a narrow building wedged between two blocks of apartments. At one point in time they had all been wings of the same grand palace, but now they were dismembered sections. The hotel's skinny five-level facade was covered in a veneer of faux pink marble, while the walls and shutters of the apartments aged honestly in chipped paint and sun-bleached stone.

The sign above the heavy glass entrance said *Hotel Memoria* above three proud golden stars. One broken half star dangled at the end.

Sebastien didn't sense disappointment in Sophie's response when the young man at the front desk informed them in beautifully accented English there was only one room available with two separate beds.

Their room was on the top floor. Double doors with glass panels led onto a tight balcony overlooking the rooftops that lined the port and the sparkling sea beyond.

The *Glacier* basked in the morning sun. Sebastien leaned against the shaky railing and examined what had been his home for the past month. It was a surreal vision from this vantage point. He could see the exterior of every deck, follow the curves of its body from bow to stern. The pyramid of the ship's funnel appeared massive when gazing up at it from Sunset Deck, but it was far less imposing from afar. The black banner his friends had unrolled for him was being drawn back by a group of white suits no larger than fleas. It didn't matter. The message was received. The staff and crew of the *Glacier* had no intention of surrendering.

He peered through the ship's impenetrable hull as though he had X-ray vision. He saw the turquoise velvet seats of the Odeon, the atrium that rose above the Agora through the core of the ship like a cavern of glass and light, the seafoam carpet of Riviera Deck.

He pictured Ilya preparing for his daily spin class in the fitness centre beneath the navigation bridge. He would have less vigour during the routine, and the smile on his face would be more strained than usual.

He imagined Diya sipping a hot mug of tea in the staff cafeteria. The casino would be closed until the ship departed from port later that night, but there would be no rest in her turbulent mind.

Rosa would be starting her rounds in the guest quarters, tossing towels into the laundry cart and shaking out duvets over immaculate beds. Much of the Filipino Mafia would be doing the same, scrubbing and sweeping like Sebastien's mother once did. They wouldn't be ready for life to return to normal, not after everything they'd learned and witnessed over the past few weeks.

Alexis and her two darlings would be eating breakfast somewhere in the open-air patios of Lido Deck before venturing into port. She would feel safe as she drizzled honey over mounds of yogurt, but little Kristo knew better. He'd be holding his mother's hand protectively, looking over his shoulder every so often, afraid to see the wild-haired man with the familiar eyes.

Perhaps Kostas would be with them, relieved that his adversary was no longer on board to expose him for the snake that he was.

Do you miss me, Father?

He wondered where Nikos would be. A shudder travelled through Sebastien's body as he pictured the young officer surrounded by the tinted glass and white sheets of their House of the Heel. There had been nothing left to say to each other when his guards arrived to detain Sebastien and Sophie. Nikos stood and watched, wordless. He hadn't been seen since.

Sebastien gripped the iron railing until his knuckles went white as he scanned the hull of the distant ship. Hidden deep within it was a secret. It festered beneath the opulence, its proximity arrogantly close to those who sought refuge from the evils of the world outside.

He pictured Athena trapped behind a guarded door. Escape for her was as likely as escaping evil. It was everywhere.

Has she given up hope? Would she be right to do so?

Sebastien would have given anything to be wrong. He wished Nikos was telling the truth. He didn't want Nikos or his father to be capable of such corruption. But he couldn't deny what he'd seen and heard.

He felt the push and pull of uncertainty. Emotion and logic were at odds with each other to the point he couldn't tell which was in control. The evidence was flimsy. He couldn't prove that Athena wasn't in fact suffering from delusions. The tattoo. The nickname. Neither proved a thing to an objective mind.

He couldn't even be certain that Kostas was involved. His father hadn't made any claims about Athena. They had been made by Nikos. The only contact he'd seen between Kostas and the young woman was that night in Sirens, when Nikos was ordered to remove her through the secret door in the wall. If Athena was telling the truth, it was still possible that Kostas was unaware of her abduction. Sebastien doubted this, but could he trust his own instincts when it came to his father? Hadn't he boarded the *Glacier* having already decided that his father was the enemy?

Then again, his own eyes had seen Kostas hand a young officer an envelope of white powder. The target had been Dominic, and the reason involved cabin A66. "They're hiding something they don't want anyone to find," Dominic had said. "Something bad."

Perhaps there was a different explanation entirely. Nikos's words echoed through his mind.

You only see people as victims or villains. Right or wrong. Good or evil. It's not that easy.

A cool breeze from the sea tickled his skin. He remembered his last few conversations with Ilya the previous day. Something Ilya had said haunted him.

There was one way that could expose the truth. If he were unsuccessful, he might never know whether he was right or wrong about Athena. But if the proof were found, he would have no choice but to face everything he had always feared.

⊗

It was nine in the morning in Petit Géant when Jérôme St-Germain assessed the easiest way of breaking into the old Goh family apartment. He stood on the narrow strip of grass that separated the building from its neighbour, staring up at the plain rectangle of glass two levels above that used to be Sebastien's bedroom window.

He had woken up to the ringing of his phone an hour earlier, surprised to discover who was calling from an Italian number. Sebastien's voice had the same familiar tenor of tenderness and intensity, but Jérôme detected an undercurrent of something else. There hadn't seemed to be much time for catching up. Sebastien had a favour to ask, one that came with clear instructions. "It has to do with my father" was the only explanation offered.

There were very few things Jérôme wouldn't do for him. He had loved Sebastien since the night of their first kiss as they tumbled across the newspaper-lined floor of Camera Obscura. It happened four years ago, but the aching in his chest made it feel like yesterday. He subjected himself to watching Sebastien fumble with how to be happy. Jérôme could have told him the answer wouldn't be found with Sophie Lamoureux. He and Sebastien had come so close to finding themselves in each other, but the chance wilted after the publicized photographs, the red paint on the storefront windows, the taunts, the insults.

Perhaps one day Sebastien would see what was in front of him. Until then, Jérôme would offer his friendship.

He placed two cylindrical garbage bins beneath the metal grate of the fire escape mounted on the side of the building. The bins weren't very sturdy, but all he needed was a boost to haul himself onto the landing that led to the second-floor window. His first attempt was a failure. The bins toppled over, sending Jérôme to the grass in a sprawl of graceless limbs. He looked at his button-up chambray shirt and slim chinos, cursing himself for not dressing more appropriately for breaking and entering.

He adjusted the red frames of his glasses before the second attempt. The bins remained upright long enough for him to grab the landing's edge. He hoisted his body forward until his lower half no longer dangled in the air.

His leather brogues pounded against the metal stairs as he climbed to the bedroom window. Just as Sebastien had described, the latch was broken and the window slid open with ease. He didn't want to soil the bed with his shoes, so he leapt through the opening and landed heavily in the middle of the floor.

The tidy room conflicted with his perception of Sebastien. The modest furniture and neatly organized belongings reflected the man's sense of order but didn't do justice to the passion inside him. The stunning photographs on the walls hinted at his talent, but the creativity should have been unleashed within this space rather than confined within frames. It occurred to him that it was his first time in this room. He had never been invited.

He wanted to linger, to smell the bedsheets and rifle through the books, but what he was searching for was in another room. Jérôme stepped into the open space that served as the kitchen, dining area, and living room. The apartment had stood empty since Sebastien's departure for Europe. The lease renewed once a year, and he hadn't had the time to find subtenants. Everything would look exactly the same when he returned.

If he returned.

Jérôme's forehead crinkled as he looked at the pile of splintered wood that used to be the family dining table.

Ruby's bedroom shared a wall with Sebastien's. He turned the wobbly doorknob and stepped inside.

The air felt different here. Jérôme tried to ignore the notion that it was because someone had died in this room.

Ruby's bed stood in the far corner beneath a window, its mattress depressed in the centre and the bronze paint chipping from its posts. A full-length mirror stood against the opposite wall, though it was angled away from the bed.

Picture frames of different styles and sizes covered the surfaces of a desk, a dresser, and a set of shelves. They displayed mother and son throughout the years. The woman was alluring, her eyes clear and present. Smiling hadn't come easily to her younger self, but she appeared to soften with age. Her face was always cloaked beneath her long black hair. One wooden frame held an image of Ruby with her young son at the petting zoo in a nearby town. They sat on a bale of hay, the mother caught in the middle of a laugh while her son held a baby goat with genuine love on his face.

Jérôme examined the photographs and watched Sebastien grow up before his eyes. He had been a chubby, happy baby, grinning toothlessly with his eyes squinted shut. He was more serious as a child, though never bored, his face alive with curiosity. Teenaged Sebastien resembled his present-day self, all lean muscle and messy hair. He'd inherited the full lips and copper complexion of his Asian mother, but the ridges of his face and alert green eyes implied European blood.

Pulling himself away from the images, Jérôme noticed something peeking out from beneath the bed. He crouched to the floor and found a checkerboard of black-and-white squares scattered with loose wooden discs.

He heard Sebastien's voice calling him to the closet, reminding him of why he was there. As he had described, several cardboard boxes were stacked on the top shelf of the closet. Jérôme placed them on the floor in the shape of a circle and sat cross-legged in the centre. There were six boxes in total. With a deep breath, he opened the first one.

Their high-ceilinged room at the Hotel Memoria was filled with the aroma of onions and anchovies. Sebastien and Sophie sat on their respective beds as they devoured their dinners. Each bed held a box of *sfincione,* the square-shaped pizza made of thick dough and sharp cheese native to the island of Sicily. He'd always admired Sophie for her unapologetic love of food. She felt no shame in ordering dessert, using extra butter, or inhaling an entire pizza, regardless of who was present.

It had been a joyless day, despite the indulgence. Sebastien had left Pétit Géant with a clear sense of purpose. Now he felt stuck, uncertain of what to do next.

Dusk was beginning to settle outside. The air that drifted through the open balcony doors was cooler than earlier. The *Glacier* glimmered in the distance, every deck aglow. A string of lights connected the mast above the navigation bridge to the enormous funnel aft. The ship was scheduled to leave for Naples in an hour. Over the course of five days, it would dock in Barcelona and Palma de Mallorca before arriving in Cannes.

Athena's fearful eyes flashed through Sebastien's mind.

"Do you love that man?" Sophie tried to appear nonchalant as she tore a piece from her pizza and popped it into her mouth.

"Nikos?"

She nodded, keeping her eyes on her dinner.

"I wouldn't call it love." Sebastien leaned back against the upholstered headboard. "Maybe it could have been in a different dimension."

"Do you love Jérôme?" She knew he knew this was the real question she wanted answered.

He turned to face her, but her eyes wouldn't meet his. Her auburn hair was pulled to one side in a loose ponytail. She licked the tomato sauce from her fingertips.

"Why does that matter now?"

"Just answer the question," she said, a measured calmness in her tone.

"I do love him, yes." It was the first time he'd admitted this out loud. "I just haven't figured out what kind of love it is yet."

She nodded again, deciding whether or not this answer was enough for her. "I know what we once had has expired," she said softly. "You were right. We tried our best. It wasn't enough. Where did we go wrong?"

He had wondered the same thing more times than he could count. "What I did to your father will always be my worst regret. Not just for everything I lost, but because I will always be ashamed of the person I was that day. I'm afraid of him." He swallowed hard. "Your forgiveness was the only thing that kept me from giving up on myself. Of all people, you should have hated me. But you helped me believe there was something worth salvaging."

"I needed it, too." She looked up, and their eyes connected. "I was so angry and confused, I needed a way to make sense of what happened, so I could put it behind me. So I could move on."

"You became the one hopeful thing in my life, so I poured everything into it."

"I did the same," she said with an embarrassed smile. "I was hell-bent on making something good from the wreckage of that year."

"And it was good." He crossed the space between their beds and sat by her side. "What we had was special. I don't know what would have happened to me if you hadn't been there. You told me I had a choice. I made my choice, and I'll never regret it. But it wasn't meant to be forever." He put his arm around her. She rested her head against his chest.

"We've served our purpose for each other," she said. "Now we learn to let go."

"No matter what happens, you will always be the woman who saved me."

She smiled. "And we will always have our final kiss, hiding from a family of three behind a statue on a cruise ship."

"You mean luxury liner," he corrected her. Laughter burst out of them and rang throughout the little room. They held onto each other as their bodies shook until their eyes were wet.

They were interrupted by Sebastien's phone. It danced loudly on the nightstand between the two beds. The smile disappeared from his face.

"It's a message from Jérôme," he said. Sophie sat upright in the middle of the bed, waiting to hear what her rival had uncovered.

Sebastien's body went cold when he opened the attached file. Everything seemed to shut down.

Jérôme had delivered a photograph of a photograph. It must have taken hours to comb through the thousands of tattered images hidden in those boxes in Ruby's closet. His search had been focused on one thing that may or may not have existed.

He had found it.

The image on the screen was of Sebastien's mother. It was taken at least two decades ago, judging by the youth that radiated from her face. It was a happier time, before graduation day, before her body would be ravaged by sickness. Ruby was laughing, eyes squinted shut and teeth bared. It looked like she was spinning. Her fingers were a blur of motion. Her long black hair was a static tornado around her head.

The bedroom mirror stood directly behind Ruby. With her hair suspended in the air, the reflection exposed a rare view of her back and shoulders. Sebastien rubbed his eyes to be sure they weren't playing tricks on him, but he knew what Jérôme must have found.

The mirror revealed something he had never seen before, something she must have kept hidden his entire life. On the back of her neck was a symbol carved in black ink. It was the same symbol he'd discovered for the first time only days earlier.

Six connected little circles.

Aphrodite's flower.

They brand their girls with that exact symbol.

Ilya's words echoed through his memory.

These criminals have been around for decades.

Decades.

Decades.

The ship's horn bellowed from the port. The thunderous sound carried over the rooftops of the ancient city and through the balcony doors of the Hotel Memoria.

Sebastien didn't say a word as he passed the phone to Sophie, the disturbing image still on the screen. He didn't feel the chill in the night air when he stepped onto the balcony. He stood there, motionless, and watched the *Glacier's* graceful retreat through the harbour. It was lit up like a funeral pyre as it drifted into the black, mournful sea.

He pictured Kostas inside the lavish halls with a smug grin on his cleanly shaven face, safe and warm, protected from the dangers outside. Sebastien screamed into the night, toward the ship that was slipping away from him. He allowed himself this release, only for a moment. As he closed his lips and his eyes, his mind had already moved on. There was so much to do.

"Don't forget about me, Father." His voice dropped to a whisper, the words touched then stolen by the wind. "I'm coming for you."

TWENTY

Spanish Snow Globe

Nobody was as feared and revered throughout ancient Greece as Achilles. Every man wanted to be like the fierce warrior, but nobody wanted to fight him. He wasn't a god, though. He was just a man, like the rest of them.

His mother loved him more than anyone else. Afraid that he was destined for a life of blood and battle, fighting for kings who cared for nothing but their own ambition, she did whatever she could to protect her son from the inevitable. This was why she dipped her baby boy into the ink-black waters of Styx, the river that meandered between the world of the living and the underworld of Hades. The water was known to make invincible any flesh it touched. It washed over the skin of the boy, except where he was held by his mother — his heel.

When Paris, Prince of Troy, fell in love with Queen Helen of Sparta, the two reckless lovers sailed across the sea to hide behind the impenetrable walls of his storied city. Her husband, the jealous King of Sparta, wasn't too pleased to have his wife swept away by the foolish young prince. After all, she was beautiful. You've heard all this before — the face that launched a thousand ships. One of those ships carried Achilles, by then every ounce the fearsome fighter he was destined to be.

Thus began the Trojan War, a ten-year siege of a city famous for its walls. The King of Sparta rallied all the forces of Greece to fight for his honour. There aren't many things more dangerous than a powerful man with a bruised ego.

Achilles couldn't have cared less about the man's honour or his wife. He was there for the glory, to have his name remembered and sung throughout the ages. He was flawed, like any man, despite his godlike presence. He could be vengeful and angry. The only person who brought him joy was his dearest friend, Patroclus.

There's no concrete evidence that Patroclus and Achilles were lovers, but it makes for a far more interesting tragedy. Everyone knew the truth, but nobody dared talk about it any louder than a whisper.

Things were looking pretty dire for the Greeks until sweet Patroclus, wearing the armour and shield of Achilles, was killed by Hector, Prince of Troy and Paris's noble brother.

Achilles was devastated and, most of all, consumed by rage. Nobody murdered the secret lover of a warrior like Achilles and got away with it. He hunted down Prince Hector and stabbed him in the throat. Avenging his lover wouldn't be complete until Achilles dragged Hector's body behind his chariot around the tomb built for Patroclus.

Now that is love.

Achilles was back in fighting form, but they still couldn't breach the monstrous walls of the city. If they were going to win, it wouldn't be by force but by wit.

One morning the Greek troops were gone, as though they had vanished overnight. *They have given up*, the Trojans thought. *They have fled across the sea, humiliated.*

On the beach outside the city was a gift left behind by the defeated warriors. It was a gigantic statue made of wood in the shape of a horse. Words were inscribed across the planks of its side.

The Greeks dedicate this offering to Pallas
Athena for their safe return home.

The Trojans couldn't have been happier. After ten long years of war, they had won and their walls remained strong as ever.

They felt victorious.

Proud.

They brought the wooden horse through the gates of Troy as a symbol of their triumph. Wine flowed freely and music played as the Trojans threw a monumental celebration in the heart of the city.

What they failed to realize was the immensity of their hubris. They had underestimated the Greeks, some of whom were hiding inside the belly of the wooden horse. As the Trojans slept, delirious from drink and vanity, the soldiers emerged from the horse and opened the gates. The Greek forces flooded the city like a tidal wave.

You're probably wondering what happened to Achilles. He was there as the city burned. He didn't even notice Paris, Prince of Troy, standing nearby with his bow drawn.

The arrow sliced through the air, piercing the only vulnerable part of his sculpted body. It was the spot his mother had held when she dipped him into the River Styx.

His heel.

As he lay dying within the smouldering city, Achilles saw the eyes of Patroclus. His heel wasn't his only weakness. He had never claimed to be invincible. He had always known he was just a man.

❖

The port of Barcelona was an alluring beacon for ships sailing across the glassy sea. The glimmer of lights lined the shore of the seductive city, a siren's call to weary sailors.

Sebastien leaned against the steel beam of a tower that rose from the wide concrete pier. His skin was damp beneath the canvas coveralls despite the chill in the air. The sun wouldn't appear for another hour. The city slept.

He spotted the *Glacier* when it was the size of a firefly in the distance. Its golden glow drifted along the surface of the water until its enormous hull dominated the harbour. It had been three days since he watched the ship sail away in Palermo. He wondered if the memory of him had faded within its decks as it travelled onward to Naples and across the Tyrrhenian Sea.

His father would be asleep in his bed, unaware of the impending siege.

This anger doesn't have to be a bad thing. It fuels our fight.

Ilya's words played in Sebastien's mind while he watched the *Glacier* glide alongside the pier with graceful precision.

It can be used for good, but only if we're smart.

The security checkpoints wouldn't allow passengers to board or disembark for another few hours. Until then, the dock would be alive with activities that guests rarely witnessed. The excess of life on the *Glacier* made it easy to take for granted the work that allowed the ship to operate. Hundreds of crates lined the pier, waiting to be loaded on board. They were stocked with food for the galley, towels for the spa, jewels for the shops, and enough liquor to incapacitate a small city. Forklifts weaved around the stacks, lifting pallets piled high with boxes wrapped in plastic skin.

A heavyset man with tightly curled hair approached, wearing the same style of coveralls. Sebastien recognized him as part of the Filipino Mafia. The man greeted him with a discreet smile. "Follow me," he said, cocking his head to the side. Sebastien lowered his cap so it covered the top of his face. They darted through the narrow aisles that separated the crates until they came to a wooden box twice the size of Sebastien's old cabin.

The man pulled a latch, and the side of the box opened on a set of rusty hinges. They were enveloped by the smell of chemicals and dampness as they stepped inside.

Ilya had explained over the phone what would serve as Sebastien's carriage into the *Glacier*, but he didn't know what to expect. In front of him, supported on an ornate base of bronze, stood a transparent globe that could fit three horses inside.

A new production was premiering on the stage of the Odeon the following evening. It was said to be an extravagant and shamelessly stylized retelling of Homer's *Iliad.* Other than the familiar characters — Achilles, Patroclus, Paris, and Hector — there was little resemblance to the classic legend. The show would feature magic of the Vegas variety and circus acts performed by exotic beauties. They would be joined by the ship's regular cast of entertainers, who had been rehearsing for weeks.

Ilya hadn't known what role this enormous prop would play in the show, except that it was meant to be a snow globe.

The man picked up a cardboard box from a corner and placed it in Sebastien's hands. "Blankets," he said. "Rosa wants you to be comfortable."

"Tell her I say thank you."

The man reached near the base of the acrylic globe and opened a hatch that was almost invisible. Sebastien climbed inside, placing his hands on the convex surface.

"Who needs a Trojan horse?" he said. "I've got a Spanish snow globe."

The man laughed and passed him the box of blankets. "Make yourself at home. You'll be here for an hour or two. Friends will meet you on the other side."

Sebastien thanked him for his help. The man stepped onto the pier, holding the side of the wooden crate in his gloved hand. He looked at Sebastien, eyes alive with hope. "We are all powerless," he said before disappearing into the darkness.

✧

The only sound in their apartment was the mechanical ticking of the moon-shaped clock on the wall. Ruby sat across from Sebastien at the kitchen table. She scrutinized the checkerboard between them with the focus of a military commander, envisioning every possible move and the resulting permutations of counterattacks. Her stack of Sebastien's black captives already doubled the height of the white discs he'd been able to capture.

Although twelve months had passed since the incident on graduation day, it didn't feel like the event was behind them. The court hearings were over and the consequences accepted, but traces of that afternoon continued to stain their lives in unexpected ways.

Sebastien wasn't removed from the mailing list of the university he had planned to attend, so brochures would arrive displaying young faces with perfect teeth and bright futures.

Ruby would ring through a customer's groceries at the Prix-Mart and be handed the business card of a "wonderful psychiatrist who could help your son with his *problem*."

Sebastien's first freelance assignment for the local newspaper was to photograph the lacrosse team that had removed him from the roster. The official statement had described him as "incompatible with our values of sportsmanship and decency."

Mother and son had each other, though, and they persevered.

"I'm going to start penalizing you one checker for every five minutes it takes for you to make a decision." Sebastien made this threat at least once every match they played.

Ruby liked to take her time, a quality her son hadn't inherited. His athletic body and restless mind were designed to move, but she thought people could stand to move less and just be.

"How many times have I told you to learn patience?" She shot him a stern look before sliding one of her white pieces forward on the checkerboard, a seemingly innocuous move. "This is why you never win. You act before you think."

"I don't never win," he said with exaggerated petulance. "Sometimes I get lucky." His face lit up as he laughed.

"And sometimes I let you win out of pity." Ruby gave him a playful kick beneath the table. "You have to think three steps ahead. And while your opponent thinks he has the upper hand, you better make sure your next move counts."

"That might work if my opponent wasn't always my unbeatable mama."

"One day you'll go against someone easier to beat," she said, leaning back in her chair to admire the man her son had become. "You seem more yourself lately, ever since Sophie visited on your birthday."

He shrugged. "She gave me some tough love, plus cake. Besides, there's no use drowning myself in my own self-pity. It's time to move on."

"Amen!" She threw up her thin hands with a dramatic laugh. "You're right. It's time to move on. I'm just happy to have my son back."

Sebastien swiped two white checkers from the board as he made his move. "Take that," he said, grinning triumphantly.

With a shake of the head, her fingers moved across the board too quickly for him to follow. "I win." She held up his three remaining black discs so he could see the evidence. "I told you. Think first, then act."

"How does a goldfish beat a shark?" It was his favourite saying after a loss.

Ruby laughed, as she always did, then groaned as she crouched forward with her arms pressed against her stomach.

"You okay?"

"I'm fine." She waved her fingers in the air to signal there was no need for concern. "It must be something I ate."

"You've been saying that for the past month. I'm taking you to the doctor in the morning."

She clicked her tongue against the roof of her mouth to make the sound that said he was being silly. "I'm fine. And change your face. You look like your father when you're worried."

He leaned forward in his chair. "Is that bad?"

"He was annoying like you." She gave him a teasing slap on the wrist. "He worried about everything. Always so serious."

"Maybe he had a lot to worry about," Sebastien said as his eyes drifted down to the checkerboard.

"Don't we all? That doesn't mean we must spend our lives being afraid. Worrying doesn't help anyone."

"You're right about that."

She stretched her arm across the table and held Sebastien by the hand. "I'm sorry."

"What for?"

A proud smile spread across her tired face. "For what I said. You are a much better man than your father could ever dream of being."

He squeezed her hand as the clock on the wall ticked away the seconds. Her smile faded before she groaned again, the skin around her eyes puckering with pain.

"That's enough." Sebastien crossed the apartment and pulled Ruby's coat from the hallway closet. "We're going to the hospital."

❖

You are a much better man than your father could ever dream of being.

His mother's voice swam through the air around him as he lay at the bottom of the transparent globe, wrapped in a blanket. The darkness was disturbed by the occasional flash of light through the cracks of the wooden crate.

With nothing else to see, his mind replayed that night nine years earlier. The peach-coloured vinyl of the waiting room chairs. The smell of liquid hand sanitizer. The doctor with the charming gap between her teeth and the fidgety hands. She couldn't stop twirling her pen and rustling the papers on her clipboard.

Eventually, they would learn Ruby's liver was failing. There wasn't one root cause but a combination of factors that had accumulated over time. Sebastien knew the stress of that year hadn't helped. He felt responsible.

Puffs of sawdust drifted from the top of the crate. Everything shook. He gripped the duvet in his hands as the freight was transported over the ramp that led into the ship. The cracks between the wooden panels became searing lines of light. The sounds outside were amplified, echoing against the steel walls. He couldn't tell where he was being taken, but the globe continued to rattle with every bump.

"You can't be serious about getting back on that ship," Sophie had said three days ago, though she knew the answer. They'd stood on opposite ends of their room's balcony in the Hotel Memoria, looking at each other, the wind blowing hair into their eyes.

"I need to see him," Sebastien said, one hand clenched around the railing. "I need to see his face when he realizes it's over."

"This isn't just about you and your revenge. You could be putting everyone in a whole lot of danger. Every officer on that ship could be involved for all we know. We need to let the police handle this."

A loud, cynical laugh shot past Sebastien's lips. "They won't be able to do a thing. The commanders won't just let them march on board. They have no jurisdiction. If we're going to take down Kostas, we need to be smarter than that. I know him. I've been studying him for weeks."

Sophie threw her hands up in surrender. Sebastien's mind was set. "Be careful," she said. "These people are dangerous."

His response sent a ripple of unease along her skin. "So am I."

Sebastien stared vacantly into the darkness of the crate, the memory replaying in his mind. Several minutes passed before he reeled himself back into the present. He could feel the crate lower, settling firmly on the ground. Everything was dark and still inside his timber box.

He didn't have to wait long before the side of the crate swung open. The beam of a flashlight drilled through the acrylic globe and into his eyes. He covered his face with the blanket.

"Sebastien?" He recognized the voice immediately despite its hushed volume. "Are you there?"

"Get me out of here, Diya!" He tossed the duvet to the side and climbed through the hidden hatch, gulping mouthfuls of air. She squealed as they held each other.

"It worked," she said with relief, patting her hands over his face as though to confirm it was really him. "You're here."

Sebastien looked around to find himself in an unfamiliar part of the ship. The ceiling soared overhead above criss-crossing gangways and tracks of spotlights. His shoes clapped against the wooden floor as he stepped toward the black curtain that ran the length of one side. Peeking between the velvet partitions, it was his first time seeing the Odeon from this side of the curtain. Rows of plush turquoise seats and carpeted aisles stared down at him, waiting for his finale. He would take a bow before long.

"Let's go," Diya whispered. "Everyone's waiting."

He pulled himself away from the curtain and faced his fearless friend. "Do you think we can pull this off?" He couldn't deny that his confidence had eroded like a beach against the tide. The uncertainty ached in his chest, but he remembered the words his mother used to say: *And while your opponent thinks he has the upper hand, you better make sure your next move counts.*

Diya stepped forward and held him by the arms.

"We've spent our entire lives running away," she said, her voice soft but unshakable. "Now we fight."

TWENTY-ONE

Premiere

―――――――――
―――――――――

"How did it feel when you hit Marcel Lamoureux?"

The woman was seated in a square, squat chair that must have been at least fifty years old, with upholstery the colour of overripe avocado. Her tangerine blouse, tweed skirt, and cat-eye spectacles complemented the seventies aesthetic that was too on-the-nose to be accidental.

Sebastien felt like a cliché as he lay on the chaise longue, itself out of place, given its sleek leather and contemporary design.

"I don't know," he said, staring at the ceiling of water-stained panels. "It was a long time ago."

"It's been a year," the woman confirmed, her voice gentle yet uncompromising.

"Might as well be a lifetime."

"I need you to work with me, Sebastien. I know you feel like you're being forced to be here, but I want to help you."

The ceiling was speckled with dots. They formed an erratic display of constellations.

"It didn't feel like anything." He uncrossed his arms and let them fall to his sides. "I felt angry before I hit him. My body was shaking. Everything was hot. But when it happened, I felt nothing. It was like my mind was severed from my body. I had no control."

The woman looked at the notepad in her lap, pen poised between her fingertips, but she didn't write anything down. It was the kind of pad he had always imagined lawyers to use, the type that flipped at the top edge rather than the side. He found it odd that his court-ordered psychiatrist used one of these pads but his lawyer hadn't.

"How did it feel when you stopped hitting him?"

His hands balled into fists, sticky and warm. "I felt tired. I just wanted to lie there. The sky was so blue. I thought my limbs would break if I moved."

"What about when you were escorted away from the field. How did you feel then?"

"Ashamed." It was the easiest question yet.

"That's good," she said, nodding as if to confirm it were true. "You knew what you did was wrong."

"I've never denied that, have I?"

"No," she agreed. "But you're not on trial anymore. There's no more pressure to answer one way or another. So it's good. Now, I want you to describe your anger. What does it look like?"

A tart little laugh slipped past his lips. "I don't know. How should anger look?"

"Close your eyes. Think about graduation day. What do you see?"

His eyelids shut with a reluctant flutter. He lay there still as stone for several seconds. The woman waited patiently.

"It looks like fire," he said. "Except it's white instead of red. It starts out small, but then gets bigger, and brighter, until it has swallowed everything."

"Does it have a face?"

Sebastien didn't realize his head was nodding. "It has my eyes."

The woman placed the notepad on the oblong table beside her before leaning forward in the avocado chair. "Do you remember what you said during the assault on the field?"

"No."

"But you've heard the accounts from the witnesses." It wasn't a question.

"Apparently I was screaming nonsense."

"That's not quite true, Sebastien."

"*Why weren't we good enough?*" His voice was flat and emotionless. "That's what I said, repeatedly, like a lunatic. At least according to the people who were there. I don't remember. You know this already, Doctor."

She nodded slowly. "Tell me about your father."

"I don't have one." He adjusted his position, twisting his shoulders left and right.

"How do you feel talking about him now?"

"Tired. I feel tired."

"Why do you feel that way?"

"Because I've already wasted too much of my life thinking about that asshole!" The confession burst from his mouth before he could stop it. "I'm sorry."

"No need to apologize," she said, her tone understanding.

"My father is nobody." Sebastien closed his eyes and softened his voice. "He's just a man who left my mother before I was born. That's all. Nothing more."

"Describe what he looks like."

He drew an audible breath, crossing his arms over his stomach. "I've never seen him," he said. "But my mother tells me I have his eyes."

The doctor reclined in her chair, analyzing the young man lying in front of her, deciphering the mystery beneath his skin.

"Have you heard of cognitive restructuring?" she asked after a prolonged silence.

"No."

"Anger is irrational. It causes people to think things they know aren't true. But the stronger the anger, the easier it is to believe these irrational thoughts over one's own logic."

Sebastien pulled his eyes away from the ceiling to look at the woman in the chair. He noticed for the first time she had a kind face.

"For example," she went on, "anger often causes people to think everyone is against them. They know logically that can't be true, but the negative thoughts make it easy to believe. It's also common to think in extremes. People are either good or bad. A decision will either lead to unimaginable success or complete failure. This is over-simplified thinking, but an angry person might not see any middle ground."

"You're talking about me, right?"

"Not necessarily." She clasped her hands in her lap. A gold wedding band squeezed her ring finger. Sebastien wondered if she was happy. "I know you've had challenges in your life. You expressed earlier that you feel your anger is justified. I'm not here to cure you or validate you. My job is simply to give you tools to manage your anger. To tame it. The most important tool is logic."

"Logic." He repeated the word as though he'd never heard it before.

"Anger is misunderstood. It doesn't need to be a weakness. The goal isn't to eliminate it, but to gain control over it." She softened her voice, allowing her human side to peek through the professional exterior. "What Marcel Lamoureux did to your mother was reprehensible. Your anger was an appropriate emotional response to that. Anger is passion. It's conviction and agency. That's what I see when I look in your eyes, not hatred. There can be power in anger when you learn how to harness it."

His muscles felt less stiff when he pushed himself off the chaise longue at the end of the session. He walked toward the door but found himself not quite ready to leave.

"Dr. St-Germain?"

She turned to him, still seated in the clutches of the aging armchair.

"Am I dangerous?"

A soft smile appeared on her lips.

"No, Sebastien. Emotion is like water. Some people keep it in a well, drawing from it by the bucket. Others put it behind a dam. But you — you are an ocean."

❖

Palma de Mallorca sizzled beneath the sun as the *Glacier* pulled into the harbour. The island's capital had come a long way since its days as a far-flung camp for the ancient Romans. It had evolved into a hotbed of all things glitzy and gaudy. Luxury yachts flagrantly crowded the harbour in the shadow of Le Seu, Palma's most dignified cathedral. The austerity of its stone walls and gothic towers had stood guard over the seaside port for the past eight hundred years. Now it was subject to the narcissism of package tourists and jetsetters alike taking too many photos of too much bare skin.

The *Glacier* had departed Barcelona the previous night, veering south to the lauded hedonism of the Balearic Islands. It was the destination's first appearance on the ship's itinerary that summer, so most officers were eager to join the guests in losing themselves in the narrow lanes of the old town or in searching for a plot of sandy heaven to claim.

The staff and crew were notified that they wouldn't be permitted in port that day by order of the hotel commander.

The mood on board had been peculiar since Sebastien was evicted. The hours that passed were uneventful, staff and crew keeping their heads down and doing their jobs with perfected smiles, but something electric simmered beneath the calm surface. The corridors in the lower decks of Hades were alive with whispers. Furtive glances were exchanged between people with no obvious connection. The resistance lived on, but for now it was kept hidden.

Kostas was no fool. He knew Sebastien hadn't acted alone, and he knew evicting the wild-haired provocateur would only elicit sympathy and anger from those who shared his hopeless mission. Kostas kept a list of people who would soon be receiving knocks on their cabin doors. The ship would be lighter when they arrived at their next port: Cannes.

Until then, he would continue to show them who was in control. The curfew remained. Neither staff nor crew had guest privileges except while on duty. The morality code was enforced so effectively that most people hid in their cabins during the evenings.

A new rule had been implemented as punishment for the black-banner stunt in the port of Palermo — the crew and staff bars now closed two hours before midnight. Kostas

almost felt sorry for them, but they had brought it upon themselves. They had taken their freedoms for granted, foolishly
thinking they were entitlements, and now he had no choice
but to show them what happened when they made demands
without power.

The bright passageway that ran straight through A Deck
was quiet as two Filipina housekeepers pushed their supply
cart past offices and storage rooms. One woman was round
while the other was thin. They wore matching grey uniforms
with pink aprons.

"Rosa, are you sure you know where you're going?" the
thin woman asked her companion.

"Trust me, Imelda." Rosa shot her a stern glance. "I've
been here many times." It wasn't true. The only other time
she'd visited the elite wing inhabited by the commanding officers was that day in Cyprus, when she delivered the special
cake to Giorgos.

Imelda looked doubtful as she pushed the large cart ahead
of her.

When they reached the locked door at the end of the hall,
Rosa pulled the plastic key card from the pocket of her apron.
It was used by her friends who were authorized to clean the
cabins and deliver food in the exclusive wing. She gave Imelda
a decisive look before inserting the card into the slot on the
door. The dot of green light flicked on.

A tiny gasp escaped Imelda's mouth when she saw the
grape-coloured floors and emerald wallpaper. Rosa's eyes
scolded her. The sound of the cart's wheels were muted as they
rolled along the carpet.

The hall was empty when they turned the corner. In front
of them stood the door they were searching for. The location
was engraved on a bronze plaque:

A66

"Good morning," Rosa said in her sweetest, most mother-ly voice. There was a broad smile on her flushed face.

Sitting on a chair in front of the door was a young man wearing the blue uniform of Nikos's security staff. His square shoulders were slouched. The hallway was blocked by his out-stretched legs. He looked at the two women with boredom etched across his face and gave them a curt nod.

"We're here to clean this cabin." Rosa's smile remained as she pointed to the door beside the man.

"Not this cabin," he said. "Go on to the next one."

The two women glanced at each other from across their supply cart. Rosa turned to the man, her smile widening. "We were given orders to clean this cabin. A66, yes?"

"No one's allowed inside," he said, the impatience seeping into his voice. "If you have a problem with that, you can take it up with Nikos Antonopolous."

"But sir —"

The man stood up from his chair in an act of intimi-dation over the shorter women. "I said move —" His eyes blinked several times as the words trailed off. He'd been interrupted, but he wasn't sure by what. Gravity pulled his chin downward, and he saw the dart sticking out of his chest. What looked like a bundle of pink feathers sprouted from the end.

He looked up, shocked. The thinner woman held a gun the size of an assault rifle in her spindly hands. The larger woman's face reflected his surprise, but the one with the gun had no hint of apology in her humourless eyes.

"You shot me with a tranq?" Scowling with disbelief, he pulled the needle from his chest and dropped it to the ground.

"These things don't work like they do on TV, you know. It can take up to an hour to take effect. You stupid bitches."

Rosa yelped as the man stepped toward them, but he stumbled, as though his legs were no longer in sync with his mind. The angry look on his face dissolved into bewilderment. His shoulder hit the wall with a thud, then he rolled over the closed door, struggling to remain standing. His eyelashes fluttered delicately before his entire body toppled to the carpeted floor.

Rosa smacked Imelda on the side of the arm. "We weren't supposed to use that unless we needed to!"

"Exactly," she said, "and we needed to."

"I had the situation under control. I could have talked our way in."

"I guess we'll never know." The thin woman looked at the tranquillizer gun, on loan from the Filipino Mafia. She liked how it felt in her hands.

Rosa crouched beside the security guard to confirm they hadn't just committed murder. "He's breathing," she said with a sigh of relief, her fingers darting across her bosom in the sign of the cross.

"He's a big sleeping baby."

"What is in these things?" Rosa held up the dart with the pink feathers.

Imelda shrugged.

Remembering their mission, Rosa patted her apron to find the key card and inserted it in the door of cabin A66. A few seconds passed, but the dot of green light permitting entry didn't appear. She tried pushing the door, but it remained locked. After a few more attempts of inserting the key card with the same result, she turned to Imelda. "They must have deactivated entry to this door," she said with a helpless look on her face.

Imelda appeared unperturbed as she scanned the hallway. She stepped over the security guard's body and disappeared around the corner, leaving Rosa standing there in a state of confusion. A minute later, Imelda returned holding one of the fire extinguishers that sat in glass boxes throughout the corridors of the lower decks. She motioned for Rosa to step aside, then grunted as she lifted the heavy silver cylinder above her head. It came down swiftly, severing the door handle with hardly a sound.

With a nod of approval, Rosa pushed open the door. She stepped into the room and saw exactly what she was told she would find inside.

A frightened young woman with long black hair and eyes as large and present as an owl's stood in the middle of the cabin.

"Who are you?" she asked, her voice shaking.

"We're friends." Rosa put her palms up in a calming gesture. "Sebastien sent us. We are here to help you."

"The green-eyed boy with the crazy hair?"

Rosa let out a sweet laugh. "That's the one."

Athena helped the two housekeepers drag the security guard by his feet into the cabin. They bound his wrists and ankles with twine from the supply cart. Rosa pulled three energy bars from her apron and removed the foil wrapping. She propped the man up against the wall and placed the bars in his lap.

"He'll be hungry," she said to the other two women.

The front of the supply cart held a canvas hamper for dirty towels and sheets. They helped Athena inside, and covered her with a fluffy duvet.

"You're safe now," Rosa whispered into the hamper. They closed the door behind them and rolled the cart away.

Laughter resounded from the table of imposing figures. Kostas Kourakis had honed his storytelling skills as a young sailor circumnavigating the globe from the swaying decks of a cargo ship. The present-day hotel commander knew how to regale an audience with the right combination of titillation and candour.

"I didn't say that," little Kristo protested, his face flushing red as he listened to the story his father had just shared at the dinner table.

"It's nothing to be embarrassed by," Nikos said. He gave the boy seated beside him a playful shake of the shoulders. "It happens to all of us. We just don't like to admit it."

The neatly buttoned shirts of the wait staff were as crisp as the linen tablecloths. It was a soundless ballet as their arms darted between the distinguished guests to retrieve plates and refill glasses.

Everyone seated at the round table was dressed in formal white-and-gold uniforms except for the two Kourakis children and Alexis, who wore a chic gown that matched the indigo sea outside. The diners were a serious group by nature, but the mood during this dinner had been relaxed. Nikos spoke more freely than usual, with some help from the glass of tempranillo in his hand. Alexis laughed at everything that came out her darling husband's mouth.

The only person at the table who didn't share the cheer was Giorgos. He had eaten his dinner silently with a distance behind his eyes. The others were becoming accustomed to this withdrawn version of the naturally joyless man.

A shining cart was wheeled beside the table by the maître d' himself. The glass surface displayed sculpted creations of pastry and icing on multiple tiers of china. "Look at those macarons," Alexis said, eyeing the immaculate buttons of muted colour.

"I want the chocolate!" Kristo reached out to grab a glass flute filled with layers of mousse and ganache.

Nikos intercepted the boy's arm. "If you ask the nice man, he'll give it to you."

Kostas laughed loudly, drawing curious glances from the guests seated at the tables around them. "Let the boy have his chocolate, Nikos."

The maître d' offered Kristo a flute of mousse before describing each dessert with practised showmanship. The *Glacier's* dining hall sprawled out behind him in an opulent setting of marble, linen, and gold trim. Two terraces filled with tables of elegant diners overlooked the main floor.

The dramatic room mimicked a theatre much like the Odeon on the opposite end of the ship. There were dining tables instead of rows of cushioned seats. The stage was a wall of glass curved around the *Glacier's* stern from floor to ceiling. Every table had a view of the ship's wake as they sailed away from the island of Mallorca. An orange glow hovered over Palma against the darkening sky.

Nikos had just put a spoonful of mille-feuille into his mouth when he felt a tap on the shoulder. The waiter slid a folded square of paper in front of him before striding away without a word.

Nikos snatched the unexpected delivery as he glanced around the table. He unfolded the paper to reveal a message written by a familiar hand.

Come find me in our House. We need to talk.

The bite of dessert felt lodged in his throat. He hid the note below the table and turned in his seat, searching for its messenger. Dozens of waiters in identical black-vested suits darted throughout the dining hall. It could have been any of them.

The others seated at the table were too preoccupied with Kostas's describing his favourite café in Cannes to notice the beads of sweat forming on Nikos's forehead.

"Excuse me," he said, his voice higher pitched than usual. He cleared his throat with a scratchy cough. "I have something to tend to. I'll see you before the show tonight."

The lighthearted expression on Kostas's face hardened. Even the green facets of his eyes had a way of darkening as quickly as the closing of a curtain. "Is there anything the matter, Nikos?" His tone was sharpened in interrogation. He knew how to read the controlled exterior of the young man.

"It's nothing." Nikos placed his napkin on the table and stood, closing the gold buttons of his jacket. He turned to Kristo. "Don't eat too much chocolate," he said with a faint smile.

The noise of the dining hall dimmed. The only sound he could hear was the dull clicks of his shoes against the marble floor as he marched toward the exit. Several guests turned their heads as he passed. They wondered why this man blessed with such youth and command appeared so tense.

A part of him felt a nervous tingle of excitement at seeing Sebastien again. It had been difficult turning him in days earlier, apprehending him like a petty thief. He had secluded himself in his office the morning Sebastien was escorted off the ship. He missed him.

His longing was overpowered by logic, though. He knew why Sebastien had returned, and it wasn't to make amends.

Instead of taking the elevator to the House of the Heel on Riviera Deck, he turned a corner and pushed open a hidden door that led down to the staff and crew quarters below. His footsteps announced his approach along A Deck. With a swipe of the wrist, he was through the locked door and striding down the carpeted hall of the elite commanders' wing, his heart pounding in his chest.

His fears were confirmed when he saw the empty chair outside cabin A66. He pushed open the broken door and burst into the room. His fists opened and closed in mechanical motions, asserting control over the wave of distress that rippled through his body.

Athena was nowhere to be seen. The guard he'd appointed was bound at the wrists and ankles by synthetic pink twine. The man was unconscious, but the rhythm of his breathing was evident in his chest and nostrils. What looked like three granola bars lay on his lap. Nikos removed the bindings and laid the sleeping guard on the floor, stretching out his limbs.

His pace was quicker as he bounded down the corridor, the emerald wallpaper creating an illusion of running through the jungle. He raised his radio's transceiver in his palm, debating how much of a stir he should cause. Calling for backup would be the sensible thing to do for an officer in his position, but he was hesitant to trigger a manhunt if he had a chance of defusing the situation himself.

As the note stated, perhaps Sebastien just wanted to talk. They had something special, didn't they?

Caught between his head and his heart, he lowered the transceiver with a reluctant jerk of the arm.

Adriatic Deck was an intoxicating swirl of lights and laughter as Nikos marched through the crowds of guests dressed in their finest. After all, it was the premiere of the new show in the Odeon that night. He weaved past tuxedoed servers carrying silver trays and musicians infusing the air with the sounds of strings and cymbals. They looked at him as though they knew exactly where he was headed.

Nikos caught the eye of the boyish photographer with the blond hair who had replaced Sebastien. He looked like he was playing dress-up in his suit, the camera held firmly in his hands.

The constant commotion of the casino assaulted Nikos's ears. Cheers erupted from the craps table as a woman in a tight pink dress and feathery hat celebrated a lucky roll. Moans came from the next table as a man in a brown suit got snake eyes.

He released a heavy breath as he came out the other side. The bank of elevators between the casino and the entrance to the Odeon was relatively quiet, the noise absorbed by the plush carpet and wood-panelled walls.

A bell chimed softly as a set of bronze doors opened. He stepped inside beside an elderly woman with a sweet face and expensive taste. She turned to him and smiled, revealing more gum than teeth. His lips curved upward reflexively.

His body was as inanimate as stone while the elevator shot upward. The same bell chimed when it reached Riviera Deck. "Good evening," he said to the lady before darting out of the confined space.

The seafoam carpet and atmospheric lighting were soothing, but his muscles were tight as he crept toward the double doors at the end of the hall. These doors once led to his sanctuary, the only place in the world he could be himself.

You can choose to be honest with yourself.

He cringed, Sebastien's words streaming through his memory.

Instead of hiding behind locked doors and hidden rooms.

He was right. Perhaps it wasn't too late to heed the advice.

The skeleton key was pressed between his fingertips while he hesitated outside the door. With a deep, calming breath, he pushed his way into the room.

The House of the Heel was warm and still. Light emanated from the tinted glass along the curved walls. The flowing white sheets that covered the furniture appeared undisturbed from the last time he was here. He pictured the scene, Sebastien pinned beneath him with surrender in the green pools of his eyes, and shuddered. The shattered fragments of the vase were still strewn across the floor.

His eyes landed on something unusual, and his body went cold. In the middle of the room was a chair covered in a white cloth. A sheet of paper lay there with a handwritten message.

IT WAS YOU ALL ALONG

Next to the note was a tablet propped against the back of the chair. A forty-second video played in a continuous loop. Nikos's face could be seen clearly. In the foreground was the back of a man's head, but he could tell by the firm waves of hair that it was Kostas.

Nikos knew exactly how the footage had been captured. He'd noticed the conspicuous silver frame on the shelf in Kostas's office the previous week. It boasted a portrait of the Kourakis family standing in front of the atrium. "It was a gift," Kostas said when asked, "from that young photographer, Mr. Goh." It had made Nikos uneasy. He remembered Sebastien holding the frame in his hands when they walked to the office together, but he would never have guessed there was a camera hidden inside. Now he knew the purpose this gift was meant to serve.

Nikos found it difficult to recognize himself in the video. The face he saw was beautiful but empty. Even as the Greek words blew past his lips, giving up Sebastien as the leader of the rebellion, knowing he'd be banished from the ship, Nikos detected no emotion in his own voice. It was flat, factual. The only hint of what was brewing behind the tightly controlled exterior were his eyes. There was regret etched into the amber.

"Put up your hands, Nikos." The voice from behind was sharp like a spear. "Turn around slowly."

He did as he was told. Standing by the door was the sandy-haired fitness trainer with a grave look on his face. He was accompanied by six men from the crew dressed entirely in black. They were armed with stun guns.

"We don't want to hurt you," Ilya said, "so listen carefully."

⌘

The warmly lit halls leading into the Odeon were packed with guests eager to find their seats inside. The premiere of a new show was a glamorous event even by the *Glacier's* standards. It was also the perfect finale for the two-week Mediterranean sailing from Athens. It promised one last night of excitement before the final destination — the ritzy French seaside town of Cannes — where these guests would disembark to make room for a fresh set of vacationers.

The ebullience had diminished in Kostas's manner when Nikos pardoned himself at dinner an hour earlier. There had obviously been something troubling the young man. Kostas had tried calling, but there was no answer.

Alexis held him stiffly by the arm as they followed the river of people slowly passing through the doors of the theatre.

"I heard there's magic in this show," Kristo said.

The boy had been withdrawn after the vandalism of their suite, but smiles were beginning to come more easily to him again. Alexis was relieved that her son was returning to his normal self, but she couldn't shake the ominous feeling that had settled in her bones. She'd discovered a new poem in her son's notebook a few days earlier. It was about a man possessed by anger. He had wild hair and green eyes. The last line had sent a cold ripple of static over her skin: "I am the man and the man is me."

"There will even be aerialists who fly over the stage," Alexis said with a smile, her hand clamped around his.

Beside the entrance was a large poster framed by the kinds of lights you'd see on a marquee. A man and woman dressed in sexualized versions of Grecian attire were trapped inside what looked like a giant snow globe. The woman's dress billowed in the bitter wind that swirled around them while the golden belt of the man's tunic was frosted with ice. The poster promised a "spectacle of ancient legend and modern magic" above the show's name: Odyssey of Ice.

Kostas grunted with disapproval. He wondered how a show in such poor taste had been cleared for performance. "This should be interesting," he said with an artificial smile.

Giorgos trailed behind the Kourakis family as they made their way down the aisle of the theatre. Their seats were in the exclusive box reserved for commanding officers and their families, a raised platform in the back of the orchestra level's centre section that could fit twenty-four. Behind their seats was the mezzanine where Sebastien and Kostas had first seen each other during the captain's cocktail party. The encounter felt buried in the past when in reality it was little more than a month ago. Tonight, the mezzanine was dark and empty.

The sweeping balcony hovered above them, evening gowns and dinner jackets obscuring the rich turquoise colour of the seats.

A hush spread through the audience as the lights dimmed. Little Kristo sat upright on the edge of his seat. The silence was heavy. Strings began to play, quietly at first, a gentle melody that eased its way into the darkness of the theatre. Then the horns countered with blasts of urgency. Soon the symphonic sounds filled the cavernous space.

Without warning, the black curtains parted from the middle of the stage like two lovers pulled away by opposing swells in the ocean. The show had begun.

TWENTY-TWO

Finale

Thunder rumbled from within the orchestra pit until the Odeon was engulfed by the storm. Flowing sheets of blue satin created turbulent waves across the stage underneath an angry sky. The figurehead of a wooden ship pierced the fog, a bronze sculpture of the goddess Athena, protector of Odysseus. Her bare breasts were thrust forward as the ship rocked amid the waves while her hair was cast behind her in golden zephyrs.

A metallic clang announced a bolt of lightning. The entire stage flooded with blinding light. Applause rippled through the audience while the brightness died to reveal that the stormy sea had vanished. In its place were the terraces and turrets of a palace. The stone walls and pillars were tinted blue, covered by a glaze similar to that on the statues that stood in the halls of the *Glacier*. The backdrop didn't

depict the sun-bleached cliffs and sparkling waters of the
Aegean Sea but a frozen valley surrounded by mountainous
crags of ice.

A young man with ashen hair coiled beneath a crown of
white laurels appeared on the stage with a striking woman
in an elaborate gown. They were Telemachus and Penelope,
the noble son and devoted wife of Odysseus. Their voices flew
above the rows of turquoise seats. The song conveyed their
longing to be reunited with the man who had abandoned
them to chase glory across the sea. Ten long years had passed
while mother and son waited. The Trojan War had finally
come to an end, but they couldn't be certain that Odysseus
would return to them one day. Still, their love never waned,
even if their hope did.

High above stage level, behind the last rows of the balcony,
Diya paced across the black floor of the Odeon's control
booth. The wide panel of dials and screens commanded the
lights, sounds, and effects of the production playing out on
the stage below.

"You're sure everything is ready?" There was an edge to
her voice.

"Everything is set," said one of the technicians seated in
front of the panel, a bearded Swede named Jonas. "You have
nothing to worry about, my dear."

"I'm not your dear."

He laughed. "I know. Wishful thoughts escaped my mouth."

A faint smile pulled at her lips as she shook her head, her
curly black hair tied back in a serpent-like braid. "We can't
afford to have anything go wrong."

The Swede swivelled in his chair to face her. "I can tell you this, Ms. Sharma. We will not let you down. Isn't that right, boys?"

The two other technicians raised their fists in the air.

"We are all powerless," Jonas said, "just like you."

❖

Far below the control booth, in the commanding officers' box on the orchestra level, Kostas squirmed in his seat. His family sat motionless, engrossed in the show unfolding before them, but he found it difficult to stay in one position for long. Inertia was his enemy. He was designed to move.

The first act was better than he'd anticipated. He didn't see the need for all the frivolous magic and fake snow, but so far nothing had been overtly offensive.

The stage by now was transformed into a frozen cave on the island of Aeaea. Giant icicles hung from the rafters above. The minimally clothed man and woman from the show's poster held each other — the hero Odysseus and the tantalizing sorceress Circe. Her long bronzed legs slipped through the generous slit in her gown while she sang a seductive song to the weak-willed man. A delighted murmur drifted from the audience as a massive snow globe rose from beneath the stage through wisps of fog.

With a sweep of the arm, Circe tore the white gown from her body to reveal golden armour that resembled metallic lingerie. She whipped the fabric above their heads. It drifted to the ground, and they were gone.

A flash illuminated the icy cave. Both Circe and Odysseus were suddenly inside the snow globe. Flecks of white swirled around them as their hands caressed each other's bodies. The music from the orchestra intensified, its crescendo gathering momentum for the inevitable climax. Circe tossed her head back in ecstasy as the snow obliterated their bodies. The white particles fell to the bottom of the globe as the music died. Odysseus and Circe had vanished.

Applause erupted throughout the Odeon. Kostas's clapping hands froze when he noticed someone new had appeared onstage. He squinted, uncertain of what he was seeing. Kristo made a choking sound beside him. He turned and saw his son was shaking. There was fear in his eyes.

The man on stage was the young photographer with the tangled hair and hateful eyes. The man whom Nikos exposed as the leader of the rebellion. The man who attacked his family, who destroyed his wife's cabin in a disturbing display of rage. The man he evicted from the *Glacier* four days earlier in Palermo.

"I'm sorry to interrupt the show," the man on the stage said once the applause died down. "I ask that you remain in your seats for an important announcement."

He stepped to the edge. The orchestra musicians looked up at him from their sunken pit. The single spotlight illuminated the proud ridges of his face and the curve of the lips he'd inherited from his mother. He was dressed entirely in black, the top two buttons of his shirt undone.

"My name is Sebastien Goh. I worked on board the *Glacier* until very recently. Over the past month, I've learned something evil is happening on this ship. There are people in command who use their power to commit horrifying crimes. You are not in danger, but there are people on board who are. We need your help."

Confusion rumbled throughout the theatre in a wave of hushed voices.

"The leader is Kostas Kourakis, the ship's hotel commander. He's been entangled in a human trafficking ring for at least three decades."

Sebastien pointed his finger directly at Kostas, who sat dumbstruck amid a protective sea of white uniforms in the commanders' box.

Kostas turned to either side of him and saw that the eyes of his wife, son, and daughter were wide with astonishment. Sweat gathered beneath his helmet of hair.

"Lies!" he screamed, jumping to his feet. "This man is the criminal." He looked at the four security guards stationed beside the exits. "What are you standing there for? Get him!"

The guards glanced at each other with uncertainty before marching down the two carpeted aisles that dissected the lower-level seats. They closed in on Sebastien, two from the left and two from the right. The guards were halfway to the base of the stage when the radios strapped to their belts hummed alive.

"Stand down," the voice declared through the transceivers. The tone of authority was unmistakable, but Sebastien could hear the veiled vulnerability. It was Nikos. "Let him speak."

The guards stood in the middle of the aisles with hands on their radios, unsure of what to do, while everyone watched them.

❧

Ilya observed the scene from behind the black velvet curtain at the side of the stage. In one hand was the radio he had taken from Nikos. In the other hand was the phone that stored the audio clip he'd created. Nikos hadn't realized six days earlier,

when he was fighting the urge to kiss Sebastien in the elevator descending from Sunset Deck, that he was being recorded.
Every word he spoke was caught by the phone in Sebastien's
pocket. It hadn't taken Ilya long to splice the fragments to
form phrases that could prove useful.

He couldn't help himself from smiling as he saw the puzzled looks on the faces of the guards, who stood paralyzed in
the aisles.

Sebastien's voice was louder as he continued. "Kostas uses the
Glacier to transport women throughout the Mediterranean
for this network of gangs. These women are held captive and
coerced into working for them. They're bought, sold, and
smuggled like human cargo." He scanned the audience, but
he couldn't see any faces with the spotlight in his eyes. "I
know this because I discovered one of them imprisoned in a
cabin hidden below decks. She's supposed to be handed over
tomorrow in Cannes. From there, we don't know what they'll
do to her."

Kostas trembled as he stood in the commanders' box.
The veins that snaked beneath his skin were inflamed, blood
surging through them. "Somebody apprehend that man!" he
barked. "I command you!"

A number of junior officers in white-and-gold uniforms
filed out of their seats and took nervous steps down the aisles.
Nobody knew what to do, but nobody wanted to sit still in
open defiance of their leader. Forcefully detaining a man on
stage in front of two thousand people was an order nobody
was eager to carry out, especially given the gravity of the
accusations.

An elegant woman in a sparkling red dress stood up from her seat near the front. "Don't touch him," she shouted with a booming voice. "We want to hear what he has to say."

The officers halted their advance as several other guests stood from their seats, voicing agreement.

"Let the boy speak!" demanded one elderly gentleman in a tuxedo.

"Don't you lay a finger on him," threatened a lady with a bouffant of silver hair.

Sebastien continued, gripping the microphone in his sweaty palm. "With the help of our friends from the staff and crew of the *Glacier*, we rescued this woman from where she was being kept. But she's not safe. Not yet. She will be in danger unless justice is served to everyone involved. Even if we were able to smuggle her off the ship and into safety, there would be more women. More slaves. That's why I'm standing here in front of you. We can't sit back and let this continue. We stop this cycle tonight." He paused for a deep breath, steadying his hands. "And if you're not sure if you believe me, listen to what the victim has to say."

Another spotlight flickered alive. Athena Vissi walked onto the stage.

Scenarios played in Nikos's mind while he sat alone with his wrists and ankles bound to the wooden chair. He didn't know what Sebastien had planned, but he knew it wouldn't end well. How had things gone so wrong?

The stillness that hung over the House of the Heel was maddening. Something serious was happening that night, and here he was tied up like an animal. The possible outcome that frightened him the most was Sebastien getting hurt. It was clear by the stun guns and tranquillizers that the rebels were prepared to use violence. Ilya had taken Nikos's radio, keys, and phone. If something terrible happened to Sebastien, he wouldn't be able to forgive himself.

The twine cut into his flesh as he struggled. Leaning forward, he was able to stand on his feet in a crouched position. With a ragged breath, he propelled himself backward into the air. He cried in pain as he landed on his back with the chair behind him.

Dazed, he looked up at the vaulted ceiling while he steadied his breathing. Lying on their makeshift mattress of sheets, tangled in each other's naked limbs, they had always thought it was the night sky painted above. Now, Nikos realized they'd been wrong. The swirl that distorted the stars in the sky wasn't air. It was water. He was looking up at the surface of the sea as though he were a drowning man.

He blinked several times, willing the tears back into his eyes.

With a jerk of the arm, he realized his painful attempt at freedom had worked. The wooden armrest of the chair lay broken beside him, still bound to him like a splint. It didn't take long for him to untie the knots with his free left hand.

He ran to the door, then stopped. Spinning around, he took in the soft light and quiet solitude of this room that had concealed his happiest moments.

He vowed to never return.

⬨

Like Sebastien, the young woman who stood on the stage was dressed entirely in black. Long dark hair framed her wary face. Her large eyes were alert but hesitant. They shifted to the side, and he responded with an encouraging nod.

"My name is Athena," she said, the microphone almost touching her lips. "Everything Sebastien said is true."

The entire theatre went silent once the mysterious woman appeared on the stage. The guards and officers stood scattered down the aisles like a parade on pause. Even Kostas had nothing to say.

"My family needed money to keep our father alive," Athena said. Her voice was bolder. "A man I considered a friend introduced me to the criminals. I borrowed money from them I couldn't pay back. The only way to pay the debt is to work for them. I didn't know how much danger I was in until I boarded this ship. They took my passport, all of my identification. I was locked in a cabin as a prisoner until Sebastien and his friends rescued me."

She flashed him a determined look before her eyes drifted to the floor.

"I was branded once I boarded the ship." She turned around, her back facing the audience, then pulled her hair up to reveal the symbol carved into her neck. Gasps echoed throughout the Odeon. Many of the Greek guests recognized the six connected little circles. Cautionary tales of what the symbol represented had been told to young girls for a generation.

"It's Aphrodite's flower," Sebastien said, "an ancient symbol now used by a network of traffickers that Kostas Kourakis is a part of. The operation has existed for decades. They branded all of their girls with this symbol — including my mother."

Ruby Goh's young face appeared on a white screen hanging above them. Her hair was suspended around her squinted eyes, her mouth frozen open with silent laughter. With the image blown up to this size, the symbol could be seen clearly in the reflection of the mirror behind her.

"Thirty years ago she met a young Greek sailor whose cargo ship was docked in her home country of Singapore. He promised to take her to France, the same country where Athena is being transported."

Sebastien paused, his lungs burning. He could feel the flames push their way up his chest. He looked out into the audience, but all he could see was his rage. It was white and blinding, a fire that burned with an intensity that was all too familiar.

"My mother didn't make it to France," he went on, the microphone shaking in front of his lips. "She escaped and started a new life in Québec. But she always had this reminder of what could have become of her, carved into the back of her neck as if she were someone's property." The volume of his voice rose, those last few words nearly shouted. "That young sailor's name was Kostas Kourakis, the man sitting right there — my father."

An anguished screech came from the commanding officers' box. It was Kristo. He screamed as he climbed over the people seated beside him before tumbling into the aisle. He charged toward the stage, limbs battering the air. Sebastien stepped out of the spotlight to see the boy's contorted face. There was no longer fear in his eyes. There was only rage. They truly were brothers.

One of the junior officers blocked Kristo's rampage down the aisle, holding him back by the chest. The boy's fists beat against him, but the officer didn't let go.

"He's lying!" Kostas screamed, delirious with anger. There was a rattle in his voice, like the tail of a snake. The skin exposed above the collar of his shirt flared into deep red streaks. "None of it is true. I've never seen that woman in my life."

Sebastien's throat tightened when he saw Nikos burst through the doors of the theatre. The deputy security commander's eyes were wide with bewilderment as he struggled to comprehend what he was seeing. His gaze went from the two black-clad people under the spotlights, to the aisles covered in paralyzed officers and security guards, to little Kristo's clawing hands.

"Nikos!" Kostas screamed in his direction. "Remove that man immediately!"

Nikos looked up at the target on stage. Their eyes locked, and for a moment everything was still. They grappled with each other despite the distance between them, grasping for a signal that they'd be on the same side in the end, that they hadn't just imagined the connection that bound them. A moment decoding what was hidden behind each other's eyes was all it took to know the truth. They both cared about their individual selves more than what they had together. Neither knew the full landscape behind what they'd so carefully shown one another.

Your move, Achilles.

Nikos broke the gaze and shouted at his guards in a barrage of Greek, pointing at the stage. They shook themselves out of their indecisive stupor and resumed their advance down the aisles.

"That's the man," Athena said in a calm, steady voice. Her delicate finger pointed directly at him. "He's the man who handed me to the criminals, the man I thought was my friend."

Nikos scowled at her. "This woman is crazy," he shouted at the hundreds of eyes fixed on him. "She's delusional. Disturbed. You can't trust a word she says."

The lights dimmed. Everyone froze as a scene was projected on the screen above the stage. The grand finale.

The video captured two men having a conversation in a white-walled office. The back of one man's head could be seen directly in front of the camera's lens, but the uneasy features of the young security commander's face were in clear view. Their words poured out of the theatre's speakers like a torrent of truth. They spoke Greek, but much of the audience could understand the lyrical words, including the sea of white uniforms surrounding Kostas in the commanding officers' box.

"You've found a great beauty, there's no doubt about that."

"We can't risk her escaping again."

"Mr. Goh has been dealt with. He's gone, and he has no evidence."

"I planted doubt. He thinks she could be crazy."

"All we need to do is get her to Cannes. She'll be taken from there, and she'll no longer be our problem."

Cries of condemnation roared throughout the theatre as the conversation on the screen came to an end.

"Get them off the stage!" Nikos screamed. Panic overthrew his tightly controlled demeanour. "What are you looking at?"

The guards and officers standing in the aisle had pivoted so they were no longer facing the stage. Instead, they stared at Nikos with judgment in their eyes.

"Now all of you know the truth," Sebastien said, his voice booming through the speakers. "And you have a choice. You can do nothing — forget what you've seen tonight and ignore the evil happening on board this ship — or you can help us stop it."

Shouts reverberated across the near-perfect acoustics of the Odeon as people stood from their seats, turning to face the two unlikely perpetrators.

Nikos continued to shout while his guards advanced on him. As they reached out to detain their commander, his fist struck one of them in the jaw. The officers in the aisle came to the aid of the blue-suited guards. Nikos lashed out at them like a lone lion surrounded by a circle of wildebeests. One of the officers tackled him to the floor, pinning him against the carpet with knees on his shoulders. Nikos was soon subdued as one of his former subordinates flipped him onto his stomach. He writhed on the floor with his wrists cuffed behind his back.

Kostas was trapped by the crowd of white uniforms in the commanding officers' box at the back of the theatre. His colleagues stood up from their seats and turned to face him, a wall of contempt. They despised him. He considered these people to be his pedestal. They held him up in his position of power. They protected him. He suddenly realized his commands were meaningless if they decided he was no longer fit to command.

"Let me pass." Kostas's tone was firm. He stared into the eyes drilling into him, but nobody moved. Alexis and Katerina stood helplessly at his side. "I said let me pass, you imbeciles!"

"It's over," one officer said as though stating a fact.

Kostas didn't know what else to do. His entire body shook as the laughter burst out of him.

"This isn't funny," said another officer who looked ready to grab him by the arms.

"Sometimes the only thing left to do is laugh or cry," Kostas said, his face hijacked by a ridiculous grin. "Let me laugh."

Before anyone could stop him, he stepped onto the arm-
rests of his seat and jumped onto the ledge that led to the mezzanine. The upper half of his body clung to the top of the short
wall while his legs kicked at the officers who tried grabbing
him from behind. The heavy soles of his shoes connected with
faces and shoulders as his arms hoisted himself over the ledge.

He tumbled into the mezzanine, knocking over several
bottles of liquor along the way. They shattered on the tiled
floor beside him with a symphonic crash. He heard people
shouting as they climbed in pursuit behind him.

Kostas pulled himself up from the floor with the help of
the long bar that ran along the edge. He stumbled around the
counter and ran across the room. It was an ominous blur of
blue-tinted statues and broad-leafed trees. At first, it seemed
as though he might make it out of the theatre. Then the pace
of his legs slowed.

Along the far wall of the mezzanine, blocking the doors
that led to the halls outside, was a crowd of people. They were
dressed in black instead of the usual turquoise and grey uniforms, but Kostas knew they were staff and crew.

Diya stepped forward. One hand rested on her waist while
the other held a stun gun the size of an electric razor.

"Where do you think you're going?" she asked, her voice
playful yet menacing.

"Get out of my way," he ordered.

Rosa stood beside Diya. The usual warmth on her face
was replaced by something as cold and hard as a slab of marble. She also held a stun gun.

"You've lost," Rosa said. "Now you are the powerless one."

A stampede of footsteps closed in on Kostas from behind.
He spun around to see he was surrounded by two dozen officers. They had followed him over the ledge of the mezzanine

and now had their hands held out in front of them, ready to use force if need be.

Kostas knew Rosa was right. He had lost.

Standing there on the tiled floor, trapped between the white uniforms of the ruling class and the black costumes of the rebels, he couldn't suppress a twisted feeling of pride. This unification was unlike anything he'd seen before. The power had shifted like a rebellious tide, and now he would be drowned by the surge. He was defeated, yes, but he was also proud.

Because he knew all of this had been set in motion by his son.

TWENTY-THREE

The Same Place at the Same Time

Kostas Kourakis was a different man thirty years earlier. The young sailor couldn't hide the sense of awe that overwhelmed him whenever they pulled into a new port. It was easy to understand. The poor son of an unwed mother never dreamed he would one day travel the world, yet here he was. His fellow Greek shipmates would poke fun at him, but the truth was they were charmed by the young man's wide-eyed wonder. It was refreshing to be around someone unjaded by life at sea — or by life in general, for that matter. They called him Gélio, the Greek word for "laugh."

The arid heat of their native Greece had done little to prepare them for Singapore. That evening their stiff white uniforms were transparent with sweat within twenty minutes of leaving the ship.

"Feels like we're in the jungle," Kostas said, unbuttoning the collar of his shirt.

"Feels like I'm between your mother's sweaty tits," said his friend Milos. The other sailors laughed as they slapped each other's palms.

"At least my mother has a pair," he said, elbowing Milos's stomach hard enough to make his friend double over.

The market was filled with the sounds and smells of Singapore. Smoke wafted into the sky from blackened grills covered in skewers of meat. Throngs of locals slurped noodles from bowls of fragrant laksa, scenting the air with shrimp paste and chilies. They sat at round plastic tables beneath a canopy of stringed lights while American pop music blared through the overhead speakers between crackles of static.

Everyone turned to look when the young sailors entered the open-air space surrounded by hawker stalls. It was the reason they wore their uniforms. They interpreted the effect as admiration rather than suspicion.

Sweat rolled down the bottles of beer the Greeks held as they seated themselves at a table near the centre of the market. The table was white like their uniforms but covered in a film of dirt. "*Yamas!*" they shouted, clinking their bottles together.

"Well, boys, we might as well make ourselves at home," Milos said, after emptying his bottle into his crooked mouth. "We've got two weeks of dry-dock to kill on this island."

"I don't mind being on land for the time being," Kostas said. "To remember what it's like not being adrift."

"Little Gélio is just hungry for pussy." Milos landed a playful punch on his shoulder while the other men howled like apes. Kostas felt his cheeks go red.

The mocking was interrupted by a loud clatter as stacks of metal pans on a counter fell to the concrete floor. The sailors turned to see what was causing the commotion.

A young woman ran along the perimeter of the market's seating area. Her long hair, black as a nun's habit, streamed behind her as the foam sandals on her feet pounded the pavement. She clutched a plastic bag in her hands.

An older man in a blood-smeared apron followed close behind, shouting pointed daggers of Mandarin. A few bystanders feigned attempts at stopping the young woman, but nobody truly wanted to see her punished for whatever she'd done. There was a resilience in her panicked eyes. Everyone could see her crime would have been committed for survival rather than profit.

The distance widened between the chaser and the chased, and it looked like she would escape the market untouched. She was only a few yards from the exit when a different man in an even bloodier apron leapt into her path from behind a stall. A guttural scream pierced the night air as she was grabbed by the shoulders. The plastic bag in her hand fell to the ground. She beat against his chest, but he held her with ease.

"Let her go!"

Kostas emerged from the seated crowd. He was neither tall nor large, and his boyish features hadn't yet matured into manhood, but he had a way of carrying himself that commanded attention. The uniform emphasized the power in his expanded chest. Nobody but the other sailors could tell he was merely a low-ranking seaman.

"She stole from us," said the man in the apron, his hands still gripped around her wrists.

The young woman didn't try to defend herself. She looked at Kostas with defiance in her eyes, not the least bit pleading or apologetic, then grunted as she struggled to break free from the man's grasp.

Kostas plucked the bag from the ground and looked inside. Wrapped in clear plastic was a foam plate of poached chicken on a bed of rice. Each segment of meat was as smooth as ivory.

Kostas looked at the man and reached into the pocket of his pants. "How much?"

The man in the apron glared suspiciously at the young sailor, but he accepted the money that was placed in his wet palm. With a sneer, he let go of the woman.

She took the plastic bag that Kostas held out to her. He offered a polite smile before retreating back to his table.

"Wait." There was a soft authority in the woman's voice. "Thank you," she said when he faced her.

"You speak English?"

An unrestrained laugh spilled from her mouth. "You westerners are all the same. This is Singapore, not Beijing. I'm probably more English than you are."

"My apologies," he said, embarrassed. He paused for a second, then thrust his hand between them. "My name's Kostas, but my friends call me Gélio."

A coy smile appeared on her face as she placed her hand in his. The skin felt softer than anything his rough hands had ever touched.

"I'm Ruby," she said, "and I have no friends."

❖

Most people spending their holiday on a ship like the *Glacier* wouldn't realize there was a morgue on board. The truth is humans have a tendency to die, and it is no different at sea.

Death on the *Glacier* was just part of the routine. Heart attacks happened. Suicides were alarmingly common. Even the occasional murder was known to spice up a sailing. The crew were trained to keep these incidents under wraps with code words, protecting guests from the grimness of reality. But the bodies needed to be stored somewhere. Thus, every cruise ship and luxury liner on the seas has a morgue, even if it is little more than a glorified freezer.

Every ship also houses a miniature prison called a brig. As Sebastien made his way to the *Glacier's* brig, deep in the bowels of C Deck, he reminded himself of how everything that exists on land can also be found at sea. A ship might seem like a refuge from the world — a suitable means of escape — but that would never be the case as long as humans are allowed on board. Wherever they go, humans bring all the good and evil in the world along with them.

"Thank you," he said to the young officer who led him through the maze of corridors to the heavy door before him. The officer gave him a dutiful nod.

The cell in the brig was the size of a standard staff cabin with all the furniture removed. The floor was covered in orange carpet, a slightly darker shade than the orange vinyl that padded the walls and ceiling. The toilet was identical to the ones found throughout Hades, except that it sat exposed in a corner. A thin vinyl mattress lay on the floor.

Sebastien stepped inside and closed the heavy door behind him. Sitting in the cell, on the mattress in the opposite corner from the toilet, was his father. The man didn't look up at the sound. The regal uniform had been stripped from his body, leaving only his white undershirt and pants.

"I knew who you were." His voice hissed like a dying fire, eyes fixed at the floor in front of him. "You thought you were so clever, but I knew who you were as soon as I saw you. The hair. The eyes. The name. It was like you wanted me to know."

Sebastien seated himself on the carpeted floor and peered through the steel bars that separated them.

"Maybe I did," he said. "Maybe I knew it wouldn't have made a difference."

Kostas raised his head. His skin was smeared with dried sweat. The rigid waves of hair were now a snarl of disheveled coils. "Why are you here?"

Sebastien rested his forehead against the metal bars, savouring the coldness of their touch. "I thought we could have a talk. Just you and me. Father and son."

"You want to sit there and gloat, that's what you want." Kostas's breathing grew heavier, the exhales more forceful than the inhales. "You may think you're better than me, so proud and so righteous, but you're wrong. I know who you are, Sebastien Goh. I see the anger inside you. And I know what you've done."

"And what would that be?"

"Marcel Lamoureux." He let the words hang in the stale air of the cell. Sebastien felt the slightest twitch in the corners of his eyes, and he hoped Kostas hadn't detected it.

"He has nothing to do with anything," Sebastien said, every muscle in his face hardening until only his lips moved. "He is nothing."

"Ever since you destroyed his kneecaps and his life, I suppose that's true." The corners of his mouth curled up ever so slightly. "I discovered a great deal about you. Some of it was easy enough to find online, but a little committed digging helped me learn who you really are. It's almost as if I've known you your whole life. So many behavioural problems. So much violence. Did the therapy help?"

Sebastien glared at him, unmoving. His fingers dug into his knees.

"You certainly didn't make things easy for your mother," Kostas went on.

"Shut up."

A whiff of lunacy surrounded Kostas as he let out a hearty laugh. "Finally! The real Sebastien emerges from behind his honourable mask. You don't have to explain yourself to me, boy. I would have beaten that man until he was ground into the dirt for what he did to your mother. They wouldn't have been able to stop my arms from swinging. There is no judgment here." He leaned forward with his arms around his knees. A calm, pragmatic expression settled over his face. "I just want you to understand that we are no different. You had your reasons for doing what you did, and I had my reasons, too. It's easy to paint people as good or bad. It's much more difficult to understand how complicated the truth can be. So don't sit there and look at me like I'm so despicable."

"Tell me, then." Sebastien mirrored his father's pose without thinking. "What is the complicated truth?"

Something clouded the intensity in the man's deep green eyes. "The truth is I loved your mother."

※

The Atlantic felt different to young Ruby Goh. The Pacific had been smooth as they sailed from Singapore to Hong Kong to Honolulu. They had encountered a few stormy patches on the way to Panama, but they were nothing compared to the constant lashing of the Atlantic. She could hear the waves pound against the steel hull of the cargo ship that had become her home.

"Don't worry," Kostas said. "This ship can take a beating. I've been through much worse."

Ruby wrapped the threadbare blanket over her shoulders, glancing around her barren cabin. "I'll be happy to get back on land. Where are we now?"

"Two days from Québec City. That's in Canada."

"I know where it is." She flicked her wrist and gave him a playful slap on the chest. "Your move."

Kostas studied the checkerboard on the table between them. Ruby had taught him how to play shortly after departing Singapore. She had been undefeated for the first few weeks, but he was slowly improving. They'd taped little strips of rubber underneath the checker pieces to keep them from sliding off the board as the ship swayed.

"You have to admit," he said as he moved one of his pieces forward. "I'm getting better."

"I would hope so," she said with a teasing smile. "We've been playing for months now." With a swift movement of her wrist, she snatched up two of his pieces.

Kostas cursed. "I didn't see that coming."

Their hands gripped the sides of their chairs reflexively as the ship struck an enormous wave. The fixtures and bolts of the cabin creaked, the sounds echoing around them.

"How long will it take to sail from Québec to France?" Ruby asked with a vexed expression on her face. "I'm not sure how much more of this I can take."

Kostas glanced into her eyes, then lowered his gaze to the checkerboard. "It should take only twenty-two days."

"What's wrong? You always tell me not to worry," she said, "but all I see on your face is worry. You haven't been the same since we left Singapore. Even when you smile, I see something hiding behind it."

He reached across the table and held her by the hands, but he couldn't find the words.

All he'd wanted was a way to escape the life he'd been born into. When he jumped at the chance to work on board a ship, he didn't realize the full extent of its cargo. He ignored the signs and pretended there was nothing sinister happening all around him, but it wasn't long before he was expected to pull his weight. He was easy to trust, a rare quality among the crew.

He didn't want anything to do with it, but he couldn't bear the thought of returning to his dead-end life in Greece. Catching fish. Drying fish. Selling fish and smelling like fish. He told himself he was merely helping these women find work, though he avoided thinking about the work itself or the conditions of consent.

It hadn't taken much to convince Ruby to leave her life behind. The prospect of travelling to France with a handsome sailor was an opportunity that would come around only once. Kostas understood her more than she realized.

The captain knew it was in the group's best interest to keep the girls pacified, which is why they were kept apart from one another. Ruby didn't know the others existed. Each girl thought she was special, that she was on an adventure to France. This dream was nurtured to be believable even when they were locked behind doors and their belongings were confiscated. The crew played their roles well. The girls would ignore their suspicions until it was too late because they wanted so badly to believe this dream. They wanted to trust these men.

The reality was always undeniable the moment the girls were branded.

Ruby hadn't been branded yet, but Kostas knew it would happen soon. With Marseilles less than a month away, it wouldn't be long before the dream was revealed as exactly that — a dream.

"I've just been tired," he finally said, straining a smile.

"You've changed your mind. You don't want me to come to France with you." It was a test. She tried to read his deep green eyes, but the man was a mystery.

"That's not true."

"I'm pregnant."

The words lingered between them. It took a few seconds for Kostas to comprehend what she had said. When he did, his eyelids fluttered and his lips parted. He didn't know what to say, but he knew then what he was going to do.

His mind was a whirlpool of thoughts when he walked down the corridor away from Ruby's cabin. He almost passed three of his crewmates without a pause before he stopped, suddenly realizing where they were headed.

"No!" he shouted, spinning around. They turned to face him. "Please. Don't do it."

"Sorry, Gélio," said the man holding the ink-stained pouch. "Captain's orders. We warned you, didn't we? Never fall in love with the freight."

The Saint Lawrence River was eerily still two days later. They seemed to be sailing across the night sky. The cargo ship pulled into the port of Québec City hours before sunrise.

Young Kostas crept into the dark cabin and shook the woman lying in the berth. "Ruby," he whispered hoarsely into her ear. "Wake up. We need to go."

"What's happening?" She swiped the back of her hands across her eyes.

"Quiet. Gather your things. We're in danger. We need to go, now."

One look into his eyes and she knew he was serious. She

changed into a pair of jeans and a hooded sweatshirt he had lent her. Kostas cringed when he saw the lines of black ink carved into the red, raw skin of her neck. She saw where he was looking and covered the mark with her hair.

"Put this on," he said, helping her into the stiff white jacket of his uniform. The shoulders were emblazoned with a single golden stripe with a diamond shape in the centre.

He guided her by the hand through the unfamiliar passageways. It was her first time seeing what lay beyond her isolated corner of the hulking ship.

Their path wound through the vessel over stairs and around corners. Kostas knew how to minimize their chance of coming across another crew member, but there was no guaranteed route. Beads of sweat dripped down the sides of his forehead. They were almost there.

The cold autumn air stunned the skin on their faces as they stepped onto the gangplank. Ruby shivered beneath the jacket, wrapping her arms protectively across her belly.

The tension that hummed steadily throughout Kostas's body melted when he saw who stood in front of them.

"What's this?" The shout came from his friend, Milos. He stepped onto the end of the gangplank, blocking their way to the concrete dock below.

Kostas motioned for Ruby to stand behind him. "You never saw us," he said to his friend. "Just let us through."

He shook his head. "Tsk, tsk, Gélio. What have you done now?"

"Get out of my way."

"I can't do that." Milos stood up straight with his chest out. He was a few inches taller with twenty extra pounds.

"She's pregnant." Desperation lit flares in his eyes. "Please. We need to let her go."

"That's not how this works," Milos said, gripping the rails in his hands. "She isn't just freight. Now she's a witness. People might ask questions we don't want answered. If I let her go, we're all in trouble."

Kostas took a step back, defeat written on his face. To the surprise of both Milos and Ruby, he laughed. His shoulders bounced up and down as if he were riding a jackhammer.

"What's so funny?" Milos asked, looking like he was afraid of missing the joke.

"Sometimes the only thing left to do is laugh or cry," Kostas said, wiping tears from his eyes. "Let me laugh."

Milos didn't see the fist swing from the side. It connected with such precision that his body nearly lifted off the gangplank by the momentum of his face. His head dangled over the edge as he struggled to regain his vision.

There was just enough room beside Milos's dazed body to squeeze past. Kostas pinned him against the railing and pulled Ruby forward. She gathered the jacket tight around her torso before pushing her way past the two men. Her shoes clanged against the corrugated metal of the gangplank.

"Let's go," he said breathlessly as he followed her. Their feet stepped onto the firm ground when they heard a roar from behind. Kostas landed on the dock with a dull thud, his chin grazing the pavement. He could barely move with the weight of Milos on top of him. His friend's arms wrapped around his stomach like an iron claw.

Ruby looked at him, her eyes frantic, not knowing what to do. He took in her beauty as she stood on the frigid pier, this woman in the oversized jacket so far from the context of her tropical home. Her long black hair danced in the wind. The skin of her cheeks blushed red against the cold, matching her name. He took a photograph with his mind, etching every contour of her face and tone of her skin into his memory, because he knew he would never see her again.

"Run!" he screamed, his voice ringing through the air like a ship's whistle. "Run!"

Sebastien eyed his father crouched in the corner of his cell and imagined how he would have looked as a young man. Like Ruby said the night she died, she had been young once, and so had the man in front of him. This story was no longer mythology. It was now part of Sebastien's history.

His father's manner had changed as he recounted what happened thirty years earlier. Every shred of pride he'd accumulated over the years withered away before Sebastien's eyes. What was left was the poor boy of an unwed mother who people called Gélio.

"Milos brought me back on board," he continued. "I thought my punishment would be death. I was prepared to die. Instead, they said they would take my ear."

He turned his head to the side. The scar Sebastien had often wondered about remained a jagged seam of hardened skin.

"They showed me mercy," he said, dropping his chin in shame. "Or at least that's what they called it. I knew then there would be no escape. They owned me."

"I have no sympathy for you," Sebastien said. The words were loaded yet quiet as a whisper. "You let one woman free because you weren't yet corrupted. But what about all the others since?"

"There was nothing I could do," Kostas said. His voice pleaded for his son to absolve him of his sins. "I never hurt them. I never once caused them any pain. My job was just to transport them. I don't even know what happens to them once they leave the ship."

Sebastien sneered at him. "They're stripped of their freedom the minute they step foot on board. They become slaves. You know that much."

"I just did what I was told. I was—"

"Thirty years!" The accusation filled the cell so wholly that Kostas shrunk in his corner. "Thirty years of doing what you were told. Thirty years of excuses."

"I didn't have a choice," Kostas said, his voice resolute. It sounded like he believed himself, but his eyes betrayed his guilt.

"You always have a choice. We all do. Everything we do, and don't do, is a choice." Calm passed over Sebastien's face. Logic gained control over emotion. "You could have chosen to accept the consequences of saying no that day in Québec. Now you'll have to face the consequences of choosing to say nothing."

Kostas inhaled deeply as though savouring the air, then accepted the verdict with a decisive nod. He stretched his legs on the carpeted floor and reclined against the padded wall. "I was sad to learn about your mother's passing," he said. It was clear he was telling the truth.

"Me, too," Sebastien said softly.

"I'm glad she had you in her life. I wish I could have been a part of it."

A contemptuous burst of air escaped Sebastien's lips. "Just stop," he said.

"I would have given anything for the three of us to be a family."

"Then why didn't you?" His voice was gentle as he stared between the bars at his father in the corner.

"I was weak," Kostas said. "I was weak, and I was scared. I can see that now, but everything was foggier back then. Young men want nothing more than to give their older selves something to regret."

Sebastien had nothing left to say. He leaned his head against the metal bars and let himself feel nothing. He passed no judgment and reached no conclusion. Analysis could wait. For now, all he wanted was to be in the same place at the same time as his father. No hatred. No blame. Just being.

Kostas looked at his son with a sad smile. "I told you once that you remind me of myself as a young man. I meant it."

"I'm not like you," Sebastien said, shaking his head. "I'm far from perfect, it's true. But I'm going to do whatever it takes to be a better man." He gave his father a sympathetic look, and it was the only kindness he could offer. "You had your chance. Now, it's too late. That's a mistake I will never make."

⁂

Nikos looked up like a wounded animal when Sebastien stepped into cabin A66. The deputy security commander's wrists were cuffed behind his back, and his ankles were bound in pink twine. He was propped in the corner of the room with his knees against his chest. His dark hair, normally styled meticulously, was matted with sweat.

He didn't say a word as Sebastien took a seat on the floor beside him. They leaned against the wall and stared at the carpeted floor at their feet.

"Do you blame me?" Sebastien broke the silence, turning his head to the side.

"It doesn't matter," he said.

"Why did you do it, Nikos?"

"I didn't do anything." The response was limp. He couldn't even believe it himself.

"You gave them Athena. She was your friend."

Nikos sat upright and looked into Sebastien's eyes. "I was trying to help her," he said, something broken in his voice. "She needed money, and I knew where she could get it. I had no way of knowing she wouldn't be able to pay them back."

"But you knew what was going to happen once they brought her on board."

Nikos opened his mouth, but nothing came out. He exhaled quietly and swallowed the words.

"You could have helped her," Sebastien went on, "but you didn't. In fact, you stood in our way when we tried."

His lips quivered. "I did that for us. I couldn't bear you knowing I was involved."

"So her freedom was the sacrifice you were willing to make?"

"Her freedom was already lost!" The tremble of his lips spread throughout the rest of his body. "I did what I did to protect you. These are bad people we're dealing with. You could have been in serious trouble. You could be, still."

"What do you know about them?"

"Not much, but I know they're not amateurs. They operate all throughout Europe, Africa, the Middle East ... You might have saved one woman, but it's nothing in the bigger picture. The *Glacier* is just one insignificant spoke in the wheel. This little victory won't make a difference."

"It makes a difference to Athena." Sebastien looked around the bare cabin, imagining the fear she must have felt while trapped within its walls. He pictured her watching the waves roll outside, wondering what awaited her on the shore. Did she reach a point when she abandoned hope?

"Kostas was the one in charge," Nikos said, his voice steadier. "I only picked up bits and pieces, but I was never part of the operation. I had no idea what they'd do with her when I put them in touch. I swear, Sebastien. You have to believe me."

"That's for the authorities to decide, not me."

Nikos let out a frustrated snort. He lay his head against the wall and stared up at the featureless ceiling.

"You used me," Nikos said, quietly stating a fact.

"No more than you used me. We both saw what we wanted to see. We invented roles for each other, then we played them. That's all."

Nikos turned to him, a soft smile appearing in the corners of his lips. "This isn't how our story is supposed to end, Patroclus. How did everything go so wrong?"

"My dear Achilles. You were mistaken this entire time. I was never your Patroclus." Sebastien leaned closer, and the smile faded as he whispered the words into Nikos's ear. "I was the arrow."

TWENTY-FOUR

Young Once

The croissant was an immaculate horn of pastry, leaving buttery crumbs on Sophie's fingertips. She chased it down with a sip of café au lait from a paper takeaway cup. It wasn't very French to order coffee to go rather than savouring it on the patio, but she wanted something to warm her hands.

The sun was just beginning its ascent over the leafy hills and ochre rooftops of the Côte d'Azur. The waves were languid as they kissed the narrow pier.

"There it is," Sophie said to no one in particular. They followed her pointed finger and saw the distant ship where the sea met the sky. She imagined Sebastien standing at the edge of the railing on Sunset Deck, breathing in the salty air as they approached land. Soon the voyage would be over, but he would relish every last second.

The French authorities were dressed in identical black uniforms with peaked caps and fitted jackets, though two of them wore traditional suits. They had crumbs on their hands from the box of pastries Sophie had passed around.

The *Glacier* loomed over the port as it docked alongside the pier, casting an ominous shadow over the pristine yachts in the marina. The ship was larger than most buildings in Cannes.

As the guests disembarked from a raised platform that connected to Adriatic Deck five levels above, a separate gangplank was lowered from the staff quarters. Two white-suited officers with matching beards emerged from the belly of the ship. They conferred with the French police before leading them up the gangplank in a monochromatic line.

"You did well," said the neatly dressed man beside Sophie. "It couldn't have been easy assembling the French." Jérôme St-Germain hadn't yet recovered from the jetlag — his eyes were pink-hued and dry behind his glasses — but his nerves were electric in anticipation of this reunion.

"I don't need your validation," Sophie said, and Jérôme winced. She revelled in his discomfort before slapping him on the shoulder with a giggle. "You'll get used to my cruel humour."

He smiled, relieved. "How did Sebastien look when you saw him?"

She gazed at the resting ship and pondered the question. "On edge, even more so than usual, but he'll be fine. I think he found what he came for."

Jérôme nodded as he fidgeted with the cuffs of his seersucker shirt. "Do you think he'll come home now?" he asked, instantly regretting it. He knew Sophie would read what was behind the question.

She crossed her arms and turned to face him, noticing for the first time how the colour of his eyes looked like rainwater.

"He loves you, Jérôme." The admission surprised them both. "Maybe you could give him a reason to come home."

The crowd of journalists nearby began to stir as figures appeared at the top of the gangplank. Kostas was the first to be led out, both hands cuffed behind his back. It was clear he hadn't slept. There were webs of red in his eyes. The skin on his face sagged, and his hair was slick with grease. He looked like an aging movie star without the team of makeup artists and flattering lighting.

The journalists thrust foam-covered microphones at him as they shouted questions and snapped photographs. He couldn't cover his face without the help of his hands. He had nowhere to hide.

Deck commander Giorgos followed. The broken man could barely walk straight as the police officer guided him toward the dock. His mouth appeared permanently closed, lips pressed so tightly together they barely existed. He hadn't put up a fight the previous night in the Odeon. He admitted to everything.

Giorgos had no reaction to the mob of reporters, but his eyes widened partway down the pier as though he'd just woken up. Standing there was Contessa Bloor, a vision of Riviera beauty in pale yellow pants and a white silk blouse. She hid behind sunglasses, but Giorgos knew the look in her eyes would be one of contempt, not sympathy. She watched him cower in front of her as he was dragged away, her face empty of emotion.

Nikos struggled the most. The once-proud officer refused to leave the ship when he saw the crowd of people on the dock waiting for him to appear. It took two men in black uniforms to escort him down the gangplank, one in front and one behind. Halfway down, he tripped and fell to his knees. His escorts hooked their hands under his arms to haul him back up to his feet.

There was no trace of the calm, cool facade he used to project. Standing beneath the glare of the sun in nothing but a sweat-stained undershirt and wrinkled pants, his fingers curled like talons on hands secured behind his back, Nikos was exposed. He had no uniform to hide behind, no secret room or locked door.

He took short, reluctant steps as they made their way through the horde, flinching at every shouted interrogation and snap of a camera. "I'm innocent!" he screamed at one point, but there was as much guilt on his face as desperation. Sophie and Jérôme stared as he walked by, but he was intent on avoiding eye contact, as though it might turn him to stone.

Sophie was silent when she placed her hand on Jérôme's forearm. They shielded their eyes from the sun. The white hull of the ship was blinding.

Standing at the top of the gangplank, his wild tangle of hair flying in the wind, was Sebastien Goh.

❖

The mood in the café that night was victorious, which was fitting for a watering hole that predated the French Revolution. Many triumphs had been celebrated and defeats dulled by liquor inside these pastel walls. Tucked inside a winding lane on a crowded hill overlooking the Mediterranean, it hadn't changed much over the past four hundred years. Some things defied the unstoppable march of time.

The wooden tables were smooth from years of touch. Every surface was covered in glasses and surrounded by people from faraway places. They huddled together, voices infusing the air with life. The walls absorbed their stories, this night imprinting itself onto the materials of the room.

This place felt like home to Sebastien.

Ilya was telling a story, his hands flying around his face for emphasis, as his audience listened intently.

A bearded Swede named Jonas tried to gain the attention of Diya, but she was more interested in the conversation she was having with Contessa. They spoke feverishly as though they hadn't seen one another in years.

Rosa and Imelda were laughing so violently that red wine splashed onto their clothes from the glasses in their hands, which caused them to laugh even more. The effect was infectious, even though nobody around them had heard the original joke.

Sebastien scanned the room to find Sophie and Jérôme at a corner table surrounded by the Filipino Mafia. They chanted and cheered as the refined Canadian man in glasses downed his beer in one uninterrupted swallow, beating his competitor from across the table. He beamed proudly as he wiped the suds from his soft lips, triumphant.

Sebastien realized he hadn't been fair to Petit Géant. It was the setting for much of the pain in his life, but he had projected that pain onto the entire town. Perhaps it never felt like home, but it also wasn't the hopeless void he once believed it was. He had been so fixated on the bad that he forgot to appreciate the good.

Jérôme caught his eye. They passed each other an intimate smile from across the room.

Grabbing his backpack from the floor, he stepped into a narrow hall that led to a hidden terrace in the back. It was quieter here, a welcome respite from the revelry. The long walls on either side were worn from time. The faded paint was chipped away in flakes of rose, revealing flashes of yellow underneath. Little clouds of dust drifted from the ceiling overhead as the rafters creaked.

What drew him to this hallway in this specific bar hung on the walls. Hundreds of photographs of people from the past stared at him, forming a tunnel of frozen memories. Some of them could have been royalty, others farmers. The faces were joyful, sad, and everything in between. He imagined each of them posed in front of the camera as the shutter closed, capturing that moment in time forever. Now, they lived on long after their faces had withered away.

Sebastien reached into his backpack. His mother was immortal behind the glass of the frame.

"You always wanted to see France," he said, a tear meandering down his cheek. "I wish I had taken you sooner."

He found the nail the owner of the bar had kindly dedicated to him. Ruby's young eyes met his from her spot on the wall, black hair blowing loosely in the wind. Her smile was faint but hopeful. He understood it better now.

The other room sounded louder than before when he returned, eyes still damp.

Ilya hooked a muscular arm around his neck. "Our fearless leader re-emerges," he said, kissing him on the side of the face. "What were you doing back there?"

Sebastien shrugged. "Just thinking about home."

Ilya flashed him a puzzled look. "You are home," he said before pulling him to a table in the centre of the crowd.

They clinked their glasses together and relived the past few weeks through their stories, each account coloured a little differently from the next. The room shook with their laughter.

The smile on Sebastien's face felt impossibly light. This was how it felt to be surrounded by family. They didn't share blood. They shared purpose.

He looked at the faces around the table, and he stored every detail in his memory. He knew that, despite his wishes, the night would come to an end. Time would move on. People would move on.

But one day, far in the future, when he was old and his reflection unfamiliar, he would lie in his bed and remember this night, and he would think:

We were young once.

We made ourselves heard.

We fought.

We found each other.

And the fire would rekindle in his deep green eyes.

ACKNOWLEDGEMENTS

This story is special to me. While I waited for months to learn if my first novel, *After Elias,* would make it to publication, I needed to find a way to channel my anxious energy. I started writing the first chapter, and very soon I was lost in the world of Sebastien as he sailed across the sea aboard the *Glacier.* I could smell the salt in the air as I poured myself into the pages, bringing me back to younger days when the world seemed impossibly big and filled with promise. Writing this story reminded me that I wish to never stop seeing the world this way.

I have many people to thank for helping me bring Sebastien to life.

Jessica Faust, my tenacious champion in an industry that's often mystifying. I'm proud and grateful to have you by my side.

Jamie Chapman and Andrea Wesley, two of the only people on the planet I'd entrust with an early draft of a manuscript. Hearing your honest and thoughtful feedback over dinner were highlights of this project.

Michelle Meade, for delivering such incisive guidance that shaped the story into what it is today. I still carry with me the lessons I learned from you.

Rachel Spence, Diane Young, Kathryn Lane, Jenny McWha, Heather Wood, Stephanie Ellis, Laura Boyle, Sophie Paas-Lang, Kendra Martin, Maria Zuppardi, Kristina Jagger, and the rest of the extended Dundurn team, for your commitment to sharing my work with the world.

My invincible 2020 debuts, for being the writing community I'd always hoped for. We survived!

Niki Khan, for the welcome feedback.

Mandy Kerridge, for helping me update my decade-old perceptions of ship life.

Judith Fournier, for your insights on life in *la belle province*.

Vanessa Butler, for being such a good friend and supporter of my work, even though you forgot the manuscript beneath the table.

My mother and father, who let me chase adventure despite preferring that I stay safe at home.

My friends, family, and everyone who supported my first book with such enthusiasm.

The staff and crew of the *Summit*, 2005, for embracing my unique brand of crazy and for not throwing me overboard.

The staff and crew of the *Pride*, 2004, to whom this book is dedicated: Melissa, Chris, Hannah, Erinn, Erin, Evan, Crissy, Ciara, Ali, Lorenzo, Andrew, Gord, to name only a few. To Claudine, the first person I met on the dock in Long Beach, who welcomed me aboard with such warmth — you are missed, but we'll never forget you.

Finally, to Thomas, for making today so bright that I no longer feel the need to escape into the past. There's so much more adventure ahead of us.

Photo Credit: Thomas Boudel Tan

Eddy Boudel Tan has been named a 2021 Rising Star by the Writers' Trust of Canada. His debut novel, *After Elias*, was shortlisted for the Edmund White Award for Debut Fiction, and his short stories can be found in *Joyland*, *yolk*, *Gertrude Press*, and the *G&LR*. Apart from being a writer and a traveller, he serves home-cooked meals to the unhoused community as co-founder of the Sidewalk Supper Project. He lives with his husband in Vancouver.